LETHBRIDGE-STEWART

BLOODLINES
HOME FIRES BURN

Gareth Madgwick

CANDY JAR BOOKS · CARDIFF
2019

The right of Gareth Madgwick to be identified as the Author of the Work has been asserted by him in accordance with the Copyright, Designs and Patents Act 1988.

Home Fires Burn © Gareth Madgwick

The character Eileen Le Croissette © *Shaun Russell*
The Nexus © *Andy Frankham-Allen 2019*
Characters from The Abomniable Snowmen, The Web of Fear and
The Dominators © *Hannah Haisman & Henry Lincoln 1967, 2019*
Lethbridge-Stewart: The Series
© *Andy Frankham-Allen & Shaun Russell 2014, 2019*

Doctor Who is © *British Broadcasting Corporation, 1963, 2019*

Range Editor: Andy Frankham-Allen
Editor: Shaun Russell
Editorial: Keren Williams
Licensed by Hannah Haisman
Cover by Richard Young & Will Brooks

ISBN: 978-1-912535-52-1

Printed and bound in the UK by
Severn, Bristol Road, Gloucester, GL2 5EU

Published by
Candy Jar Books
Mackintosh House
136 Newport Road, Cardiff, CF24 1DJ
www.candyjarbooks.co.uk

For Stan, Margaret, Mel and Glen.
Wonderful grandparents who could all tell a far better
story of the war years than I ever could.

Massive thank you to: Alison Hall for a thorough read through. Alyson Leeds for helping me straighten out Matthew's career. Gareth Barns for geology. Andy Frankham-Allen for the chance and helping make it a far better book than I started out with. And lastly my wife and children for putting up with Saturdays out spent with Daddy staring into space, while he tried to work out the next scene in his head.

FOR A BRIEF moment there was stillness, and the causal nexus of reality rested. Everything was in its place; time was on track. No more anomalies, no more paradoxes. It was a rare moment, for time was always being played with. So many races interfering, thinking they knew best. Only one species had ever truly understood time, but other than a handful still out there, these self-professed lords of time no longer existed. One still served as time's protector, but he was damaged, no longer the man he once was. A hero turned warrior, and now so heavily wounded by the single worst war in creation, that his protection barely mattered.

But, for a brief moment only, time was still.

It was not to last.

Throughout the causal nexus of reality there were fixed points; moments in the timelines of the multiverse that could not be changed. Despite the best efforts of so many, these points always resolved into their default pattern. Always the same course of events, always the same outcome. They were the invisible threads that ensured the causal nexus never reached the point of ultimate temporal collapse. But for every ten fixed points, there was a fracture point. A moment in time that was especially susceptible to interference, where, with the slightest alteration, an entirely new timeline could be created. Such fracture points were the biggest threat to the causal nexus, constantly pulling at the tapestry of the multiverse. For, despite the assertions of the greatest minds of corporeal beings, the multiverse was not infinite. There were not endless possibilities. Some possibilities were a threat to the very nature of the multiverse. Too many divergent timelines and even the fixed points were in danger of unravelling.

There was one fracture point in Earth's history that was, according to these lords of time, the weakest. It had always been under close scrutiny. It was a tipping point in the history of the galaxy known to some as Mutter's Spiral. A moment that could either secure mankind's role in the future of the galaxy, or it could mean the ultimate destruction of mankind. Where the decisions made would either create the greatest enduring legacy of Earth, or they would determine Earth's place as the wasteland of humanity.

That fracture point was known, by the authorities of Earth, as the London Event.

But the lords of time were no longer watching, and so, as it often was, that fracture point was under severe strain.

Time cried out, and once more it splintered.

A form appeared in a void simply known as the quantum nexus. The being did not normally need to take form, for it was a being of pure energy, existing on a quantum level. But there were moments when it needed to interact with corporeal beings, and in those moments a physical form was necessary.

For a brief time it stood there, immobile. Watching the tapestry of time, in particular two threads – the bloodlines of two human families. Throughout time and space they intersected, two threads so intricately linked that if one was to be severed then the fracture point would be destroyed. As was happening now.

The Guardian of the Quantum Realm needed to consult with a corporeal being. There had to be a way to fix the threads before they were irrevocably severed.

'Where the devil am I?'

The Guardian turned its whole form to face the corporeal being it had called forth.

'You!' the man snapped. 'The Accord. What the blazes do you want now?'

The last time they had met, the corporeal being had found it harder to grasp the being that was sometimes called the Accord. That time the corporeal being was needed to find the right quantum point to fix Earth's enfolded timeline.

The Accord walked towards the corporeal being, and split

into three forms. Each talking as one, its voices overlapping, in much the same way as its three forms phased in and out of each as they walked.

'I need your help, Brigadier Alistair Lethbridge-Stewart.'

The Brigadier regarded the Accord. 'Why are there three of you?'

'There is but one, but you now perceive three as what we must discuss involves what is, what was and what should be.'

'You mean the past, present and future?'

'As you understand such things, yes.'

'I see. Well whatever it is, I've done my bit. I'm retired. All I want to do is enjoy my time with my grandchildren. In fact, my granddaughter has just been born. They called her Lucy, you know, and...' He stopped talking, a curious look on his face. Bewilderment. 'Why am I even telling you this?'

'You must help me. I cannot interact with the corporeal world, so I need a being such as you to act as my agent. Your entire history is on the verge of collapse. And not just yours, but that of the Traverses.'

'Travers? You mean Anne is in danger, too?'

'Not just her, but her whole timeline. The entire history of her progenitor and descendants. Just like yours, they are integral to the...'

The Guardian's explanation trailed off as the corporeal being that was Alistair Lethbridge-Stewart fell apart on the temporal winds.

The Guardian of the Quantum Realm considered the two threads. The bloodlines of two families, destined to intertwine, to unite at that fracture point. Already the damage was severe. The fundamental timeline from which the Brigadier had been pulled, the timeline from which all other quantum realities in the multiverse branched, was unravelling. He was too intricately connected.

The Guardian needed another agent. Someone connected, but whose own timeline was not dependent on either the Lethbridge-Stewarts or the Traverses.

The Guardian searched the entire history of Earth in the moment between seconds. Searched for a moment where the essential timeline was still stable...

Yes. She would serve. Her human compunction called duty

would compel her, and the Guardian would send her to the first moment where the Lethbridge-Stewarts and Traverses time-threads unknowingly crossed...

PROLOGUE

FLIES BUZZED in the late day's sun as he ran his hands over the branch, feeling every knot and whorl along its length. It was a good piece with no weaknesses. A new scythe was needed and come harvest time it would do them all some use. He held his hand-axe in one hand, the branch balanced against his leg, and slowly scraped the bark back, letting the woodlice and centipedes holed up inside run down the shaft and escape into the corners of the workshop. They hid in a million tiny cracks of the dry-stone wall that had been home to generations of insects and rodents.

The bark and shavings had fallen around his feet like snow. He gripped the branch between his thighs, held the axe to the top. He brought both down firmly, not so much that the wood would split, but enough to cut into the top of the branch. The axe still came away easily when he tugged it free. He moved it a fraction to the side and repeated the action. The wood was splintering now into a good-sized slot at the top of the branch.

He took a knife, ran the blade against his fingernail and noted the white line that it left behind. Running the blade within the slot left by the axe cleared the wood splinters, like cauterising a wound, cleaning it of infection. He ran his eyes across the now bare wood, a thing that had grown for years, feeding on soil and sun and earth and growing to now reach its end as this.

It was not fully the end. One day, the wood would rot, the blade would rust, and the scythe would cease to be a tool again, becoming food and shelter once more. It gave him comfort to think of it as he looked at the twisting shape of his new scythe, glowing in the amber light that was slowly setting past the hills, letting motes of sawdust dance around the workshop.

He picked a blade as long as his arm from the rack. Again, he tested it with his fingernail; it was easily as sharp as the knife, all along its length. It fitted perfectly into the slot he had cut in the scythe handle. He held it with one hand as he reached with the other for the drill, which would create the holes for the bolts to hold it in place.

That was when he heard the footsteps approaching. Egcbert and Arian on their way back to the farm.

He stepped out of the shed, rubbing a woollen cloth across his brow to push the sweat back from his eyes, so that he could see better down the lane to watch them return. He knew they wanted to explore, to see some of the world beyond the farm. He always worried when they went. The world was now far more dangerous than when he had been young. The planes that buzzed overhead and the searchlights that could be seen in the surrounding cities told him so. He was happy to leave it all alone, and wished his children would follow suit.

Through the dust of the evening and the sun against his eyes he saw their silhouettes approaching, but between them…?

His heart sank. They had been there before, many, many years ago. This was a mistake, it had to have been a mistake. He dropped his tools and they clattered to the floor in the rocky dust by his feet. He called for the rest of the community.

Section Officer Eileen Le Croissette snapped to attention in front of General Dornan's secretary.

'You're keen,' the grey-haired woman observed, gazing over the rims of her glasses. 'Not many sticklers for military discipline down here.' She glanced around the dark bunker, checking that the various officers were out of earshot. 'Not many sticklers for most rules down here.' She motioned towards the office door. 'He's free. Best go through. You'll find that anything that needs doing here, needs doing quickly.'

As she stepped through the door, Eileen reflected that fast-paced work was no different than the Filter Room, before Professor Edward Travers had recruited her to the Home-Army Fourth Operational Corps. Before Gulliver Base. Her new role felt like a strange dream, the trappings of military service were still there, but dealing with things from space, with rockets and other strangeness. Was that really for her?

She snapped a salute to Dornan as she stopped in front of his desk. The papers scattered across it and the chaos that it entailed were a change from her previous role. Dornan followed her eyes.

'Mr Churchill has changed his mind again. That means that all hell breaks loose on my desk as I try to close off his last big idea and start work on the next one.' He glanced back up at where she still stood stiffly, arms by her sides. 'Sit down, Section Officer.'

She picked the chair with the smallest pile of papers on it and sat down, perching them on her lap. Dornan pointed at his wastepaper bin.

'Best send them over there. Our funding will never stretch to that. What with the way the North Atlantic is looking.' He grabbed another page from the pile in front of him. 'You've not long joined us, Section Officer?'

'No, sir.'

Dornan grunted, his eyes fixed on the sheet in front of him. Eileen remembered applying to be an Intelligence Officer once. Her CO had seen to it that her interview got cancelled without her even being told. Was this meeting another dead end?

'It's time for your first assignment.' She swallowed. That was more promising, but she felt barely ready for this. So much in Churchill's secret scientific corps caught her by surprise. 'You'll be out of the Home Counties. Might get a few full nights' sleep without an air raid.' He watched her, looking for a reaction.

'Where will I be going, sir?'

'Up North. Sheffield to be exact. We're not happy about a downed plane in the moors nearby. We've got one of our scientific boffins on site dealing with that aspect, but we need you to go and look up some possible book-cooking at one of the steelworks there. There's more going in than we're getting out for the war effort. The owner is a foreigner, from Canada.' He handed a sheaf of papers over. 'I want to make sure there's no connection to the plane.'

'You want me to run through their books?' As a first assignment, this was not looking like the most difficult thing to deal with. She flicked through the papers. They contained a lot of ledgers with numbers and unfamiliar names all over them.

'Ye gods, no.' He handed her another list, this one of names. One in particular was circled. Hilda Graves. 'Recognise her?' he asked.

'She was on the same Filter Room training as me,' Eileen said, pondering for a second before adding, 'Sir. She dropped out after a couple of weeks.'

She remembered Hilda; a tall girl, quiet but practical. She was also a girl who preferred to be working with her hands rather than dealing with the high-paced mental somersaults and communication that made up the Filter Room. She had finally had enough and ran out of the training room one day after breaking down in tears. Eileen had kept in touch. From one of the letters, she knew that Hilda had eventually been discharged from the WAAF. The letter had stuck in the mind. She had read it shortly before the fateful shift in which she had spotted a rogue craft in the Filter Room. The rogue craft that had turned out to be from another world.

'They only take the best.' Dornan looked at her sideways, a strange half smile on his face. 'But she is still doing her bit after dropping out of the WAAF and being declared a mobile worker. This is a list of the workers at the Pickering Steelworks. Mostly women, I'm sorry to say. These are dreadful times.'

'You think that she's involved, sir?' Hilda was headstrong in her way. The kind of girl who would go her own way.

Dornan pursed his lips. 'I doubt it. She's a welder. But what I need you to do is meet up with her, spend a couple of nights up there. I know how women can chatter. This is our chance to find out as much as possible about what's happening in there. A perfect use of your skills. Make sure you report back to this office anything that you find out and we'll see you back here in a few days to review. I would get a telegram sent now if I was you. Miss Roberts will help you.' He went back to his paperwork, shuffling the piles around his desk.

He barely even acknowledged Eileen's salute as she left.

She quietly closed the door behind her and sighed. This was not the sort of assignment that she had anticipated. Her nerves had evaporated to be replaced with frustration. Moreover, although she wouldn't say so to his face, she was far from convinced that Dornan's assessment of her abilities was remotely accurate.

She would much rather have been involved with the boffins that were dealing with the scientific aspects, whatever that may have been.

She waded through the smoke from Miss Roberts' cigarette to dictate the telegram.

CHAPTER ONE
The Search by the Professor

MIDSUMMER APPROACHED and the early day sun was flooding the little valley when Professor Edward Travers alighted from his train at what he hoped was Edleton Station. After changing at Sheffield, he had nearly jumped off at Hope, before the train guard had shook his head with a, 'Next one, sir.' The lack of signs made travel to unfamiliar places difficult, and his concentration was not helped by three hours spent on scratchy threadbare seats as the sun had slowly climbed past the backs of the red-bricked houses that lined his route from London. A London that was empty now that so many children, Anne and Alun included, had fled to the countryside. Margaret, alone, had waved him off from her bed.

At least no bombs had blocked the line. Things were improving as the war dragged on. Fewer bombs didn't always mean better living mind. Rationing was biting hard and it was a rare street that didn't see the telegram boy on a regular basis.

Like so many rural stations, Edleton sat some distance from its corresponding village. The army driver laid on by the Fourth Operational Corps was there to meet him off the platform. Travers' heart fell when he saw that it was Corporal Felix Cownall.

'Professor Challenger. They always said you were beyond Hope.'

'Very droll,' said Travers. 'Have you been briefed on this?'

Cownall gave a curt nod, his face falling. 'Came down up there.' He pointed up at the hills that hemmed the town in on all sides, promising peaks and delivering nothing but black peat bog.

Travers remembered them well from youthful expeditions

as he allowed his eyes to follow the man's arm. The locomotive whistled and pulled away, leaving behind a silence that seemed to weigh heavily.

He recalled General Dornan's briefing. The Home Guard on night watch had reported unexplained bursts of light in recent months, emanating from the hills around. Hundreds of feet high in brief flashes in otherwise isolated areas. Pillars of flame.

So, a reconnaissance plane had been sent over, a Bristol Blenheim. It had travelled across at night, keeping an eye out for any reason for the sudden phenomena. He'd seen the radio transcripts. A lot of chatter and flirting with the girls on the ground. Then the radio operators had reported gasps of surprise, then nothing. The plane had been found the next day, scattered across the moorland. The bodies of the crew, missing. That's when the higher ups had decided to send the Fourth in.

'Found anything since you've arrived?' Travers asked.

'Our digs. Not too shabby. The Home Guard have the local inn, so we get a house to ourselves. And I thought I'd found an eyewitness to the crash.'

Travers stopped short.

'Thought…?'

'He was just a child. He told the Home Guard he'd seen it come down. They passed his name to us to look into it. Trouble is, he vanished two days ago. I've got the local bobby coming round in a bit. He should know a bit more.'

Travers let his eyes drift across the landscape. Fields gave way to rock which gave way to twisted heather clinging to the moors in bunches, still brown. Occasional splashes of purple rhododendron in the heavy summer air. He was troubled. Something that he couldn't put his finger on had caught hold of him as soon as he had stepped from the train.

'Right, let's go.'

He settled himself in the passenger side of Cownall's Austin Tilly, a cheap car converted to a flatbed for wartime use. He placed his fedora on his lap.

'Is this the best they can offer?'

'I tried to get a Rolls from the staff car pool at the nearest base, but since neither of us is an officer, here we go.'

Travers tutted. Cownall gunned the engine and spun the wheel with one hand; the Tilly juddered and started shaking itself down the lane leading away from the station, squeezing between the dry-stone walls that marked it.

'I used to come spelunking up here,' Travers mused, looking out of the window at the ridge of hills that divided this valley from the next.

'I'd keep that to yourself, Professor. There's laws you know.' Cownall was clearly trying his best to keep a straight face.

'It means exploring caves, Corporal,' he snapped back. 'As well you know. So, it's time to play hunt the child just to find out what's going on.'

'It would be boring if we got the answers before we've even started wouldn't it.'

Travers grunted as Cownall started to whistle Colonel Bogey.

'You might not be in a hurry to finish the job and go home, Cownall. I get little enough time with the family as it is. I'll give that boy a good talking to when I find him.'

'Without asking for tenure first? You're getting generous with your time, Prof.'

The village was a dead end. A collection of grey stone houses, an inn, a post office and a shop nestled among the verdant green farmland. The kind of place that barely needed an ARP Warden because no lights would ever show, where the Home Guard joined up for a chance to meet their friends of an evening.

The digs were an empty police house. Its occupant had received his call up papers and met his end in Crete. All perishables had been cleared, but Travers could see that the house retained much of the boy's belongings. A series of pulp paperbacks lined the wall. *The Shadow* and *Secret Agent X*. Good reading for a young copper, Travers mused. Soap and cologne still sat in the bathroom alongside a monogrammed towel reading 'BP'. A gift from a mother to her son as he flew the nest? Houses like this would soon dot the country again. The lives lived here lost far away. Meanwhile, the cities were levelled by the bombs and families sat on the street.

Travers knew that he was now living in a dead man's house. But was his own house any more homely? With Anne and Alun away staying with his in-laws and Margaret laid up in bed with a succession of doctors and experts tutting at her refusal to suffer from anything they could deal with easily… She spent so much time in hospitals that he felt he had lapsed back into his bachelor days. He should probably be grateful to Toby Kinsella for matching him to a well-paying job to pay the medical bills. Truth be told, he would rather, on many days, be poor and have his family around him again.

A loud hammering from the doorway caused him to jump. He heard Cownall rushing from the upstairs rooms.

'Got it!' shouted Travers.

He preferred to have some autonomy. The second worst thing about military life after being given orders was being responsible for the command of others. He flung the front door open.

A constable stood in the door, holding a sheaf of papers that looked to have been kept under the teapot for the last week. He was an older man, like anyone now still in civvies, a darting pair of eyes behind a craggy mask of indifference.

'PC Armthorpe, sir. I've been told you're taking this over. I don't know why it's falling to the Army. I thought you'd have more on your plate than a missing boy.'

Travers grabbed at the papers. 'He's a means to an end. Come in, give me the debrief.'

The man wiped his feet as he entered.

'Good house this. It's a shame young Parkin won't be coming back to it.'

Travers shrugged. 'War is hell.'

The constable nodded sadly. 'I was in the last one. Two many mates in this valley just a name on the memorial at the crossroads in Hope. More to add to them before this one's out no doubt.' He showed himself to the parlour and sat down in one of the armchairs. 'Edleton got lucky mind. No memorial here. Poor Parkin is the first loss in war this village has had for…' He trailed off. 'To tell the truth, I really don't know.'

'Brew, sir?' asked Cownall.

'Please, son. I'm parched and our ration ran out yesterday.'

'British Army's finest coming up.'

Travers took the other armchair. 'Not a patch on what they have in India. But it's all we've got now.'

The policeman made no reaction to Travers' reference to his travels. He'd likely never left this village except to go to the training college and then get himself posted straight back. Well, if that's what made a happy life for him, let him be.

'Right,' said Travers. 'Let's hear it. What's happened to the boy?' He put the papers to one side. Plenty of time to read them later.

'Not a lot to tell. Charles Peeves. Nine years old. Lived with his mother. Father away with the Forces. No brothers or sisters. He was playing out in the afternoon one day and didn't come home. The mother came to find me the next day. We've had the men left in the village hunting high and low for him. Checked all the fields, the caves up on the edge, we've wandered the forests. There's no sign.'

Travers kept quiet; he was no expert on missing children. The age was a concern, he felt. A young child might get lured away by an unpleasant sort. An older child might run away from home. But for a nine-year-old to simply walk out of the house? Unless the child was of limited intelligence, it struck him as strange.

'What was his school work like?'

Armthorpe looked confused. 'Come again?'

Travers cast around for the right turn of phrase. He settled on being blunt. 'Was he dim?'

The policeman shook his head. 'Far from it. One of the brightest ones. Probably heading for a good position. Maybe even a scholarship boy.' He gratefully took the proffered cup as Cownall returned. Cownall, in turn, settled himself down by the windowsill.

'Go and check the blackouts, Corporal.'

A look of daggers and the man was gone. Travers tapped the arm of his chair absently.

'Anything you know about his home life?'

'Nothing untoward,' Armthorpe said. 'Seemed like a happy little family. Obviously, he's not seen much of his father since it all kicked off, but no sign of it sending him off the rails like a few others around here I've had to give the odd clip to.'

'Suspects?'

14

The officer shook his head again and took a sip. 'None that I think did away with him. Dashed strange business.'

Travers leafed his way through the paperwork. It was a long list of people that hadn't seen anything. It was amazing how long people could spend telling a policeman nothing of any use. It must drive them mad.

'Has anyone mentioned anything he said about seeing the plane go down?'

The officer shrugged. 'Only in passing. I know he saw it, but you know…' He sighed. 'Planes from every side come down a lot these days.'

'You've got search parties?' Travers folded the papers carefully, the better to read later.

'We do. Another one being organised in an hour or so. We meet in the village green.'

Travers pulled himself upright. 'Good work, constable. I'll meet you and the rest when you start.'

Although recent experiences had left him a Jack of all trades and an expert in robotics, Professor Edward Travers would be the first to tell anyone that listened that his primary field was anthropology, the study of people. There was, to his mind, nothing so full of texture and meaning as the inhabitants of a typical English village when they were gathered to a common purpose.

He looked at those gathered around the well at the centre of the village green, where Armthorpe stood with a list and a map. Farm labourers, retired old men, shopkeepers, publicans, a jowly vicar with eyes sunken into his face. Bleary-eyed Home Guard and ARP Wardens fresh from watch duty after a very short sleep. He identified their commander immediately. A vacant looking man that seemed almost bewildered to be there wearing sergeant's stripes. He approached and coughed.

'Can I help you?' His accent was surprisingly refined.

No sense in flashing authority around for now.

'I'm just trying to see if I can help,' Travers said. 'Did you ever meet young Master Peeves?'

'Do you know? My men and I are actually all from out of town here. We only came up to do some night-time manoeuvres with the locals, and now we've been roped into finding this boy.' He rubbed the back of his neck. 'Actually, come to think of it, I think he may have been the one that approached us the morning after the crash. Said he'd seen it or somesuch. For the life of me I just couldn't make out his accent. I think he was talking about circles or somesuch.'

Circles. That could mean anything. Damn the Englishman's instinct to ignore any words he can't understand.

'It must be unusual to see planes brought down around here.'

The sergeant fixed him with a quick glance. 'These hills are a graveyard. Not all suspicious of course. A lot collide with the crags around Kinder. The navigators don't expect it to be there.'

Travers agreed sadly, made his excuses and cast about for another target. A vicar might know more about his parishioners than others. He ambled towards the man of the cloth to be met with a glower.

'Did you know the missing boy?'

The vicar nodded. 'Oh yes. I knew that family only too well.'

'Indeed?' Travers tried to leave enough space for the man to give him something, anything, more for him to go on.

'Who are you anyway?'

Travers coughed as he thought quickly. 'I'm ah… working with the authorities. A scientist. Seeing if I can help. Edward Travers.' He extended his arm for a handshake.

The vicar looked down at the hand, keeping his own firmly at his side. 'Reverend Carter. Don't see much call for scientists out here. Either we find him or we don't. That is God's will.'

Travers knew a tough nut when he saw one. 'I'm only here to help.'

Carter fixed him with a glare from his deep-set eyes. 'I'm pretty sure that boy is beyond any help you can offer. Why else would I be wasting my time on his family? Excuse me.' He pushed past.

Travers turned to Armthorpe as he watched the vicar stalk off across the green. 'Well. That went well.'

Armthorpe pulled a face like a man biting into a lemon. 'For a man of God, Mr Carter is quick to judge. He's not too keen on poor young Mrs Peeves.'

'What did she do to him? Take the last slice of Victoria sponge?'

'Not my place to speak ill of ladies. Perhaps you'd better ask her yourself.' Armthorpe pointed at the young lady sat on a bench by the well, dressed in grey knee-length dress offset by a bright scarlet turban. Such things were the style now that hair products were scarce.

Her chin was raised in defiance at the bustle around her. As the men dispersed to search the area, Travers approached the mother and lifted his hat.

'Mrs Peeves?'

She nodded curtly, her lips pursed.

'Professor Travers. Here to assist the authorities. Can I sit?'

She made space on the bench.

'I don't know what you can do that the rest can't. They already think he's been killed. That's why old Armthorpe has forbidden me from joining the search for my own son.'

'What do you think?' Travers hadn't meant to be so blunt, the words just fell out.

She looked into the middle distance. 'He's not here anymore. He's not dead. I know that much, but he's not going to come running around the corner like the little boy I used to know, with a smile on his face and a bunch of flowers for his mummy.'

Travers swallowed. 'A charmer already, eh?'

'He was.' Ouch. That past tense hung in the air between them.

'Like your husband?'

'He's gone too. Out there on the Atlantic by now. He'd never seen the sea before he joined. It's so hard to keep track of who is where now. The tide's just not turning for us.'

Travers thought of his own work behind the scenes, of the various experiments that the Fourth had on the go at any one time. If people like Mrs Peeves knew the half of it, they might pray for an everlasting stalemate.

'It must be difficult on your own?'

'We coped.' She sniffed. 'If you're trying to imply that I couldn't control my child on my own, you are sorely mistaken. We are an upstanding family in this village.' She stood.

'Excuse me.'

As she walked away, Travers puffed his cheeks out. So far he had managed to upset everyone he spoke to. A good start. But then, what else did he expect? A man of fighting age, a scientist at that, tramping around a village, poking his nose in and exercising authority that no one believed he had. Sometimes he wondered if Dornan knew what he was doing by sending him, of all people, on this kind of task.

The men of the village had dispersed. Armthorpe ambled over.

'They've been dispatched. No sense making a big speech. They know what they're doing and all they need from me is a location. Let's hope this is the last morning.' The policeman pulled a flask from his pocket. Obviously his tea ration had been supplemented by Cownall's Army supply. Even Travers' driver was ingratiating himself better than he was.

'The mother isn't keen to speak to me,' said Travers, dropping himself down next to the policeman.

'She won't be. She's got a lot to keep to herself that one. Mother died at childbirth. Father, well, he's over there.' He nodded towards the church yard. 'Drank himself there after his wife passed.'

'Husband at sea and son swallowed by the hills,' Travers finished, gesturing around him. 'And then some busybody from God-knows-where is asking questions about them both.'

Armthorpe smiled and offered a spare cup. Travers took it. It was, by rights, his damn tea after all.

'I'm a bit of a beginner at this,' he admitted. 'Not really my bag. Any idea where I'm best off starting?'

'You could try the kids that young Charles used to play with. With the war, they've been roaming the countryside around here unchecked all morning while they wait for the evacuees to finish with the school house. Always possible that they've found some undiscovered cave or something that no one else has seen yet. Tunnels run everywhere around here. There's that huge network under Eldon Moor. Or they might have walked all the way to the reservoirs and drowned, found an unexploded bomb... So many things that parents and policemen don't get told; a stranger might be more fortunate. Might be worth checking to see what you can get out of the tykes.'

Travers mused that as children, he and his brother Vincent could keep secrets from each other, let alone a passing scientist. Still, until the men returned, it was definitely worth a shot. Armthorpe gave him the directions to the nearest child's house.

'He'll be anywhere but there mind,' he said. 'But that's your best starting point.'

Travers approached the address. A stone cottage like any other, roses and ivy intertwining above the door set deep into the wall next to miniscule paned windows. It was the kind of place that appeared in newsreels with a plummy propaganda accent telling the cinema that it was 'what we're all fighting for'.

Travers banged briskly on the door, to be met by the hairnet and beady eyes of its occupant.

'Mrs Lander? Is Jacob at home?'

The eyes took in the whole of Travers as he stood there, flicking across his leather boots and tough outdoor flannels.

'Who's asking?'

He had rehearsed this one after his experiences so far in Edleton. As he opened his mouth to speak, she cut across him.

'Don't bother, young man. I know who you are. The chap from the military that's been poking his nose in where it's not wanted and upsetting Mrs Peeves.' She tutted, hugged the edge of the door closer as if to deny him entry. 'Jacob's down by Gibbet's Woods. That's where he last saw Charles. There's no help he can give you, mind. And if you upset him, you can best get out of this town as quick as you can move.'

The door slammed in Travers' face.

CHAPTER TWO
If You Go Down to the Woods...

BETWEEN THE village and the woods, the grass rippled like water as it was caressed by the wind and bathed by the sun. Above, a pair of crows marked Travers' path, cawing as he crossed fields marked by dry stone walls, covered in yellow lichen that made them look diseased and infected. He followed a barely marked path through thickets and brambles. The crows leaped from each tree and bush he passed along the path. Gibbet's Woods sat in a hollow, behind one of the walls. Thick trunked trees, twisted hawthorn and elm, clustered together, surrounded by a dense hedgerow. Lichen grew on the trunks and branches too, making the wood look as dead as the stone. The brambles of the hedge caught his eye. He looked closer and caught his breath. He could see pieces of flesh and skin hanging off the spikes, patches of red blood on the twigs. One of the crows landed and tugged at a scrap, snapping it with its beak and then thrusting up to a higher branch to consume it.

Travers held his hand to the fragments and pulled one of them off. The dry material tugged slightly and then gave. Thin skin covered in a fine black fur, the same as a thousand identical pieces across the rest of the hedge.

Travers shivered; this place held the stench of death. He thought of tribes that he had studied, rituals surrounding the blooding of animals. Sometimes there would be a cross-over. If an animal was not a sufficient sacrifice, he swallowed, a human would have to do.

A stick snapped behind him and he whirled around, his heart hammering in his chest.

Reverend Carter stood there, his clerical collar visible even in his outdoor clothes. He held his hands up.

'You look shocked at this little display.'

Travers held the pelt up to him. 'Hardly the sort of thing I'd have expected a man of the church to condone.'

Carter laughed. 'On the contrary, Professor, I was going to ask them to do the same to the vicarage garden.'

He chuckled again at Travers' bewildered expression.

'Moles, Professor. The trapper gets paid by the farmer. He works early in the morning and late at night. He hangs them here to show the farmer that his money had been well spent.'

Travers threw the miniature pelt away into the base of the hawthorn, swearing under his breath.

'How can a man be so well versed in the ways of the universe but so ignorant about what is on his own doorstep?' Reverend Carter asked. 'It does, of course, beg one question.'

'Where did the moles go?'

'Exactly. Good to see an enquiring mind can emerge from the laboratories.'

'And a sense of humour from the seminaries,' Travers said. 'What are you doing here?'

'Searching. These woods would be a good start, I think. Good strong branches to attach a rope to.' He made to walk through the kissing gate that led into the trees.

'You seem convinced this boy is dead. That he killed himself.' Travers followed the man, picking over the shoots of wild garlic that littered the floor between the towering and twisted trees.

'Sin and cowardice come naturally to him. It's an obvious route to take. It's in his blood.'

'In his blood?'

The vicar stopped short. 'See, this is why I don't like people like you poking their noses in. People think that a vicar's job is to keep his flock on the straight and narrow, but you see, the Lord alone knows that is impossible. My job is to keep any deviations out of sight and mind. That's what keeps a parish happy.'

'I'm not here to cause a problem. I just have to look into what's going on.'

Carter looked at him, really stared into Travers' eyes until the younger man felt uncomfortable.

'There's something you're not telling me,' Carter said carefully. 'There might be things in this village that I don't want you to know, but until I know who you are and why you want to know, I'm saying nothing to you.'

Travers made to walk further in the woods, where the elms gave way to only the curled trunks of the hawthorns. Carter followed.

'And yet,' said Travers, stopping. 'You are going to follow me.'

'You're a stranger here.'

That was the vicar's only response. Travers didn't know if he meant to protect him, or keep an eye on him.

Tracking an unsuspecting boy through an English woodland should have been child's play after his time travelling the world in anthropological pursuits. Although he hadn't done that in a while. It all kind of died out after Tibet and the Doctor... and that was eight years ago. It didn't seem so long.

He looked for tracking clues. The child would likely have fled away from the sound of his and Carter's voices. The grass underfoot was slightly flattened and had less dew when he followed it deeper into the woods. Footprints obviously only happened in Agatha Christie's novels, but there was enough evidence for Travers to start looking in that direction. He grunted and motioned to Carter. They set off through the trees, Travers keeping his eyes on the ground. Above his head, he heard the crows continue to follow from tree to tree.

After a few hundred yards, he saw a change. A clearing in the trees, a hollow of bare earth in the forest floor with broken, snapped trees all around. It was a bomb crater.

A lonely relic of a German plane that had come back from Liverpool or Manchester without emptying its bomb bay. In the centre were a collection of little mounds, like burial chambers. Travers knelt in the hole and started to pull back the earth with his hands, feeling through the loose soil and letting it flow between his fingertips. Then he felt it, a solid shape, slight and fragile. He pulled it out.

Velvety black skin, oversized claws and almost blind eyes stared back at him from the corpse.

'You've found them then,' said Carter. 'But who buried them?'

Travers turned and put a finger to his lips.

'Right!' he shouted. 'You had better come out now.'

He heard the crunch of sticks behind him.

'There you are,' he said, turning around.

The boy must have been just eight or nine, standing there in his short trousers. His face had the sullen look of a child secretly scared.

'The Lander boy.' Carter folded his arms. 'And what are you doing here?'

Travers sighed. 'That's enough!' he snapped. 'I'll speak to this child. You keep looking for the missing boy.'

Carter tutted. He turned and lumbered off into the forest. Travers waited until he was out of sight. He turned back to the boy and held his hand out.

'It's all right,' Travers said. 'I'm just looking for Charles. If you've got anything to help me, that would be wonderful.'

The boy looked down and took a careful step towards him.

'These moles have been given a proper Christian burial,' Travers said, trying to encourage the lad. 'Did you do it? Did you say prayers for them?' Was he edging into mockery? He wasn't sure. Children were never his strong point, even Anne and Alun. Like all fathers, he struggled with any child older than his own. 'It's okay. I won't tell the farmer. I'm not too keen to see them strung up like that anyway.'

'It weren't us as buried 'em!' the child blurted out.

Travers sat down and patted the ground next to him. 'Jacob, isn't it? Sit down, start from the beginning. Who is us and who buried them?'

The child sat. He still looked away as he spoke.

'Us. Me an' Charlie, we come 'ere all the time. It's our fort over there.' He pointed at a dense bush that had been buttressed with sticks and branches from the fallen trees.

'I see.'

'But two days back, there was a coupla new uns 'ere. Boy and a girl. I can remember them being odd.'

'How so?'

'I don't know. They just felt, sort of, wrong.'

Travers sighed. 'Well, what did they look like? How were

they dressed?'

'Looked like they were in a play,' Jacob said. 'The girl had a long skirt on. I remember that because it was dragging through the leaves. They were all stuck to it. She had all her hair covered in a bonnet too. Boy had old clothes and a big old hat. And long trousers. I ain't had long trousers since cloth went on the ration years ago.'

'I see. Anything else?'

'Well, they weren't playing. They were just wandering and talking like. Least, I think it were talking. You couldn't hear them but they was nodding and acting like they was.'

'Did Charles speak to them?'

'Yer, he did. Likes going up to folk does Charles.'

Travers was sure of this at least. That was the reason they were all now here. 'What did he talk to them about?'

'This and that. He wanted to find out where they were from. I think he had a thing for the girl. Kept guessing things like as them being Jew refugees or German spies.'

'What did you think?'

'They weren't no Germans. But they was weird. Didn't wanna say much to us. So Charles sort of followed them out of the woods, that's when they saw the moles on the hedge. Then they got even more weird.'

Travers thought. Were they not acting odd enough before?

'It was like they'd found their own relatives there. The girl was beside herself. Weeping like a running tap. The boy pulled 'em all down off the spikes, laying them on the ground. She put them all in the sack. Charles said he knew where to bring them, he brought them, back here. And then...'

Travers leaned closer. This felt key. 'What then?'

'Well, that's just it, you see. Charles went up to them; I can remember him holding his hand out to take one of the moles. Then they both took his hand. One on each side, but that's it. I can't remember anything else that happened.'

Travers jumped up.

'Well, what do you remember?'

'I dunno. I been trying to work out what came next in me head. I think I was next in my own bed. But I can't remember how I got there.'

Travers could remember nights like that when he should

have been writing his dissertation. He was pretty sure that nine-year-old children shouldn't have experiences like it.

'And Charles?' He had a sinking feeling that he knew the answer to this.

'That was the last I saw him.'

'When was this?'

'Afternoon, two days back.'

So, that was it. This boy was the last one to see the missing child alive. If Travers had any doubt that this was a job for the Fourth, it was dispelled. They had to find the strange children.

He stood and looked around. He couldn't see Carter. He imagined the man was long gone. As much as he clearly enjoyed interfering in lives, he was far too proud to eavesdrop.

'I think you need to get home.' Travers shivered, despite the sun. 'There's something close to this wood that I don't trust.'

But there were other leads, other things to think about. As he got back to the house, he yelled for Cownall.

'Professor?'

'Get into the War Office and County Hall. I need these details.' Travers handed him the list.

'What if they don't give me anything?'

'Use your initiative, man. You're supposed to be working for a top secret special ops team answerable directly to the PM. If you can't throw some official weight around, you should probably ask for a transfer.'

'That's what got me into this mess in the first place.' Cownall stuffed the list into his top pocket. 'I'll hit County Hall directly, Prof.' Travers winced. 'See you by the evening.'

As the chap left, Travers headed for the kitchen. A piece of hard bread and a painfully small amount of cheese remained. Cownall had taped a notice to the top of the corned beef and potatoes that they were waiting for the night's supper.

Travers thought of the curried meats and sweetened bread he had enjoyed on his travels through India and China. What he wouldn't give to be back out there now. He hastily made and consumed the sandwich before heading out again.

In every village in England, you could be assured of one

25

man that always knew what was going on.

From the outside, *The Black Boar* looked far too big to be a village pub, with its two wings and multiple outbuildings, it was clearly an old coaching inn, designed for a more sedate time.

As he entered the bar, the illusion of history was shattered. Khaki covered half of the available seats, along with a cluster of rifles in one corner, wallpaper – unchanged for decades – peeled from the walls.

There was one solitary patron, an elderly lady sat at one of the tables, her beige suit mixing well with the discarded army issue bags. She looked vaguely familiar, although Travers couldn't place from where. Her walking stick leaned against her table as she nursed a small bottle of stout. That was certainly a rarity.

The landlord caught his eye. Travers approached the bar. He turned back to see if he could catch the name of the lady's drink.

Her table was empty.

The landlord must have mistaken his look of surprise.

'Home Guard, having an exercise on the moors. They use this place as a base.'

Perhaps he had been mistaken. The woman's clothing had looked a little like the kit bags strewn around. Then there was the sudden shift from the bright sunlight outside to the gloom of the bar. Easily done.

'Are you open?'

The man paused from wiping the bar. 'Until two. What will it be?'

Travers checked his watch. 'Half a mild.'

As it was poured, the landlord left an expectant silence in the air, a dare for Travers to fill it. He didn't. For once, he felt that it was best to let silence soak into the room and let someone else start the conversation. He wasn't Poirot.

'Investigation going well, Professor?'

Travers could swear he had encountered close knit primitive tribes in Asia that spread news slower than this village did.

'Reasonably. My job is more an observation. If there are

any criminal matters, that role lies with the police. Short of enemy action obviously.'

The landlord nodded and pushed the pint over. 'Something brought the plane down. Only young Peeves saw it. If it was the usual altitude mistake, I daresay you wouldn't be here.'

'There is one thing,' Travers said. 'I'm wondering if there is any history of this kind of thing; children going missing and that sort?'

The man shrugged. 'How much history do you want? Us Thatchers have been running this inn for the last three hundred years.'

Travers smiled. 'I'm an anthropologist. Three hundred years is a good start.'

The other man laughed, and extended his hand. 'Derek; pleased to meet you. I know your name, Professor Travers. Come with me. I'll show you something.'

He came from behind the bar and started towards the stairs leading up to the inn's rooms.

'Leave the beer, it's quite safe here.'

Travers took a sip and regretfully agreed.

Derek led him up the narrow stairs, past woodchip wallpaper to the landing. With no lights on, they could barely see from the limited glow left by the tiny paned windows. The walls of this ancient place bulged inwards as Travers was led down the corridor, past rooms full of Home Guard kit, spare radios and camouflage nets. The feeling was of being in a building liable to, not so much collapse, but constrict the two of them inside itself.

At the end of the corridor, Derek opened a further door, using his keys. 'Watch your step,' he said.

Beyond, Travers finally felt that he was in the seventeenth century coaching inn that he had seen from outside. Plastered and whitewashed walls enclosed a narrow oak staircase. The light dimmed further as they climbed up the steps, hearing the creak of little used beams as they went.

They emerged into a room, the dim light from the stairs showed it to be a good sized one, but with little in it, except a wardrobe and an old bed with a tatty eiderdown barely covering the mattress.

Travers looked about him, ducking his head under the oak beam that stretched through the room from end to end. Derek pulled back the blackout blind on the small dormer window to let some light through.

'We don't use this place much. Only when rooms are really tight. To tell the truth, the soldiers know this place and they prefer to kip on the floor downstairs.'

'Go on,' said Travers.

Derek Thatcher sighed and looked out of the window. 'It happened years back, when old Vic was on the throne and my grandad was a lad. Big bustling place this inn was back then. The road from Manchester to Sheffield was still in use. Landslip took that road away thirty year ago. Left us at the bottom end of nowhere with a pub that's so big that it's a bugger to keep the rats out of. Pardon my language.'

Travers had heard far worse from squaddies and indeed mountaineers. He merely smiled.

'Getting back to it, the Smythe family came to stay here, Mister and Misses and little Jonathan. Not long married and doing well from the cotton industry. Stopped off on the way to Yorkshire to catch a night's sleep before the next stage. My great grandma gave them this room. Best room in the house back then, it was.'

Travers thought of his own family holidays. Truth be told, there hadn't been much of that so far, but as Alun and Ann grew, well, it was always hopeful that this terrible war would end and some kind of normality could come back. Imagine that, holidays on a beach with no sea mines floating off the foreshore.

'That night, no one knows what happened,' said Derek. 'My grandad told me he remembered being woken up by a scream. Not just any scream, something unnatural, something primal. My great grandad got his sword and he ran for where it came from.' He paused. 'It was this room. You want to know what he found here?'

Travers placed one hand on the low beam for support and nodded. After Tibet, nothing was too outlandish.

Derek continued. 'Mr Smythe curled up in a ball under that bed, whimpering and pointing at the window. There was no bedspread on the bed though. Mrs Smythe had tied it round her own neck and used it to hang herself from the same beam that you're leaning on right now.'

At this, Travers, despite himself, jumped back slightly. He looked at the beam, at his own eye level.

'How tall was she?'

Derek nodded approvingly. 'Looking for holes in the story? She was a normal size, I think. It takes a lot of determination to hang yourself from a low point, doesn't it? But she went through with it. Whatever she saw out of that window, she didn't want to see again.'

'And the boy? Jonathan, wasn't it?'

Derek pointed at the window. 'That's the thing, never seen again. The window was open, no sign of his having fallen out and hurt himself. Whoever and whatever terrified Mr and Mrs Smythe took their son and never returned him.'

'The husband?'

'Never spoke again. Never truly functioned again. Got carted off to an asylum somewhere in Wales. They say he used to draw pictures of devils on the walls whenever he got hold of a pencil.'

'And you believe this?'

Derek looked at Travers in dead seriousness. 'In all of his life, my grandfather never lied to me once. If this is what he says happened, this is what happened. I'm not saying it was the same thing that took young Peeves. But you asked about missing children. He was a missing child.'

Travers looked out of the window, over the fields. Could it be? Yes. Gibbet's Woods, a direct line of sight from this window of all windows.

'You know the strangest part?'

'Let me guess,' said Travers, trying to get a handle on the distance from here to the woods. 'The little boy's ghost still runs up and down the corridors.'

Derek laughed. 'You think I'm having you on. Well, the strangest bit is that there's no ghost. Not of that little boy. You can still hear his father's scream some nights, or the creak from that beam as his mother's body swings from it. She keeps me awake as she rocks back and forth. But little Jonathan Smythe? If any trauma befell that boy, it happened far from here.'

Travers shivered, despite himself. 'Who owns that woodland?'

Derek followed Travers' pointing hand. 'Gibbet's? No idea. All the kids play down there. It's not far from Owd Hob's Mead. The folk that live there might have it.'

'Do you know a boy and a girl that go there often?'

Derek snorted. 'This is a small village without much to do, Professor. If you want a boy and a girl that disappear together into the woods frequently, you'll have to be more specific.'

Travers ran the conversation back and forth. Something bothered him.

'Owd Hob's Mead... The Devil's Field?'

'That the name? Well, it suits them. The folks that live there; we've always called them the Boggarts. I ain't ever been up there, but they never come down neither. Must be the most incestuous family going. Pretty sure they ain't got no children. Least, never seem 'em in the village with them.'

'Thank you. You've been most helpful.' Travers turned to go back down the stairs.

Behind him, Derek carefully replaced the blackout blinds.

CHAPTER THREE
The Search by Miss Le Croissette

'WHAT A BEAUTIFUL place Sheffield would be, if Sheffield were not there.' It was an old quotation that Eileen had heard once. She hadn't truly understood it, thinking that someone had just really hated a particular town up north. Now, as she advanced up one of the hills that rose above the factories, shops and theatres below, she understood better. Many years ago, this would have been a land of rolling countryside separated by valleys full of charming brooks and streams, like the neighbouring moors of the Peak. Now the hills served to bring her high above the smog that permeated the air, draining into her throat as she walked. They also served to cause her muscles to ache in a way they hadn't since she'd enlisted.

She had never been given orders to socialise by a superior before. But then, she'd never before been given many of the orders she now got in the Fourth. Mrs Roberts had taken the telegram to Hilda from Eileen. In it, Eileen had played the pure innocent. Two long separated friends meeting in the middle of a war, and then she would try and find where the missing Ministry money and resources were going. Because it certainly wasn't leaving the factory as steel parts for Avro Lancaster and Spitfire crankshafts.

Her plan was that she would have a walk around the city first before arriving at Hilda's house, to give her a chance to get the lie of the land, as well as to clear her head on her first assignment with the Fourth. The little walk around the city was the part that she was regretting.

She was nearly at the house, up a series of steps that led from the street to a parade of villas set up and away from the street. Nothing in this city could possibly be on the same level as anything else.

She let her bag fall off her shoulder to reach the knocker. The door opened a crack to reveal a defiant lady, in her housecoat and holding a duster in one hand.

'Whats'a want?'

'I'm looking for Hilda?' Eileen wasn't sure why she was asking. 'Is she in digs here?'

A nod. 'She's got a room here. Not back yet.'

'Can I wait for her here?'

A sniff. 'Careless talk, love. I don't know thee from Adam. There's girls from all the Services and factories living here. Can't trust thee without one of them speaking up for thee.' The door closed in Eileen's face.

Well.

Eileen picked up her bag. *Let's think about this logically.* Hilda had said that she'd be back at three. It was now four. If she wasn't at home and she knew that Eileen was due, there was only one sensible place to start looking, and that was the factory; Pickering's Steel Works by the River Don.

As she set off back down the hill, Eileen tried to contain the thought that if Hilda wasn't home in time to meet her, something was already seriously wrong.

The clock set in the archway above the compound entrance read quarter to five. The steelworks had taken some work to find with no road signs, yet the sign above Pickering's works remained. Eileen approached the gatehouse.

'Is Hilda Graves still here? She was supposed to finish at two but didn't meet me.'

The guard put away his copy of the *Star* and took a deep drag on his cigarette. 'No idea, love.'

'Could I come in and look?'

He sighed. 'Tha knows how many people work here? About three 'undred. Tha knows how many I know by name? About ten. And any one of 'em ten would sack me if I started letting thee wander around poking tha nose in where it's not wanted.' He pointed back out into the street. 'If I were you, I'd go wait for her. She's probably shacked up with some GI somewhere. You know what they say, "Overpaid, over…"' He coughed. 'Well, you know the rest.'

Eileen turned, hiding her red face. It wouldn't be like Hilda to shack up with anyone, least of all an American soldier. Still, it had been a couple of years since Eileen had last seen her. Eileen walked away from the archway that marked the entrance, waiting until she got around the corner before she stopped.

One missing friend and some dodgy accounting was no reason to go breaking into a factory that was assisting the war effort. She trudged away down the street, heading in no particular direction around the perimeter of the steelworks, walking on the pavement opposite the walls of the works, past parked flatbed lorries.

There was a further gate. An enormous wooden affair clearly designed for vehicles, with a small hole through which the padlock was threaded. She looked through it. Beyond another large, green liveried truck a few yards from her peep-hole, she could see nothing.

She looked around and let a sudden smile wash over her face. There was certainly some advantage to the hilly terrain of this city.

From there, she could see down onto the steelworks itself, a square, brick wall compound surrounded massive sheds built in an impossible to follow labyrinth of lanes, extensions and bridges, in which hundreds of men and women worked shaping the metal. Eileen knew from experience how quickly extra planes were needed. She remembered hearing that a place over by Chester had built a Wellington bomber in just a day. Sometimes, she felt that her role in the Filter Room had been the easy one to take. While these girls worked in dangerous, back breaking labour to get the planes back up, she and her commanders had directed them into a position where some of them must surely be shot down in flames. Places like this supplied the meat behind the pieces that the girls pushed around the boards in the Ops Room.

The works were quiet as she looked down from the small hillock. There was nothing stopping her from being there. It was just a patch of wasteland, a remnant from a bombing raid months ago that had been cleared, ready for redevelopment when the country got a chance to breathe again. She could see one of the sheds was larger, hulking at the back with a pair of huge steel doors across its entrance, a contrast to the simple wooden doors the rest of the buildings had. Out of use? Or was something in there that shouldn't be seen by prying eyes? She could see that the lorry which had blocked her view earlier was parked with its back end to the shed's loading bay. Clearly the place was in use.

Eileen made up her mind. She was going to head back up to Hilda's digs and see if she had arrived back yet. If not, then it would be time to speak to the local constabulary and start to throw the Fourth's weight around.

Later, Eileen sat in the pub opposite the house, *The River Cottage*. Four years ago it would have been unheard of for a respectable woman to sit alone in a place like this. Times had changed. A group of girls fresh off their shift had already gathered by the bar. There were no military bases close by either. Eileen supposed that kept the standard up. It appeared decent enough: clean, respectable, if on the whole elderly clientele, and a place that was happy to furnish her with a cup of tea. She was, after all, on duty. She'd asked and discovered that they had a room free. The landlady of *The River Cottage* had believed her when Hilda's own landlady had near enough chased her from the door again. So, Eileen at least had a room for the night, if she wanted it. As the piano started up and the folk songs began, she wondered how much of it she would be able to sleep through.

The smoke rose off the tables to swirl around the lights of the ceiling and Eileen watched it, trapped between the blackout blinds and illuminated by the amber lights and red cigarette ends. Was this so different to being inside the steelworks themselves?

The crowd began to build, women and men, some fresh off their shift and covered with dirt and grime. She felt out of place, a fraud and trapped.

She had to leave, just five minutes and fresh air and she would feel better. She stood and headed for the door.

'Mind you close the inside one before you go out, love!' shouted an old gent by the door, ARP helmet on his table.

Eileen nodded, keeping her counsel. He wouldn't have

treated her like such an idiot if she were in uniform. In any event, it was June. Nearly the longest day. It was brighter out than in right now.

Outside, she felt free of the atmosphere in the bar room. She still had her overnight bag with her, and her respirator of course. She resolved to stay here, to perhaps walk around and clear her head. She'd felt a sense of almost panic rising as she contemplated a strange city without a friend to stay with.

She looked from side to side. Could it be? Yes! There was Hilda, her walk hadn't changed in the time since she'd last seen her. That slight lolloping gait, like someone with springs in her heels.

'Hilda!' she called. 'Where have you been?'

The figure in front of her stopped. Eileen could see that she was still wearing her overalls and had streaks of black dust and grime across her face. The other woman paused, staring at her, then her face cracked into, not exactly a beaming smile, but at least an interested one.

'Eileen! Eileen Le Croissette! What are you doing...?' She trailed off. 'Of course, you were coming to visit. You're in the area. At Finningley.' She sighed. 'Look, it's a bit of a bad time. The factory is running right on capacity now. We're throwing everything at...' She paused again. '...Our current product.'

'Wonderful, you can tell me all about it over a brew.' Eileen motioned towards the house.

'There's not a lot of time. I'm just back for a few hours kip. Then I'll be back there tomorrow morning. I'll set the camp bed up for you. I'm sure you're used to worse in the WAAF. We both were. Then, you should probably get back to base tomorrow.'

Hilda was distant. It wasn't like her. Eileen could remember the days they had spent together in the training huts. Eileen's head had always been for numbers, but Hilda was the practical one. She had always been the first to get weapons drill.

But there was no joking in Hilda's eyes. Eileen was getting used to that. As much as this war brought people together, it fundamentally changed those who were apart. You had no idea what might have happened to a friend in a year or two years. When you met again, there was too much going on to catch up and explain. Everyone had a hundred stories that they would never tell. You simply had to take the stranger standing in your friend's shoes and build a connection with what was given to you.

'Well, I'll walk down to the factory with you tomorrow anyway. It's been a long time.'

Hilda started for her door, then turned quickly. 'There's nothing there to concern the WAAF. Come on, I need some sleep.'

'Well they are our planes, Hilda...' Eileen started but Hilda pushed past, striding for her house.

Eileen recovered enough to follow at a scamper, just in time to follow her friend inside. The landlady was just reaching the hallway and saw Eileen. She sniffed.

'Good to see tha were an honest 'un. Mind tha feet on t'tiles.'

Eileen dutifully stepped out of her outdoor shoes and followed Hilda up the stairs.

Hilda was true to her word. She set up Eileen's camp bed with minimal talking, had a very swift wash at the sink, scrubbing to try and get the worst of the grime off and then took to her own bed.

'What's it like in the steelworks?' Eileen asked. If she was going to be kicked out of here tomorrow, she needed something to go back to London with.

Hilda turned in her bed. 'Hot, loud, dirty. Like nothing you've ever seen before. You learn a lot of new language from the men that stayed on as well. Luckily my section is all women. Mr Huxtable likes it that way.'

'What do you make in your section?'

A sigh from the bed. 'I shouldn't talk about it. Wartime secrets.' She rolled back over. 'How is the WAAF now?' came her muffled voice. It sounded like an exercise in politeness.

Eileen told her what she could. She was using her head, getting to put her maths skills to the test. She didn't mention the Filter Room, it may have been an open wound still. She stayed very clear of Gulliver Base and her meeting with Professor Edward Travers a few months ago. She was still looking for her place in the Fourth and feeling like she had been drafted in to keep her under watch. After Gulliver Base, she knew too much.

'Do you prefer it to what we had before?' Hilda had turned back to her.

'Prefer the war?'

Hilda gave a half laugh. 'Sort of. Do you prefer it now? We're working, getting a wage. Not much but something. Trusted to do the work that the men were doing. We can go out, have a drink, see a show without anyone raising an eyebrow. The streets are ours now.'

'I'd prefer not to have the raids,' said Eileen. 'I feel like I'm doing my bit and doing it well.' She didn't know what it was like in the steelworks, but she knew that in the Filter Room the top dog was certainly not in a WAAF uniform skirt.

'Yes. It was just a thought.' Hilda sighed. The conversation was clearly over.

Eileen lay in the darkness, listening to her former friend's breathing. She still felt that something here was definitely amiss. The idea that the WAAF should be kept from the factory that made their own planes was a bizarre one. Eileen had signed the Official Secrets Act in the WAAF. The Fourth sat a level above the Act. They were above top secret. It had been made quite clear to her that if she opened her mouth about what she saw in her new role, she would be locked up. 'Not in a military prison mind you,' the sergeant showing her around the Fourth's HQ had said. 'If you told anyone outside of here about what we do, they'd stick you in an asylum.' Eileen thought he was half-joking. Still, it effectively meant that there was little of the conventional War that was out of bounds to her. Or at least, little that should be. She owed it to her new employers to investigate the factory further.

She turned, hearing the springs of the camp bed squeak and groan as she did so. She lay still, an uncomfortable position but a better one than she had been in.

Suddenly self-conscious and vulnerable in this room, with its peeling wallpaper and a stranger lying next to her. Her every instinct was to get out and sleep elsewhere, however, she simply had to follow Hilda tomorrow.

Something was in those sheds.

Finally, as the red light started to spread from behind the pub, creeping slowly up the walls, Eileen woke and sensed movement across the room. She almost held her breath as Hilda stood, pulled her overalls and boots on, tied a scarf across her hair and thumped out the room and down the stairs. She didn't even stop for breakfast. Eileen pushed the covers back and got up to follow her.

Even as she pulled her civvies on, while running down the stairs, Hilda was almost out of sight down the road by the time Eileen managed to leave the house. This early in June, the light first thing was bright enough that she could see her friend's back retreating down the tree-lined avenue towards the factory. Staying far enough back that she could duck into doorways should Hilda turn around, Eileen followed.

The women and men from the steelworks were out in force, leaving their shifts, going to their shifts, overalls covered in grime, ash and soot, the men flat-capped, the women with hair tied back with scarves in a hundred brightly-coloured patterns. Symbols of rebellion against the conformity that war inflicted. The steel mills here never stopped. Thousands of men and women keeping them going every hour of the day, leaving sleep and their families, the steel mills kept turning, hammering away all night long through sun, rain, darkness and air raids.

At the foot of the hill, Hilda walked into Pickering's Steelworks, but Eileen didn't even attempt to follow her inside, she knew that she was never going to get in the doorway. The only thing to do was to watch from her bombed out vantage point.

Unlike the other steelworks, she saw that there were few workers inside the Pickering compound at that time in the morning, and those who were moved with a certainty of purpose. Why so few?

Eileen watched as a group of girls, Hilda included, converged on the single building she had seen earlier, set apart from the rest. A large, almost hanger-like structure with two huge iron doors across its entrance that swung open as they approached. Eileen peered closer, trying to get a look at what was inside. A framework of geodesic designs and metal. Blue and yellow sparks flared from somewhere within. She could see nothing more before the doors slammed shut behind the girls.

The yard was now as quiet as the grave again.

What was in there? And why set it apart from the rest of the works? Every other building was connected, presumably to allow for materials to be craned or conveyed around. The one Hilda had entered was an island.

Eileen was still coming to terms with being backed by the might of the Fourth and their powerful benefactor. Even so, waltzing in and demanding to see this, that and the other wasn't a good idea. Firstly, Fourth or not, she remained a Section Officer in the Woman's Auxiliary Air Force and was unlikely to have the clout to get anywhere. Secondly, it would likely only lead to important evidence going AWOL, something General Dornan would take a dim view of.

But Hilda was in there and Hilda was not herself. Hilda was acting, she hated to say it, German. She reminded Eileen of the German workers she had seen scurrying around Bonn shortly before the war, living only to work and sleeping as little as possible.

She knew then that she was going to have to go undercover to get in. But before she did so, she needed to alert the Fourth. If she didn't come back, someone was going to have to find her.

As she turned, she saw a man that was watching her.

He stood, staring back at her, his back, ramrod straight, like a colonel, but dressed completely in civilian clothes, a black suit and tie. A pair of binoculars were held in one hand.

'What are you doing? Are you watching me?'

He shook his head. 'I could ask you the same.' A clipped accent, just a trace of Scots. 'I'm checking this position for future development. We're short of factories after all.'

'Well,' Eileen said with a huff, 'I was just looking for a good view of the city.' That was a weak excuse. This was a public place. She didn't have to justify herself to this man.

She marched away from the edge, through the rubble. The man stood back, arching an eyebrow as he did so, to let her pass.

'Watch your footing, young lady. These bomb sites can be dangerous.'

She continued down the street. She found a phone box and

put a call through. A message for General Dornan.

'Worried that birthday boy will see what is in his present. Will wrap it in brown paper to be safe.'

CHAPTER FOUR
Agent Le Croissette

EILEEN STOOD in front of the archway again, its huge clock face looking down at her. There were no workers trooping in and out at that moment; it clearly wasn't a shift change. She approached the guard again. She'd done her best with her hair to get it looking as different as possible to the previous day, found clothes that looked as unlike yesterday's clothes as any could do in the middle of a war. She showed him her WAAF ID card. He raised an eyebrow.

'No planes here, love.'

'I've been told my numbers aren't up to scratch.' God, it hurt her to say this. 'They think I should find an alternative for the duration. I'm just waiting for my papers to come through. I'd really like to work on something that still involves the planes. Can I please look at what the work here is?' She could see that he was wavering. Just a little further push. 'Please. You can see that I've done top secret work before. I just want to see if this is right before they start sending me out to the country to plough fields instead.'

That seemed to do it. He motioned to her to go through the gate, closing it behind her.

'Head for that shed over there,' he said, pointing. 'That's t'machine shop. Probably safest part of t'works. Can't get burned to death in there, just lose a limb or two. Ask for Jane. She's my niece. She'll show you around. Got a good head on her shoulders but at the end of the day, the line could probably do with a break from her to keep it running smoothly, if you get my drift.'

Eileen feigned a brief laugh and started to head towards the shed. She turned, to see if he was still following her. He was. A smile and a nod. She was going to have to walk into the suggested shed. The one she wanted to look in, the sealed one that Hilda had disappeared into, was the other end of the site. It would take some serious work to make it all the way there without being challenged. *Harder still,* she thought, *to make it out again.*

Her stomach rang hollow. This was it. All she could think was: *They shoot spies, don't they?*

Inside the shed, sunlight still shone down through holes in the roof, interspersed with the arc lights. The roar of a generator and about a dozen women hammering and drilling at steel filled the air. There was no way that Eileen was going to get hold of 'Jane' in here. She would never hear her. There was, of course, the silver lining that everyone was so devoted to their tasks that there was no way that they would notice a short, inoffensive little lady. She quickly crossed the floor, heat from machines causing sweat to drip down her neck.

Once this place would have made steel for cutlery, automobiles and locomotives. But with the men gone to war, the women working here were left to make it for bombs, bullets and planes. The men made steel for peace, the women for war.

A hand grabbed her wrist. She turned.

Not all men were gone. It was a foreman. Clearly too old for call up or too skilled to be allowed to leave. He released her and stood back, arms folded.

'Where do you think you're going?' he shouted over the din.

'I'm looking for Jane.' Eileen repeated her story, willing the man to believe it as she flashed her ID again. He turned and pointed.

'That's her over there. Grab her quick. That's the second batch that's had to be reforged this week. When your papers come through, don't be surprised to take her place.'

Eileen started towards the slight figure with her blonde hair pulled back behind a scarf. She glanced behind her; the foreman's eyes followed her steps. A shame, she would be better without Jane on tow.

The girl looked up as Eileen approached.

'You look lost.'

'Oh, I am,' said Eileen. 'I'm probably going to be kicked out of the WAAF. I'm just seeing what this place entails. The chap at the front said you could show me around.'

Jane nodded enthusiastically. 'Happy to.' She looked up at the foreman who clearly indicated that she could go. 'Come on, let's start at the beginning.'

They started in the next shed along, near the front of the factory and next to what looked like a pile of scrap metal. From inside came a roar that caused the ground to shake like a beast aching to escape. Jane pushed open a side door.

'It's pretty noisy in here when it's running,' she said.

Inside, the machinery stretched the length of the room, and the noise it made felt almost solid from wall to wall.

'It's an Electric Arc Furnace. The scrap metal gets loaded in the far end and melted down. Then...' Sparks exploded from the top of the furnace, a bright flash flickering against the walls, the high-pitched crackling pounding Eileen's eardrums. '...A current passes through the molten metal to reduce the carbon.' Jane was shouting now. 'It comes out the far end as good quality steel, ready to be shaped into sheets, rolls, bars. Whatever is most appropriate.' Her breath running out, she pointed back out of the shed for both of them to leave. 'The men say that Mr Huxtable replaced the old Bessemers with this thing when he took over from the Pickering family. State of the art, you see. Better control of the final product.'

'What's Mr Huxtable like?' Eileen asked as the noise died down.

Jane's face took a faraway look. 'Look around this place. There's some men, but Mr H was happier than most to take women on when the rest of the men went off to war. Special projects is all women, I hear.' She smiled. 'And unlike the rest of the works in Sheffield, he made sure to top up the conscription wages with his own money. We get paid the same as the men. That's unheard of! I mean, we're all conscripts, aren't we? But we landed on our feet at this place and no mistake. You won't hear a bad word said about Mr H in these walls.'

As they stepped out into the yard again, Eileen pointed

toward the large shed at the back, the double iron doors firmly closed. 'What's that one for?'

Jane looked at it. 'Special projects, innit? You're not allowed in there unless you've been selected. Totally different shifts to the rest of us.'

'What do they make there?'

Jane shrugged. 'Something top secret, I think. For the War Office. To take out the Jerries. Right,' she said, 'once we've got the steel bars or whatnot, it's over to the forge to be shaped into something useful.' She started to walk towards another shed. 'You need to know that if the siren goes, we keep working. I was on a crane during a raid once. They left me up there for the whole raid. I could hear the bombs dropping around me.'

Eileen thought of being trapped up there, the thumps of the bombs drawing closer, knowing that every moment could be her last. It was bad enough underground during her time in London, seeing all the terrified faces peering out of steel bunks in the tube stations.

'You must have been brave,' she said.

'I was a wreck. I didn't have a choice. I was trapped up there, shaking and crying. That's when they put me into the machine shop.' Jane sighed. 'It were a terrible raid. Last year.'

Eileen remembered the bombed-out wreck that she had used as a vantage point. 'Were the steelworks badly hit?' she asked.

Jane shook her head. 'Missed most of us. Hit the town centre. Lorraine was off that night though. They hit her street. I don't think she were ever found. They really hit us hard. We knew it were coming. Too important to miss.' There was almost pride in her voice.

Eileen thought of that image in her mind's eye as the bombers flew over London, that sick feeling in her stomach at the noise they made, lower as they approached, and the look of them in formation, never knowing when they would release their payload and who it would land on. It could be a favourite shop, a neighbour. Or it could be you.

She followed Jane through the rest of the works, the rolling mills, casting, heat treat and fettling. Each one dangerous in a different way, by fire or smoke or shrapnel or edge. But they avoided 'Special Projects', almost as if Jane couldn't even see it.

Finally, they stood outside again, the morning sun rising higher now and filtering through the high sheds and the gantries and chimneys that they sprouted like a nest of spiders.

'Thank you,' said Eileen.' You've been very helpful. It's given me a lot to think about.' She looked around. 'I think I know my way around now. I can probably find my own way back if you wanted to head back to your post?'

Jane was only too happy to leave her. Eileen watched her go, feeling terrible for taking advantage of such a trusting woman. As the blonde girl turned a corner, Eileen faced the lonely, isolated shed of 'Special Projects'.

'Right,' she said under her breath. 'Let's see what you're hiding.'

The high, iron doors were tightly closed. Carefully, Eileen looked around them. No keyhole, just two slabs of metal. She needed to see what was happening inside. She thought quickly and listened to the door. Inside, she could hear no conversation, but the sounds of hammering and welding. Something was being constructed in there, and the Fourth needed to know what.

She sighed. How to get inside without kicking up a fuss was the tricky bit. So, the girls went in at set times. The last shift had started hours ago when Hilda had gone in, but probably wouldn't be ending yet. But what did they need beyond labour? The steel. This was the worker's entrance. Where did the material go in?

She paced around, searching around the outside of the shed. There it was. The large works truck with huge bars of steel ready to be reversed into the loading bay, just as she had seen through the gate. It was a huge stroke of luck. The driver was already climbing up to the cab.

Please, thought Eileen, *let this be the blanks going in and not just a stack of really large forged parts heading elsewhere.*

She crept towards the loading bay, a shelf at head height leading into the shed, closed off now by wooden shutters. She kept close to the wall, low and out of sight behind the crates that littered the floor.

As the van backed in, the shutters were raised, clanking chains rattling as the crane was winched out over the Bedford..

Despite the noise, Eileen kept her breathing steady. She crouched under the lip of the bay. *Watch the workers*, she told herself. They hooked up one steel bar to the derrick, and it was lifted off and into the shed. Eileen counted under her breath. She got to thirty-two before she heard the muffled clang of the bar hitting the ground inside, followed by the clattering of chains as the hooks were brought back out. Half a minute to get in. Always assuming that no one was watching the entrance for that half-minute and the girls didn't get quicker with each load.

Eileen could see the driver's feet on the other side of the Bedford and the tell-tale wisp of smoke coming from beyond the cab. She was having a crafty cigarette. Good, keep her distracted.

As the second bar was lifted, Eileen waited until it disappeared through the loading bay doors, then leaped into action. Using the rear tyre as a boost, she scrambled up into the lip. A quick look around, she was on a concrete platform. The steel bars were being stacked to her left, the two girls dealing with the operation had their backs to her. Another stroke of luck. The pile to the right was full. Had they still been filling that one, she'd have been seen.

She dived off the platform, behind the pile of steel. Breathing hard, she looked around her. She could only see a part of the shed from here, none of the girls or foremen. There was a large pile of scrap, further along. That was much less likely to be a target for anyone to find her. Keeping low again, and glancing to her left to make sure no one saw her, Eileen scampered for the pile.

As she ran, she saw the rest of the factory, girls with their heads down working the forge, polishing the parts, welding them together. Skeletal frames dotted the floor in various states of construction, looking like nothing Eileen had ever seen before.

Behind the pile, Eileen tried to get a better look at the rejected objects. There was a box, the size of a small child. A strange weapon as well, a perfectly square cross section and a long rectangular shape; the interior fittings looked like a

Sten gun. There was a single ball-shaped object, but with pyramidal decorations jutting in almost all directions, like a Christmas star.

'They've been rejected, my dear.'

Eileen slowly turned.

'As really, should have been your application to join any covert operation. That was some terrible infiltration work,' said the aristocratic woman facing her.

In shock, Eileen realised that the woman only had one eye, a patch covered the other one. She had clearly made it herself because it matched her overalls.

'Come on, my office.' She turned and led the way. Eileen stood in shock for a moment. 'Well come on, girl, I haven't got all day.'

They crossed the floor, past numerous staring eyes, to a small wooden cabin in one corner. Inside were ledgers, pens and tallies. An accountant's stock in trade.

'See, my dear,' said the woman, dropping the blinds on the windows around the room and turning to Eileen with a face like a school mistress. 'Some of us were prepared to put the hours into spying. It's a lot easier to do it from the company accounts than crouching behind a scrap metal pile.'

Eileen felt a flush across her face, as well as anger. She really should have been better prepared, both by herself and General Dornan, before being dumped in at the deep end.

'So, who do you work for? And who are you?' Eileen asked.

The woman turned to her, a sceptical look on her face. 'I think, in all the circumstances, I should be asking the questions, don't you?'

CHAPTER FIVE
Suffer Little Children

PROFESSOR TRAVERS could see the hedge again; it stood a hundred feet high in front of him, the spikes in the brambles as long as his arm. Shapes hung from it, not moles this time, familiar forms; they seemed to shift as he approached, but they were clearly human.

More than just human, they were children, hundreds of children, pinned to the vegetation by the thorns, stabbing through their limbs like a pagan crucifixion by the hundreds. He couldn't help but come closer to those still forms, so innocent in the bright moonlight.

The closest one had a familiar shock of dark hair. He didn't want to, but his body drove him on, he reached out a hand to lift the chin up and see the face.

Anne's lifeless eyes stared back at him.

He woke with a yell and lay in bed, breathing hard. This mission was getting to him. It wasn't even his job to find the child. He should be looking into the downed plane.

Travers pulled himself out of bed and splashed water onto his face. He thought of the last time he had seen Anne and Alun, playing in the evening sun in the Goff's garden. A formation of planes had flown over.

'Look!' Anne had shouted. 'Halifaxes. It's all right, Alun, they're ours.' Alun had crawled out of his den laughing.

Travers hoped to be back with them soon, once he finished what he was doing here.

Cownall had returned just slightly too late last night for Travers to use the information that he had found. Yet, he had sufficient time now to be able to deal with the village's inhabitants on less of a back foot. He thought back to his last visit of the day before. The farm that lay just closer to the village than Gibbet's Wood. The farmer had greeted him in the surly way that he expected from everyone that worked there. The farmer had leaned against the door jamb of his farmhouse and grunted at Travers' introductions and background. No, he hadn't seen the child that had gone missing. Yes, he was sure. Then Travers had moved onto the subject of Owd Hob's Meade.

'The Boggarts? Yes, I know them well. Properly called the Hobsons, I think. Keep themselves to themselves and never speak to the rest of us. Been there as long as my own family have farmed these fields. Father used to say they were witches. You look at those fields of theirs. They grow crops on slopes. Arable hill farming year after year with nothing lying fallow. It's not possible.'

Travers' curiosity had deepened. He had spent so long out in the world chasing creatures of folklore. He should have stayed in England. Boggarts, he knew, were a mythical creature in northern English folklore, dark, mischievous, like the trolls of Scandinavia. Now, his curiosity in this task was piqued by something more than simply a missing child.

Moreover, it was the moorland high above that farm where the Bristol had met its end.

His first stop after breakfast was Mrs Peeves. She was already awake, bustling around her house, getting ready to head out to join the search parties. She greeted him coldly by the door at his request to enter.

'What have you got to offer me?'

Once, Travers would have barked at her about her obtuseness. Perhaps family had mellowed him.

'Right now, madam, nothing.' He fixed his eyes on her. 'But I am here to try to help. Please, can we speak?'

She let him in and directed him to the parlour. Tea was already in the pot. Silently, he was offered a cup. He poured a small amount, treading the balance between rudeness and not taking too much of her ration.

'To the point, Mrs Peeves. Did your son know that his father, Petty Officer Gerald Peeves, has deserted?'

She was silent. The clock ticked over the mantelpiece as she stared down at her own cup. Finally, she lifted her eyes, over to the window, searching for escape.

'How did you know?'

'A contact at the War Office.' More than that. A direct line.

'Men from the Navy. They visited to speak to me. To see if I knew where he had gone.' Still looking away. She placed her cup down with a careful chink. 'I never told Charles that his father had run away. He wouldn't understand.'

'Did you? Did you know where he went?'

She shook her head. 'Of course not.'

'Did you speak to anyone?'

She sighed. 'Only Reverend Carter.'

Ah. He let that sit in the conversation for a moment.

'Probably not the most sympathetic ear?'

She laughed with a short, sharp, bark. 'That man is not fit for the clergy. Since you've been digging into my past, I imagine you know why?'

Travers nodded slowly. 'I do. He obviously has strong morals to take issue over a difference of just a couple of weeks. Not that it should matter anyway.'

'Maybe,' she said. 'It would probably have been better if we hadn't kept Charles hidden from him until after the wedding.'

Despite himself, Travers laughed. 'Like the witch that did for *Sleeping Beauty*. What a conceited man.'

Mrs Peeves smiled at Travers, naturally. 'It's good to get an outside view of village life sometimes.' Her face hardened as her smile froze. 'But how can any of this help you?'

'I'm not sure. When did you last see Gerald?'

Her eyes snapped over to him, then back to the window. 'A week before they came to see me. He was home for a couple of days.'

'Where did he go while he was home?'

She was quiet for a long time. 'You need to understand. He's not the man he was before the war. He's different now. And food is so scarce. He just wanted to do something for his family. Every man does, don't they?'

Travers understood. 'He was a poacher. And he found you

something?'

She shivered. 'I didn't like it. It was only a fawn. Can't have been away from its mother for more than a few minutes. I wish he went for the old and sick ones. But he says the taste is too tough. I mean, there's a war on! You can't be too picky.'

'What did you do with it?'

Tears came to her eyes, quickly. 'Hung it in the larder; it's good to let them hang. I was going to butcher it and share the parts out with my friends. But then...' She swallowed hard. 'I came down the next morning and opened the larder.'

'It was gone?'

She shook her head, her eyes screwed up and cast downwards. She motioned for him to follow. He stepped into the kitchen, crowded with copper pans and wooden utensils. A farmhouse kitchen. A wooden door lead to the larder. She had bolted it and now drew the bolt back slowly, her hand shaking.

Inside was a husk, blackened and charred, its rear feet tied and suspended from the ceiling hook. Travers could see the empty sockets where the eyes had burned away. It had been hanging here for weeks, a dead black thing swinging to and fro.

Travers rubbed his chin. 'How'd it get burned?'

'I don't know. Go on, *Professor*, explain that. You can't, can you? The explanation is simple. This family is cursed.'

'But you left it here? For a week or more?'

She turned away, swung back and shut the door on the dangling corpse.

'It was the last thing my husband gave me. And besides, what else can I do with it? I'd sneak it out of the house and hide it, but every man for miles is spending every day searching for bodies in the moors and fields.' She slammed the bolt back.

She led him back to the parlour and took up her tea again, a shield of respectability against the truth he knew.

'Is there any way that Gerald could have contacted Charles after he disappeared?' he asked.

She snapped at him, tea spilling as she did so. 'And not me? Not his own wife?'

Travers drained his cup. 'Point taken, Mrs Peeves.' He

stood. 'Thank you for your help. You've given me some valuable background. I will see myself out.'

'Do you know what's happening here next Sunday?'

He gave his head a slight tilt. Unwilling to show ignorance, but wanting to her to speak further.

She sniffed.

'A well dressing. You don't have them where you come from, I shouldn't think. The children will all come together, all of his school friends, and decorate the well. Stories from the Bible. It won't be much with this war on.' She stared into space. 'I should like to know where he is before then.'

He left her sitting in her chair, hands gripping the arms in a futile attempt to retain control of a life that was rapidly slipping away from her.

When Travers arrived at the vicarage, the curtains were open, and the door locked with no reply. Clearly Reverend Carter was up and out. Down the road was the church, square spired and surrounded by an oversubscribed and overgrown graveyard.

As Travers stepped through the lychgate he could hear the organ inside. Clearly a practice session, but the unmistakable sounds of *Abide With Me* wafted across the churchyard. Travers paused for a moment. He was not given to religious thought. At times, the religions of the Far East having more draw to him than the established Church of his own country. It was a thought that didn't seem strange after his time at Det-Sen, the Monastery of the Second Dharma King.

He stepped out of the bright sun into the chill closeness of the church interior, his eyes taking a while to adjust to the sudden gloom. The music continued and Travers, drawing on his memories of long ago school assemblies, began to mumble along: 'Earth's joys grow dim, its glories pass away, Change and decay in all around I see…'

Slowly, the chords of the organ faded away and Travers advanced past the empty pews, sunlight catching them. Reverend Carter stepped away from the organ, approaching to meet him, as if to deny him the chance to enter deeper.

'Can I help you?'

Travers brought himself to a halt.

'I hope so, Reverend, I really do, because so far, you haven't. And you've given precious little help or hope to Mrs Peeves.'

The reverend sighed, cleaning his glasses on his cassock. 'You are here for a purpose I hope, and not to simply give baseless insults in our Lord's home?'

'Well, firstly, I think I have all the information I was hoping for about Gerald and Vivian Peeves. Their slightly untimely marriage being the basis of your rather irrational dislike, I understand.'

Carter shook his head. 'It was not, I think, the marriage that was untimely.'

'Well, if it bothered you so much, you should have found them an earlier slot,' snapped Travers. 'And then of course, there is Gerald's disappearance himself.'

'The man is a coward. Absent without leave. He left his ship shortly before it set sail. If the boy found out about it, he likely decided the shame was too much.'

'Well, I thought that might be something, but then I asked for his war record as well. Do you know his posting at the time? Engineers. Specialised Non-combatant role. He was servicing the ship he travelled on. What did he have to run away from? I think we have two disappearances, don't you?'

Carter sat down in a vacant pew.

'Maybe there are two disappearances. Both from the same family. What can I do about it?'

Travers stood over him. 'You can help me, finally. I've done the legwork to get the information that you could have told me. What it mostly amounts to, is that you don't like the family for rather pathetic reasons. There have been other disappearances, haven't there? Not recent.' Travers tapped his feet. 'I know about the Smythe family's boy at *The Black Boar* many years back. There must have been others.'

'Professor, I have served this parish for fifteen years. I cannot be expected to have an encyclopaedic knowledge of every tearaway and stray that is littered here.'

'I think you know more than you let on, Reverend. For instance, what do you know about the family at Owd Hob's Meade?'

Carter turned to Travers with a strange look in his eye.

'The Hobsons? What have they got to do with anything?'

'The boy was last seen with two children near the farm. They wore old style clothes, like something from the last century. They wept over dead vermin. The boy that saw them lost his memory. Sound strange to you?'

Carter sighed and shook his head. 'No.' He stood. 'Very well, follow me.'

He led the way into the vestry. There sat desks and bookcases, dust coating the shelves and tomes like an overcoat. Carter opened one drawer using a key.

'My predecessor kept this.' He withdrew a map and unrolled it. 'This is the parish of Edleton. Drawn about a hundred years ago. You see this outline?'

Travers followed Carter's finger to the fields and buildings surrounded by a thick black line. They lay the other side of Gibbet's Woods from the village.

'I was told that line is where God's reach ends.' Carter tapped the label that read: *Owd Hob's Meade*.

'And you believe that, do you?'

Carter shook his head. 'I believe a great many things, Professor. I don't believe that God's reach is limited on this Earth. But I am one man. If they wanted to be a part of my flock, the door has always been open.'

Travers grunted. He thought of the Peeves family and kept his own counsel.

Carter withdrew a small, leather bound book with a sigh. 'He also kept this. I haven't had cause to fill it. It's what you appear to be looking for. A list of souls that the vicars of this place could not lay to rest.'

Travers leafed through it. Names, ages, many of them young, going back to the seventeenth century and the Restoration. Parents were listed, sometimes children as well. Occasionally, not often, an entry would be crossed out and replaced with 'Found and laid to rest'.

But the majority were lost, simply names in these yellowing pages.

'I hoped never to fill it in,' said Carter. 'But as the days go on, it appears that there is evil here that has not gone away.'

'You know the derivation of the name, of course?'

'The Old Devil's Field. Of course I do. I had an education. But it goes further than that, doesn't it? You've no doubt heard the villagers call them the Boggarts?'

'I have.' Travers pulled his military issue Ordnance Survey map from his pocket and started to use a pencil to trace the outline of the Hobsons' land on it with a pencil.

'Well, Owd Hob is, according to folklore, the forefather of the Boggart creatures. A horned figure with the legs of a goat. The derivation is clear.'

'It is.' The sudden image appeared in Travers head. The Devil himself at the Smyths' window in the dead of night, stealing their son and driving them insane with fright. A flight of fancy. 'But I'm hoping that I find something more rational when I get there. What's that?' He tapped on the OS map. A feature marked 'stone circle' high on the hills behind the Hobsons' farm. It lay close to where the Bristol had come down.

'What it says. A circle made of stones.'

'I can read, Reverend. I meant what type; double circle, single, altar stone?'

'No idea. I tend to stay away.' Carter shrugged.

'Have you never been curious, man?' Travers banged a fist against the stone wall. 'About a Neolithic worship site in your own parish?'

'It might have been once. Now young men sleep out there on their last night as a bachelor.'

Travers rolled his eyes. 'Why the devil would they do that?'

'Tradition. Let's them sleep it off, I guess. Now, have you finished with that priceless parish artefact?'

Travers grunted and handed it back to Carter.

'What about burned livestock?'

'I beg your pardon?' Carter slammed the book back into its drawer.

'Animals. Burned to a crisp, no obvious source of ignition.'

Carter shrugged. 'I'd put that down to incendiaries. Not seen any, mind.'

'Right, time to pay a visit.'

'To Owd Hob's Meade? Good luck.' Carter gathered the map back up, folding it carefully.

'Thank you.'

Travers folded his own map and placed it in his jacket pocket. As he did so, he checked for the reassuring lump of his revolver. A man could never be too careful.

CHAPTER SIX
Trees

THE CROWS followed him again. Travers avoided the woods by taking the lane that ran directly to the house. It was a road that had been here a long time, twin ruts that had sunk below the level of the surrounding fields. The hedgerows on each side stretched to form an arch over his head, leading Travers to walk down a tunnel that led away from the modern world and its warfare. Every time the branches cleared to show enough of the sky, he could see the black birds settling on a nearby tree or branch.

They finally alighted on twin stone gateposts, covered in a soft damp carpet of moss. The farmstead beyond looked like a place out of time, tiny windows in a stone cottage that was so covered in vegetation itself that from a distance it appeared green. Wooden barn doors hung open on other buildings, revealing only darkness inside and no life of any sort. An old trap lay on the corner, the spokes on its wheels rotten and splintered and no horse stabled to pull it. A hand plough stood next to it. It was in better shape, but still appeared rotten. The yard was bare of the musty odour of animals and the stench of their muck, nothing underfoot but stone and earth.

'Hello!' he called. Nothing. 'My name is Edward Travers!' He doubted that would work, but good to get the introductions in early.

Entering the house would be a foolhardy opening gambit. He picked an outbuilding, one with an open door. He pushed it further, letting light fall inside. Nothing but grain. Bagged up and in stacks against the far wall. Somehow Travers doubted this selection would make it to the war effort. He thought of his earlier breakfast of stiff, hard bread and felt a sense of rising anger. Why had these people slipped beneath the radar so much? And where were they now?

He looked further around the farmyard. The neighbouring farmer he spoke to yesterday had been right. In a hillside community, bordering a famous grouse moor, these people had managed to create an entirely crop-based farm. It defied logic. It defied science. Even crops needed manure.

Then, he heard it. A child's laughter. High and unconstrained, before it was abruptly cut off, as if stifled by a parental hand. It had come from behind the farmhouse.

As he approached, he could see that the farmhouse did not stand alone. Tall walls extended away from it, enclosing some sort of outdoor space. A courtyard or a garden. He heard scuffling behind that wall, hisses and the sound of children trying to stay quiet.

He would have to go through the quiet, dead, farmhouse to get to that hidden garden. He placed his hand on the bare wooden door, sunk into the cracked and crumbling stone frame.

He felt rather than heard the steps behind him. He turned, not knowing what he would see.

They stood in a semi-circle. More footsteps joined the first, more figures moved in, their clothes old fashioned, shawls and bonnets, and broad hats above Edwardian-style beards. But there was something more, their hooded eyes fixed on him, gazing out of deeply lined faces. He felt pinned to the spot, that frustrating feeling of being in a dream and struggling to move or speak, feeling that anger and frustration build.

He tried to speak, tried to ask the questions he had, words would not come out.

He stood in the doorway, facing a semi-circle of something other, something that he felt simply did not belong. He dug deep, forced his mouth to form the words.

'Ch-Ch-Ch…' he began. His mouth struggled to form the words.

It was no good. They encroached on him. Footstep after footstep. Not carefully, but deliberately.

'Charles!' he finally managed. 'P-Peeves…' It was easier now. 'Charles Peeves. Where…?'

The figures stopped, and just for that second, Travers saw

something more, something beyond the clothes straight from a Thomas Hardy novel, he felt the primal urge to run and never stop, to curl into a ball. To be judged and found wanting.

The lead figure, a small old lady, merely five feet high, pushed back her bonnet and Travers realised what the Smythe family had seen through their bedroom window all those years ago. No wonder the poor Victorian family had gone mad.

His mind closed off, his vision darkened around him and was replaced by flashes of light, of starscapes, and the feeling of someone rooting through his brain, rummaging.

He saw Anne and Alun, saw Tibet, the monks facing off against robotic, fur covered enemies and the Doctor, a bizarre little man who could stand up to an evil older than time.

He screamed again, railing against the invasion of his mind, trying to throw up barricades, mentally punching out at them, and feeling like an infant that beats its tiny fists against a parent when it can't understand.

The figures remained, their faces locked onto his. Those faces had changed, they weren't the simple men and women out of time that he first took them for, the features had changed. He tried to focus and couldn't as the background behind them shifted. Those weren't stars he recognised, there was something about these people, something old, but they had travelled far to be here, a very great distance.

Then, he wasn't standing in the farmyard anymore; he was lying on his back looking at the sky.

His neck hurt, like the pain of sleeping in a bad position. He drew himself up and realised two important things.

Firstly, he was lying on a large flat rock. Secondly, the light was now very different. Instead of the early morning sun shining on the wet grass, it was now high in the sky. Beneath him, the rock was warm, like something that had been under the sun all day.

He checked his watch. Gone one o'clock. He had lost nearly two hours. What had he seen?

He remembered there were people. He remembered the fear. But where had the fear come from? All was distant, untouchable.

He looked around him. Purple heather stretched in all directions and scented the air with its sweetness. He was clearly up on the moors, above Edleton. A closer look showed that his new resting place was not the only rock. At regular intervals in a circle around him were other monoliths of every size and shape.

He was lying in the stone circle, a simple ring of misshapen boulders hewn from local gritstone, decorated by lichen and weathered in the sun. The kind that could be seen across the country. With the characteristic flat sacrificial altar at the centre.

A call above his head pierced his ears. He looked up. There was a kestrel, hovering, directly above his face. As he watched it, it pulled its wings in and dropped.

Travers rolled quickly off the rock, avoiding the creature's snapping beak. As he scrambled to his feet, he pulled out his revolver, pointed it in the air and pulled the trigger, hoping to scare the bird off.

A click.

He checked the chamber. Empty.

The message was clear.

We can see you, we can follow you, we can control you. You can't harm us.

He picked at a pebble and lobbed it in the kestrel's general direction. It missed, but the bird backed off.

It was a long walk back to the police house in the village. He still had his map, but paths clearly marked on paper would split, hide or simply disappear under the advancing peat bog that steamed in the hot afternoon sun. The heather caught at his feet, tearing and snapping as he forced his way through it.

As Travers approached the edge of the moor, and the path that he hoped lay across the escarpment, his heart hammered as, without warning, a loud, thumping squeal erupted from the undergrowth ahead of him and a red grouse, disturbed by his progress, leaped into the air in a rush of feathers. As it glided away, the thumping continued at the edge of his hearing, a familiar sound that he knew from previous raids.

The sound of disinterested chaotic destruction heading his way.

Unusual to hear it in cities in daylight, but out here, with less ack-ack guns, it was a different matter. He turned to see the familiar shape of the Junker skirting low over the heather, heading for him. And why wouldn't it? The only human being for miles around. The pilots must want the target practice. Did the Boggarts know it was coming when they stranded him out here?

The peat served to muffle the sound of the bullets as they hammered near him. Too far, yet, to draw a clear bead on him. Travers took off, heading straight for the edge.

The engines' noise grew as the plane bore down on him and another burst of fire whistled past him, this time ricocheting off the gritstone boundary of the moorland. His heart began to pound in his chest as he raced against the oncoming vehicle.

Finally, Travers reached the edge. Having no idea of what lay on the other side, he nonetheless scrambled past the rocks, scraping his hands on the rough grit as he did so, and dropped to the other side. He was fortunate. The drop there was only a short few metres and he rolled, scrambling under the overhang as the German bomber buzzed over his head, not changing course. Once past, he heard the familiar drone of its engines. It was unladen. Its bombs had already fallen and it was heading home.

He should feel honoured, he mused. They'd taken time out of their flight just to have a pop at him.

In front and below him, the village waited for his return.

'Professor Travers!'

His route through the village back to the police house had taken him past Mrs Peeves' cottage. She, of course, had been outside, hoeing the garden ready for more planting. PC Armthorpe stood next to her, leaning in the fence. It was he that had called out.

'Ah! Constable, Mrs Peeves.'

'What have you found?' Mrs Peeves stood, leaning on her hoe and staring at him coldly. Travers was taken aback by her directness. 'And where in God's name have you been?' She looked at his clothing, stained with peat and ripped by thick heather.

'Owd Hob's Meade. And then, more recently, the stone circle. And nearly to an early grave after that. How I moved between the two is more of a mystery.' Travers decided to be blunt. He wanted to see the reaction of the village to what he felt was almost certainly the reason for the disappearance of Charles Peeves and many others through the years.

Armthorpe shook his head.

'You shouldn't have gone up there without speaking to me. That's a dark family. What did they do? Get you a club over the head?'

'More than that, I think. Some sort of psionic control…'

'Satanic!' said Armthorpe. 'That's exactly what they are. I've been suspecting for some time they've been involved up on that circle, sir.'

Travers stayed where he was.

'I think more than just Satanic. That family may be the source of large tracts of folklore. Even just their names; you call them Boggarts, they reside in Owd Hob's Meade. Now, Owd Hob was the progenitor of the creatures called Boggarts, horned and cloven hoofed according to legend. I think that family can take a form that inspires terror in all who see it… Damned if I can remember it, it's buried at the back of my mind…'

He trailed off at the looks that the two villagers were giving him.

'Are you feeling all right, sir?' asked Armthorpe. 'Satan worshippers I said, but you're going off into the deep end here. I'll round up some chaps and we'll head down there and have a look. You best get yourself to bed.'

Travers shook his head.

'I'm going to get some reinforcements in. On no account is anyone to go to Owd Hob's Meade until then.' He paused. 'And that is a military order.'

Mrs Peeves had been quiet, but then, her voice rose.

'Satan worshippers and demons!' she snapped. 'Do you have children, Professor?'

He nodded.

'Well then, imagine them, keep them in your mind's eye, and imagine that one day, they weren't there.'

Despite himself, he did. He saw Alun and then Anne, he remembered her eyes shining as she told him she wanted to be a scientist, as she scampered around in his laboratory.

'Think of that hollow feeling in your stomach when you lose sight of them for a second or two and they run off on a walk through a park or by the boating lake. Think of all the nightmares you've had of finding them floating face down, or buried under earth or not breathing in their bed, and now imagine that any of those things could happen at any moment and are more likely than ever seeing your child again.' Mrs Peeves took a deep breath as Travers scrambled through his mind to try to think of anything but Anne and Alun. 'And now, Professor Travers, think of that tiny dash of hope. That feeling that at any moment the child might come walking around the corner and run straight into your arms shouting for his mummy. Then the crushing reality that as much as that could happen, *it won't*. That tiny little sliver of hope is worse than any certainty you can give.'

'Mrs Peeves…'

'And then, Professor, double it all for my husband and…' She broke off. 'Just tell me this. If you could speak to your missing child, how would you reconcile that the man wanted to go chasing ghosts instead?'

Travers thought long and hard. He looked up at the sky and then back down.

'I'd tell her to try to find out exactly what makes the *ghosts* tick. I hope that she would. And that, madam, is exactly what I am now going to do myself.'

'Cownall!' he called when he got back to the digs. 'Where are you, man?'

The corporal appeared from the kitchen. 'Professor, I…Where have you been?' He took in Travers' mud marked and tattered clothes.

'Never mind. Had a run in with that Juncker that went overhead. He didn't like my face. The feeling was more than mutual. Look, man. I've discovered something incredible, right here in the heart of England.' His terror was gone but his excitement had built.

'Something has come up. I was about to…'

'It can wait!' said Travers. 'A whole community. Possibly not even human. They've got incredible psionic powers. Look, they might even be the source of the flares that have been seen

63

out there. Likely brought the plane down. Imagine it… If we can harness that energy from psychic power alone?'

'I think you should…'

'Probably. But even more, these could be the actual source of some of British folklore. Imagine that. Maybe even Nordic as well. This was a Viking area, wasn't it?'

Cownall sighed. 'I have no idea, Professor. I was trying to say…'

'Look, they've probably got that boy too. I think he's still alive. I've just bumped into his mother. Poor girl's distraught and I don't blame her. First priority, we find him, then we can worry about these people. The bottom line is, we need to go back there. Clearly they have a strong psionic defence, so I'll need the strongest minded members of the Corps. A full squad, I think. Put a call in to them. Where are our nearest troops?'

'That's what I've been trying to tell you. They're all miles away. That's just become a major problem, because Section Officer Le Croissette has gone missing while investigating a matter in Sheffield.'

Travers stopped short, memories of his meeting with the down to earth young lady at Gulliver Base. He knew that she had joined the Home-Army Fourth Operational Corps, at his recommendation, but not that she had been assigned so close.

'Eileen? Then why didn't you say so, man. Come on.' He turned and went for the door. 'There's not a moment to lose. Make sure we've got a squad on its way anyway. We need all the help we can get.'

CHAPTER SEVEN
The Girls That Make the Thingummy-Bobs

'I DON'T think I'm at liberty to say,' Eileen told the woman who was now sitting behind her desk.

'Hmm. You're too incompetent to be German. Too loyal to be Russian. Am I right to assume that you are British and spying on your own factory?' As Eileen stood in silence like a scolded school child, the woman tutted. 'Just nod, dear. I have a hunch that my brother-in-law's work resulted in you being called in. He doesn't trust the military, mind you. Don't ask me why. So here I am.' She tapped her eyepatch. 'I'd been invalided off from conscription, took some blast shot in the eye from the furnace. Not the best thing for a young lady. I was resting at home and always fancied myself as a spy. Couple of string pulls later and here I am. Took a couple of months to work my way inside this section. And then you turn up and threaten everything. Matthew might have had a point about soldiers.'

'So, you're working for…?'

'The Ministry of Aircraft Production, yes. But more precisely, family. The Bodians to be exact. Beatrice Bodian,' she introduced herself. 'Pleased to meet you, Miss…?'

'Le Croissette. Eileen Le Croissette.' Eileen recognised the woman's family's name. She'd seen it so many times. 'Wait, don't you make…?'

'Cutlery? Yes, dear. At least we did. We're in bayonets and bullets for the duration.' Beatrice stood. 'Right. Best bring you up to speed. You've no doubt realised that this section is where all the money is disappearing from. Correct?'

Eileen nodded.

'This is where Huxtable brings all his best workers. His

most loyal and most efficient. He tells them that this is a top secret government project to create a new weapon. One that the Germans and Russians will kill to get hold of. It keeps them all loyal and desperate to please. You've met him?'

Eileen shook her head.

'A shame. You'd understand the hold he has.' Beatrice paused for a moment. 'Come here.' She walked to the door of the little office, opened it a crack. 'There, you see that man over at the far end, by the pillar drills?'

Eileen peered through the door and across the maze of machines and furnaces. There was a man, standing on the balcony overlooking the girls methodically drilling the holes in steel girders and gears. Tall, almost svelte. A jaw like a matinee idol and a mop of blond hair swept to one side.

'He's the owner?' Eileen had been expecting an old, wealthy industrialist. 'He looks like a film star.'

'He's very young to be owning a factory, and full of charisma. Bought the place off the Pickerings just before the war. Replaced a lot of the plant machinery.' Beatrice carefully closed the door. 'We should wait here until he is finished for the day. Can't have you being seen wandering around.'

Eileen set herself down in a spare chair in the office. She was at least, apparently, on the same side as this woman.

'And what are they making? Where is all the War Office money going?'

'That's the difficulty. The way these places work, each girl gets taught to make or do one thing. Helps stop our tiny minds overloading you see. It also acts as a useful security measure. We don't know how it fits together.'

'But that ignores the one thing women do that the men don't. Talk to each other.'

'Exactly,' Beatrice said with a smile. 'And as the accounts manager here, I've done a lot of talking. Then I got hold of this.' She unrolled a blueprint on the desk, pinning it down with a pair of mugs. 'I shouldn't have this. It doesn't relate to the accounts, but I nabbed it from one of the foremen.'

It showed a squat shape, oblong, with one of the strange Christmas star balls at the top. Underneath were two support struts, looking almost like little comical legs.

'What on earth is that?'

'That's something I simply don't know. The name is strange. It's a word I've never heard before. I've looked it up. It's a German term for a type of soft cheese.' She let the thought sink into the muffled quiet of the shirts and hammers outside.

'*Quarg*?' Eileen asked.

'Clearly your German is better than mine. But no, not *quarg*, although almost... *Quark*.'

'What?'

'Exactly. Why be so blatant as to use a German word, and then why *that* German word? It must have another meaning.'

'I'm fairly sure this is no cheese mould,' said Eileen. 'Could it be some kind of armour?'

'Look again. It's a steel frame with fabric stretched across it. Like a Wellington.'

'Boot?' Eileen was confused.

'Plane.'

Eileen remembered what she'd heard of those planes. They really were constructed out of steel frames with a covering of fabric to get them airborne. That made the planes themselves surprisingly resilient, some managing to fly and land while literally on fire. Bullets themselves went straight through them, mind, mostly missing the unfortunate men inside, but not all. Not a good design for armour, but a good design for something that needed to be made cheaply and quickly.

'So, who fires the weapons?' asked Eileen.

'What weapons?'

'These bits.' She pointed at the pair of folded oblongs in the stocky bulk of the thing. 'I saw them in the waste section. They're some kind of machine gun.'

Beatrice looked at where Eileen was pointing.

'So. Definitely a weapon,' Beatrice said, tapping her teeth. 'I'd been wondering about that.'

'Where do the finished articles go when everything is ready?' Eileen tried to remember the layout of the manufacturing floor outside.

'That's the thing. Apart from creating the actual steel next door in the furnace, everything is done here, the forging, the welding, all construction. Final assembly takes place in a locked area at the far end of this shed. The testing house.'

'Then that's where I'm going to look.'

Beatrice closed her eyes for a moment or two. 'If Huxtable grabs you, I had nothing to do with this.'

Eileen smiled inwardly. That was tacit encouragement in her book.

'I'll do my best. How do I get in there?'

Beatrice thought for a moment. She sat down and sighed. 'There's no key and that door stays locked unless parts are taken in there. Huxtable's office is there too. It's a tricky one.'

'You've just found me,' said Eileen. 'Sneaking around. Clearly spying.'

'True…'

'Then take me to Huxtable. Gives you your story. Gets us both in there. He'll be furious, but we'll be in the right place.'

Beatrice shrugged. 'Worth a shot, my dear. Not done any good acting since fifth form. Let's do it.' She dropped into her office chair, however. 'But we need to wait for him to finish his walkabout. If there's one thing Mr Huxtable enjoys, it's keeping an eye on his staff. Probably too close an eye for comfort.'

'You think he doesn't trust his workers?'

Beatrice made a strange face, like someone who had just bitten into an onion. 'The thing is, my dear, my family runs its own factory. We know how much you need to watch people to keep their eyes on the job. You can't do it all the time. It's a waste of effort.' She puffed out her cheeks. 'But I don't think that's what Huxtable is doing. He's not watching the girls for mistakes; there's almost a look of glee on his face. He enjoys simply watching people doing their work. It's like he has never been in a factory before.'

Eileen leaned forward. This was interesting.

'And when you speak to him, does he sound like he is new to the business?'

Beatrice drummed her fingers, then worked them through the cuts and grooves scratched into her desk by generations before her. 'He does and he doesn't. He asked what a fettling shop was once. I had to explain it was where we buffed and polished the steel. Now, it's a Yorkshire word I'll grant you…' She rubbed her chin. 'Do you know what he reminds me of more than anything else?'

'Go on.'

'A little boy. No, don't laugh. He reminds me of a little boy that has been playing with trains and reading about trains and has now been given the run of a train shed.' Beatrice shrugged 'And I'm just as baffled about his excitement. Stinking, hot smoky machines are the same anywhere.' She looked lost in thought, her hand reached up towards the patch.

'You did very well to come back after losing your eye,' said Eileen.

Beatrice rubbed at her eyepatch. 'In a strange way, I had to. I had to come back to somewhere like this in order to make peace with myself.'

An hour later and Eileen was dragged back through the workshop. She could almost imagine that Beatrice was enjoying it. Ahead, she could see the partitioned area that Beatrice had spoken of, built of thick brick with large 'Keep Out. Danger' signs across the doors. No guards, just a locked door of normal size next to the larger double doors for taking the parts in. Beatrice hammered on the door.

'Come on. Open up!'

It was opened a crack. A woman's eye peered through. 'It's not shift change yet.'

'Doesn't matter,' Beatrice said. 'Found this skulking in the bins. Is His Nibs around? He's going to want to talk to her.'

A pause. Was she going to buy it?

She did. The door opened and the two stepped through. As the door closed behind them, the sound of the factory behind it dulled. In here the lights were lower too and revealed little, dark shadows at the edge of a cavernous space. One girl was working in the centre of the floor. The sparks from her welding, danced in her face mask and across the floor, as she put the finishing touches to… something.

Well, Eileen simply didn't know what it was. It looked like the blueprint that she'd seen earlier; a squat, metal frame. A quark, she supposed. The spiked globe on top looked like a head, but the size was that of a small child. What possible purpose could this thing serve? The girl working on it stood back. Within the frame, Eileen could see hydraulics, wiring and ammunition.

The girl put one hand to her head and lifted her face mask off. As she stepped back, Eileen recognised her gait before she turned. It was Hilda.

Hilda fixed her with a look of shock, developing to anger. 'Eileen,' she began, 'You shouldn't be here.'

And that's when all hell broke loose.

'Glove box, professor.'

Travers rummaged around at Cownall's suggestion. He found a flask, scrunched up paperwork, biscuit wrappers and an AA map of Sheffield. 'What possessed you to bring this?'

'Nearest city, isn't it? Can't just rely on the tourist pamphlets if I wanted to go there. Can't stand the countryside at the best of times.'

Travers held on to the door handle as the Tilly hit another bend far faster than it could comfortably handle.

'There's no need to take it out on the hedgerows. When did you last change the tyres on this thing?'

'Rubber shortage, prof.'

'That wasn't an answer, Corporal. Right. What was Miss Le Croissette doing at this factory? I need a full briefing.'

'With respect, prof, Section Officer Le Croissette and I are both members of the military arm of the Fourth. You're just attached to us for advice.'

Travers tutted. 'And I was given to believe the Fourth was primarily a scientific outfit. Tell me, Corporal, have you ever actually been in a firefight?' A stony look from Cownall. 'Thought not. You got called up and shipped straight into our Corps, didn't you?' He thumbed through the map sheets, searching for River Don Lane. 'In any event, as I am a scientist, I think the PM would probably give me more authority than you're willing to allow.' He stabbed at the page. 'Found it. Now, background, Corporal.'

'Request from Government to look into anomalies in the finances of the Pickering Factory. She called in with a coded phrase to tell us she was going undercover. Not reported back since. Still in there as far as we can tell.' Cownall rattled off the explanation as he went.

'Financial anomalies are not usually something for us,' said Travers.

'The fire pillars and the downed Bristol over here gave the higher ups some concern. They decided to take this one just in case. Good first assignment for Miss Le Croissette.'

'But you're not tell me what they were doing. Wonderful. Skulduggery for the sake of it, and now we can't help each other.'

The city rose into view as they crested the ridge, just visible through a gap in the hills. Closer than the landscape hinted were chimneys belching smoke into a continual smog across the rooftops.

They arrived outside the Pickering Steelworks, the clock above the archway showing it was now late afternoon. Despite its position sheltered among the hedgehog-like city of furnace chimneys, the street outside remained deserted as rumbles and hammers came from inside. Cownall drove past the entrance until they were out of sight of any windows, before he pulled to a stop.

Travers was first out, looking around him.

'Recce first,' said Cownall as he joined him. 'Can't be too careful.'

Grudgingly, Travers agreed. They split up and each went his separate way around the compound. Travers knew something of steel making, but struggled to match his recollection of the various and varying processes with the sounds and vibrations that came from the other side of the wall. This was only one factory, a small one, compared with English Steel and Vickers elsewhere in the city, thousands of men and hundreds of machines combined in this beating heart of the war effort.

The road was sandwiched between the Pickering works and the surrounding industrial buildings, high red bricks reaching above his head. He looked up, seeing occasional glimpses of bright blue beyond the chimneys and smoke, searching for a way up or in to save him going through the main gate.

'Lost?' said a voice. Clipped and confident.

'Looking around,' said Travers turning to its owner. A tall, clean shaven man in a smart suit. 'You're not a steelworker.'

'Neither are you.'

Both stared at the other, daring him to make the first move. Finally, Travers went for broke and produced his papers.

'Professor Edward Travers, on attachment to the military.' He didn't mention the Fourth.

'Matthew Stewart. Assistant Director at the Ministry of Aircraft Production.' Stewart handed his own papers over and paused. 'I'm the one that spotted the financial anomalies that brought you here. That was a difficult task after the mess that Beaverbrook left the place in. Got a man inside have you?'

Travers smiled. 'A woman. New, but one of our best.'

'Likewise,' said Stewart. 'Couldn't trust you chaps to do the job.'

Travers paused. He often had similar feelings on the military capability. Particularly when resources were as stretched as they were, but personal was personal and the Fourth was now his home, such as it was.

'I suppose you've cleared this with your superiors?'

Stewart gave a half chuckle. 'Like heck. This is all in a few days' leave. There would be hell to pay if they found out I've sent my sister in-law in.'

'There will be hell to pay *when* they find out,' corrected Travers.

Stewart shrugged. 'Needs must. And you haven't met Beatrice. She was a Suffragist way back, and, thanks to a shortage of good gentlemen of her status following the last war, she'll be an old maid if she sees this one out. Her father has his reservations and I agree with them, but she knows how to look after herself. She'd already started in the works before being laid off for losing an eye. And did that ever irritate her...'

'It's still grossly irresponsible to send a civilian in,' said Travers, feeling his blood rise. 'Even if this was a safe area, the damage she could do to the surveillance operation...'

'What do you mean "even if"?'

'Our girl's been gone seven hours,' Travers pointed out. 'She should have reported five hours ago.'

Their conversation was halted as Cownall appeared around the far corner and hurried over. Travers made the introductions.

'We're going in then,' said Stewart.

'We?' Cownall turned to him. 'This happens to be a

military operation, sir. I need to ask you to stand back.'

Travers placed a hand on Cownall's arm. 'Actually, I think an appearance by a high-ranking bod from the Ministry is far more likely to give us safe entry than going in guns blazing. You're in uniform, Corporal. I suggest you hang back until it sounds like you're needed.' He turned to Stewart. 'Come on, Assistant Director, time to take your scientist colleague on a tour of your facilities.'

CHAPTER EIGHT
In the Factory

'**WHAT DO** you mean, we can't enter?' Stewart shouted at the gatehouse. 'I happen to be a senior civil servant within the Ministry of Aircraft Production. We're responsible for this place. I will report you to the owner of this establishment.'

Standing behind him, Travers could not help but notice a single, throbbing, vein in Stewart's neck.

'Well,' said the man at the gatehouse, drawing on his cigarette. 'That's just the thing, in't it? I see that owner every day, and he gives me very clear instructions on who to let in. And he an't mentioned your name. You're not expected.'

'We control what you produce, you ridiculous little man. We are always expected.'

The man shrugged. 'Apparently not.' He jabbed back out of the archway with his cigarette. 'Reckon you should head back that way.'

Travers tapped Stewart on the shoulder. 'Let me speak,' he said. He leaned into the man on the gate. 'Right, we're after a lady called Eileen Le Croissette; do you know her?'

The guard shook his head.

'Probably waving around military documents. Claiming to be from the WAAF...?'

The man swallowed.

'The thing is,' said Travers. 'She's not well. Not well at all. In fact, she's criminally insane. She tends to infiltrate into organisations, isolate the young pretty girls and then...' He drew an imaginary knife across his throat. 'So, if you've let her in, anything could be happening in there. We need to go and find her. Only we know how to help her. Now, if you have let her in...' He raised a finger to stop the man replying. 'Don't tell me, but if you have, it's going to be a very black mark against you. Possibly even criminal matters for giving a woman like that access to a sensitive site. But if you let us through now, Mr Stewart and I will be the soul of discretion, as long as we can find her and get her out with no harm done. How does that sound?'

The man took a long, shaky drag on his cigarette. 'Go on,' he said. 'But be damn quick in there. Mr Huxtable is on the warpath today.'

Travers nodded his thanks and led Stewart past the barrier.

'See,' he said once they were out of earshot, 'this is what worked so well in Tibet eight years ago. What you've got to do to gain someone's favour is find someone else to make them afraid of. Works every time.'

'I do read the news, Professor,' muttered Stewart. 'I think the world is learning that lesson right now.'

'Yes, well, I think most things are more virtuous on a small scale than a large one.' Travers waved his hands around the compound they stood in, vast brick-built structures all around and a maze of roads threading between them. 'You've done the homework, I'm fresh from chasing missing children in Derbyshire. Lead on, McDuff.'

'"Lay on",' Stewart said. 'And that was the precursor to a fight.' He pointed down the central lane that led through the complex. 'The most secretive area, and the one Beatrice is now working in, is the back shed; "Special Projects". This way.'

Occasional staff members were out and about, but most of the activity was taking place inside the closed doors of the vast halls. Glimpses of furnaces and forges, blazing with heat and the vibrations of rolling mills and heavy hammers made Travers feel uneasy, a sense that they were walking through some kind of man-made volcano, ready to erupt at any moment. Matthew Stewart was much more relaxed as he strode through, pointing out the processes and actions around them.

'You get used to these places,' he said. 'I have to visit them so often, a lot of them just blend into each other. You can always spot the very old. They've got terrible layouts like this one. Steelworks expand by adding new bits as they need them, no overall plan. That's why you get this bizarre patchwork of buildings stuck on to each other. No wonder the Germans missed the place, they must have mistaken it for a slum district, compared to their ultra-efficient factories.'

'You haven't always been a civil servant, have you?' Travers asked.

'What makes you say that?' Stewart stopped dead.

'You walk like a man used to being on the parade ground and talk like a man used to commanding one. I can tell by the gatehouse business that you aren't used to having your orders disobeyed.'

Stewart turned away. 'Not everyone wants to talk about their military service, Professor. I presume you haven't served?'

Travers blew air into his cheeks. 'Beyond my current press ganging, you mean? No, I missed the first round because I was off to university at the time.'

'The search for knowledge more important than serving King and Country? I started off at university. Bristol, sadly. Then my father laid the law down and I was off to clear up the mess in France.'

'I like the King and I like the Country. It's the men in the middle ordering me around I have a problem with.' Travers started walking again towards the double metal doors at the far end. He could already see both doors shut tight.

As he reached them, he pushed against them, then ran his hands across the point where the doors met, searching for the keyhole. It was blank, no way to open it, simply blank ironwork. Travers stood back.

'Right. Beats me. Must be locked from the inside. That also means that it is constantly manned, like Number Ten. Now what do we do?'

'We could look for another door?'

'You think they would leave an unguarded, unlocked door elsewhere after making this one so impregnable?'

Stewart shrugged. 'It worked with the Maginot Line.'

'I fear we are dealing with someone with far more cunning than the French government here.'

Stewart leaned forward. 'Right,' he said, 'Nothing ventured, nothing gained.' With that he used his fist to hammer smartly on the door with five, brisk, rapid taps.

Travers gaped at him.

'Well,' said Stewart, 'if all else fails, act like you own the place. In many ways, I do.' There was a lull in the sound inside. 'Aha!'

There then followed a sound that was to Travers like rain falling on a pane of glass. He struggled to place it, until, suddenly, it clicked. Feet, a lot of them. The doors gave a creak.

'Mr Stewart,' Travers said, his voice rising in panic, 'move. Now. Any direction should do.'

They each dived to opposite sides of the doors as they were flung open, metal hinges straining and screeching as a crowd of women shoved through shouting incomprehensible things to each other until all were past.

'What's happening?' shouted Travers.

'Weapon malfunction in the testing house!' shouted one girl over her shoulder. 'Bullets spraying everywhere. Wait until they've stopped.'

As one, the two men peered through into the vast space beyond with its now empty drills, lathes and furnaces. In the far end came a sound, a rattle of loosely grinding cogs followed by the unmistakable sounds of ricochet. Stewart's face paled.

'Machine gun,' was all he said.

Travers nodded and withdrew his revolver. It might not achieve much, but its weight was somehow reassuring.

Inside the testing house, Eileen dived behind a pile of packing crates as the bullets had started flying from the incomplete quark that Hilda had been working on. Beatrice jumped after her. Bullets hammered into the walls, showering them with splinters of brick. Tiny lumps of flattened metal dropped to the floor next to them with a gentle metallic sound like loose change dropped from a pocket.

A high-pitched noise echoed around the room; clearly words. Eileen concentrated. She'd always had a skill at linguistics. The thing was shouting in English, a strange accented and bizarrely inflected version, but clearly English.

'Reveal yourselves. Come into the open.'

Maybe not German then... If so, what was it and, she thought as another hail of bullets rained red dust on her, why was it firing at her.

Think, just before it started to move, Hilda had shouted something. *She said that I shouldn't be here.* That was it; the thing was acting like a guard dog, protecting its home.

Beatrice tapped Eileen on the shoulder; the door they had walked through was just a few yards away. Yet, there was no cover between it and their position.

'We've got to try,' Beatrice said.

'It's a death trap. Literally no man's land.' As if to illustrate Eileen's point, a shower of wooden splinters flew through the air as the machine strafed the packing crates.

What's in them? Something must be stopping the bullets to protect us.

Cautiously, she reached a hand up. They'd been stacked slightly off set and were open at the top so she could get her hand into them to look inside. Metal parts, large blunt spikes. She rummaged and pulled out a couple of the strange spiked heads. She handed one to Beatrice.

'We can use these to distract it. I'll throw one over there.' She pointed away from the door, into the darker sections of the testing house. 'Hopefully it will turn and shoot at it, then you run for the door. When you get there, lob your head over to the far side, that will give me a chance.'

Beatrice nodded. 'Good luck,' she said.

'You too,' said Eileen.

She scrambled to the far end of the pile of crates and, trying to remember her game mistresses' advice on a far-off playing field on how to shot-put, threw the head as far as she could away from her. She heard it clatter into the darkness.

A spray of bullets followed it as the machine whirled and tracked it. Eileen turned to see that Beatrice was already running for the door. She tensed, ready to follow as soon as the further distraction was provided.

It never came.

'Quark! Cease search and destroy function. Guard the entrance.' The human voice, clipped tones, echoed around the space as if made by loudspeaker.

Eileen heard the bullets stop and high, fluting tones trill, 'Order obeyed.'

Beatrice was out of the door now. Eileen didn't know if she still had the head, but she saw the little, child-like, metal framework lumbering after Beatrice. She knew that exit was now closed to her. At least Beatrice had escaped.

'Right,' said the voice, 'I think you'd better come out now.'

Eileen stayed where she was, barely breathing.

'I've ordered the quark to stand down. I don't want to harm you.' A pause.

Eileen peered around the corner of the box. Huxtable stood there. He wasn't wearing his pinstripe suit, but rather some sort of boiler suit of a strange, almost shimmering material. Despite the grime of the works that was already clinging to Eileen's skin and clothes, it looked spotless. In one hand, he held an obvious weapon. Some sort of pistol, made of clean lines, no obvious breach or barrel, but with concentric rings surrounding the tip.

'I need to talk to you about how you can help me,' he said.

Eileen didn't trust him and stayed resolutely still.

'About how you and the War Office Special Support Group can help me.'

Travers and Stewart approached the far wall of the works shed from which they could hear the sounds of gunfire. They moved quickly but stayed low; Travers by instinct, Stewart clearly by some sort of training. Travers wondered again at the man's military experience. What had led him to leave it all for the civil service and not return even in a time of war?

As they approached the little, open door to the testing house, the bullets ceased to the sounds of some sort of command inside. A woman ran out, wearing overalls but with a patch over one eye. Stewart threw an arm around her shoulders and bundled her to safety behind the pillar drills. Travers followed.

'Beatrice!' Stewart said. 'What's going on?'

Still breathing hard, the woman raised a finger and pointed at the doorway.

'That,' she said. 'It's what they are making here. We've upset it.'

It stood there in the doorway. The size of a child, but Travers could immediately see that it was some sort of robot. The frame that held it together looked like it needed to be covered in something more, some kind of armour, but within

Travers could see the hydraulics and wires that kept the thing moving and ambulatory, all set perfectly in their place.

'Brilliant,' he breathed. 'Such precision engineering. Incredible work here.' He thought of Anne and her new ambitions to be a scientist. 'And all built by women too.' A thought caught his mind. 'Wait, where's Miss Le Croissette?'

Beatrice shook her head. 'She gave me a distraction to get out. She was supposed to follow, then Huxtable called that thing off and placed it on guard. It's called a quark. I thought that was a joke name at first.'

Travers grunted. 'I'm not laughing.' He looked around him. 'What can we use to disable the thing?'

'It will cut you to shreds, you fool,' said Stewart.

'We have to get Eileen out.' Travers stood and dashed into the central walkway of the works, raising his revolver and aiming at the quark. He squeezed off a couple of quick rounds at it, feeling the recoil from the gun shaking his arm.

The response was immediate as a hail of bullets thundered out from the quark, spraying across the workplace, creating a racket as they pinged off pillar drills.

Travers took cover behind a metal desk until the onslaught died down.

'Satisfied?' Stewart shouted over. 'We need to get out of here and get reinforcements.'

'I'm not leaving a member of staff in there!' yelled Travers back across the passageway.

'She'll be safe,' Beatrice shouted. 'Huxtable sounded like he wants to talk to her. In any case, the damn thing's shooting at us.'

Travers hated orders at the best of times. At least these were being called by civilians. He didn't have to obey them and that made him feel more inclined to at least listen. He also doubted that his revolver or Cownall's rifle were going to achieve much.

'Reinforcements then,' he called, and started retreating back towards the main doors by weaving under and through the machinery and desks. Stewart and Beatrice followed.

They emerged into the sun to see a familiar figure approaching, armed and in uniform.

'How did you get in, Cownall?' Travers asked.

'Heard the gunshots and walked the opposite way to everyone who was running. Think the gate guard took me for someone in authority. Where's Section Officer Le Croissette?'

'Captured.' Travers sighed and rubbed his eyes. 'No point running in there. There's some kind of robot; equipped with machine guns. Deadly to infantry.' He saw realisation dawn on Cownall's face. 'Where to now?'

'Our family's house,' said Beatrice. 'Well, it's pretty much mine for the duration. My parents have shipped out to the summer house in the Lakes.'

Stewart nodded. 'We can regroup there. Get some support in. What resources can you chaps call on?'

Cownall rolled his eyes. 'We're primarily a scientific corps, so hopefully the professor can rustle up a couple of Bunsen burners and a flask or two...'

'Shut up.' Travers face hardly moved a muscle but clouded over nonetheless. 'You think I'm enjoying being stranded here playing soldiers? Kinsella has a lot to answer for. Particularly if we're going to see harm coming to WAAF girls on secondment.' He turned to Stewart. 'Back to the house then.'

CHAPTER NINE
Master of the Universe

MATTHEW JUMPED out of the Jaguar almost as soon as the Bodians' butler trotted out to the driveway. It was maybe a waste of petrol coupons, but he would deal with any repercussions when it came to it. Beatrice stepped out to follow, breathing a sigh of relief as she gazed around the front garden and driveway of her family's house.

'Get a room ready, we're having a conference,' Matthew said. 'And make sure there's space, we're expecting military company.'

Jeffers held up an envelope, his facial muscles barely changing. 'Letter for you, sir. Redirected from London.'

Matthew took the slim, cream envelope. He recognised the family crest immediately. 'I'll take this in the study. Make sure everyone else is comfortable in the dining room.'

Jeffers looked at Beatrice for confirmation. Matthew saw that she nodded as he jogged past. It was hard to remember that Beatrice was providing her assistance, and indeed this house as a base of operations, purely from family loyalty. His wife's family had certainly been good to him.

He entered Mr Bodian's study. It was empty, following his father in-law's retreat to safer areas.

'Let the King and Queen look the East End in the face,' he had told Matthew. 'I've done my duty, and discretion is the better part of valour.'

Matthew took the silver letter opener from the desk and slid it down the length of the envelope. He let the paper fall out. He recognised the signature. His own brother, Gordon.

He swallowed and looked out of the window. Travers and his driver had just pulled up in their Tilly. Jeffers had approached them and appeared to be pointing around the corner to the tradesman's entrance. Matthew would have given anything to hear Travers' reply, but got the gist from the expansive arm gestures the man was making.

Matthew turned his attention back to the letter. He was putting off reading it. He already knew what it would say. He forced himself to unfold it and smooth the paper down to begin.

His brother had been visited by their father. Conversation had naturally turned to the war and Gordon's exemplary service in the RAF. Matthew obviously had no such service. He had taken the decision not to rejoin the military and decided to do his bit from Whitehall. He had also taken steps to try and distance himself from his last command. This is what had particularly caused his father's ire.

You would not have liked to see him, Matthew, Gordon wrote. *He was as angry a man as I have ever seen him. You know how important the family name is to him.*

Matthew did. That was one of the reasons behind his decision to put that name to one side for his time in the War Office. 'Why are *you* here?' was a hard question to answer. Matthew had known that his father would disapprove, but then, he had also known that his father was desperately disappointed after France. He may have miscalculated, however.

Matthew, you know that Father has long considered that Glen Cladach must go to you as the first born. However, he asked me something yesterday I never thought to hear. Could I see myself taking the Estate and handing it on to Alistair?

The words welled up in front of him. It didn't say so, but disinheritance was the implication. The loss of the Estate that he had been prepared for, bred for. Was his father so devoted to a military career that he would change the line of inheritance? He knew the answer to that.

The family was a military one. The Estate had come to them many years ago after Waterloo, but was no more than a welcome bonus. They were soldiers first and gentry second. Matthew, as far as his father was concerned, had let the side down. The change of name must have been a last straw for his father, for him to even consider that course of action. Lethbridge-Stewart; it carried with it an impressively great weight.

The letter finished: *My brother, while I can still call you such, please speak to Father. Mary loves her life in Bledoe, despite the loss of James, which she still feels most dearly. As does Alistair. I am not willing to uproot them, nor am I yet prepared to take on responsibility for our birthright.*

Matthew believed him, but he also knew that changing his father's mind was an impossible task. Violet and Beth ran through his mind and into the fields around Glen Cladach, playing on the summer days that they spent there. That could all be at an end. How long before children played there again? He carefully folded the letter. His own difficulties were a minor matter in the scheme of things. First priority had to be the Pickering steelworks.

Travers held the floor in the dining room when Matthew arrived.

'Robotics!' he said. 'But with no armour. What use is an unarmoured robot?'

'It looked unfinished,' said Matthew, sitting down.

Beatrice shook her head. 'Based on the parts and materials that I could see were allocated to it, it was as near as finished as it was going to get. Some fabric needed, pretty rough stuff I believe, given rationing, but that's it.'

'That would serve to keep the dust out of its moving parts, nothing more.' Travers massaged his temples. He seemed to be struggling, perhaps the encounter with the quark had hit him harder than he cared to admit. 'So, form follows function, especially in war. This thing is designed to take on an enemy that doesn't shoot back, doesn't inflict blunt trauma, needs to be attacked with machine gun fire and poses a threat sufficient for Huxtable to deploy robots against it.' He dropped into a dining chair. 'Robots are never an easy option. They are only used when there is no other choice.'

'Like your contraption at Gulliver? I heard about that,' said Cownall.

'Walls and ears, Corporal!' snapped Travers. 'But yes. Exactly. Orville was able to operate where a human pilot couldn't, because of the intense heat. Where can these robots go that humans can't? Somewhere that doesn't need speed or armour? And where does Huxtable come from anyway?' He turned to Matthew, who raised both eyebrows.

'His background checks out. Canadian,' Matthew said. 'His family did well before the depression. Struggled through it and he came over when our economy picked up faster than theirs.' He reached for his briefcase and handed the paperwork to Travers, who grunted.

'I suppose you've checked with the Governor General's Offices over there?'

'The High Commission now. I've checked and checked again. If he's fake, then he's gone above and beyond with his preparation. But of course, genuine British subjects can still be fifth columnists. We've got prisons full of chaps detained under regulation eighteen-B.'

Travers handed the papers back. 'Of course. Any connections with Moseley?'

Matthew shook his head. 'Clean as a whistle. There's cabinet ministers with dirtier fingers.'

'That doesn't surprise me. How did he get hold of the factory?'

'He bought the Pickering works,' said Beatrice. 'The place needed modernising and he had the capital. We knew the Pickering family. I'll be honest, it was somewhat of a surprise that they sold it.'

'That's why I dug further into the output of this place,' Matthew pointed out. 'I knew the resources were going elsewhere and not into the war effort.'

'I think that we can conclude that mystery as solved. We know it was going to someone's war effort. The question is, whose?' Travers rubbed his bristly chin. 'And who are their enemy?'

'Why don't we ask the women that work there?' Cownall turned to Beatrice. 'Surely they've been gossiping like fishwives.'

Beatrice sighed. 'They do. But the thing is, most of the girls there are there because they have to be. Mostly what they talk about is getting their children's teas ready.'

'It's as if they haven't got cooks to do it,' said Matthew with a raised eyebrow.

'Your point?' Beatrice glared at him with her one good

eye.

'That you expect too much of them. Women with rights is all very well for your class and generation with money to burn and not enough men to go around...' The spectre of France swam across his mind again. '...But the working classes have better things to be doing, like looking after their families.'

'That still doesn't help us, dear brother in-law.' Matthew smiled inwardly. He enjoyed these bouts even if Beatrice didn't. 'The fact remains that Huxtable is a mystery and we don't know his intent for these quarks,' she finished.

Travers banged the table. 'Cownall! How far off are the troops?'

The corporal shrugged. 'A few hours, prof. They were out on manoeuvres when I called. One of your experiments must have got loose again.'

Travers sighed. Matthew assumed that this was the usual banter that soldiers had; he was familiar with it from his brief service. He could see from Travers' irritation that it was now no longer appreciated, if it ever had been.

'Just make sure they've got some grenades and sticky bombs please.'

'Will do.' Cownall nodded.

Travers leaned back, before jumping up. 'Of course. They're connected!'

'What's connected?' Matthew said.

'Huxtable and the quarks. They're connected to the Boggarts.'

Matthew and Beatrice sat in silence for a moment or two, looking at each other.

'The what?' Matthew asked, finally.

'The professor thinks he has found a bunch of satanic trolls living on a farm in the High Peak,' said Cownall. 'Although why he doesn't just use their surname I don't know.'

Travers glowered at him. 'Because their surname, "Hobson", is an obvious modern derivation from the name of their homestead, which in turn derives from the folklore associated with them. Until we know how they describe themselves, we will have to settle for the folkloric term.' He started pacing and rummaging in his pockets for a map. 'Their chief defence and attack appears to be psionic. Psychic. They attack the mind. So, what would be the perfect weapon against them? It's obvious: a robot. It has no mind to affect.'

Matthew shook his head, trying to lodge this information inside. 'So how do they obey orders?'

'Oh, you don't need a mind of your own to do that. Just look at Hitler and Mussolini's followers,' said Cownall.

'Well, exactly,' said Travers. 'So, we've got a group of dangerous psychics and a group of dangerous robots.'

'Which one is on our side?' Matthew wondered.

'Do either of them have to be on our side?' Beatrice asked.

'Look at the world. There's only two sides to anything now.' Matthew thought for a second. 'And Franco.'

'The enemy of my enemy,' said Travers. 'I think I need to get over to Owd Hob's Meade.'

'Don't be stupid,' Cownall said. 'The last time you went there they knocked you out, sent you out to the moors and, for all we know, sent a German bomber to meet you.'

Travers was almost oblivious now, absorbed in his planning. 'We need to turn to folklore. How did people deal with these creatures before we had robots? Any ideas, anyone?'

'Billy goats!' said Cownall.

'Not helpful.'

'It's midsummer's eve today. Midsummer's day tomorrow,' said Matthew. 'Has that any relevance?'

'Nothing to our favour I fear.' Travers clicked his fingers. 'We need iron. This is a steel making city. There should be tonnes of it.'

Beatrice shook her head. 'You'd think that, but best grade steel comes through electric arc treatment of scrap steel now.' She nodded behind him. 'Or you could try that.'

Matthew laughed as Travers turned. Behind him was a full suit of armour.

'The helmet is solid iron,' Beatrice added. 'I wouldn't recommend walking in it for long.'

Travers lifted the headgear down carefully and placed it over his head. It fit, albeit rather loosely.

'This might work. If my own theory is correct.'

'Won't you need the rest of the armour, Professor?' Cownall was beaming at the appearance of the distinguished scientist in the medieval headgear.

'It's to protect against mind control, Corporal. Unlike you, I keep my brains in my head.'

Matthew tensed. Discord in the military rarely played well in his experience. Yet Cownall took the barb in his stride.

'I'll give you that one,' he said.

'You can give me the Tilly too,' said Travers.

'Oh no you don't. I've signed it out, I'm driving it. Gotta stay here to help the squad get to the steelworks too.' Cownall grinned. 'But if you look under the tarp at the back, you'll find a Triumph motorcycle that's signed off in your name.'

Travers smiled as he lifted the helmet off his head and lowered it. 'That will do nicely.'

'Cup of tea? Coffee?'

Huxtable had led her into his office. It was like nothing else that Eileen had seen. There was no paperwork, no typewriter, secretary, counting equipment, ledgers, inkwells or anything she expected. The desk sat in the middle of the room was a steel slab, no ornate carving or leather writing surface. Around the room were cabinets, steel again, some glass, but opaque, impossible to see through. Maps were pinned to the front of the cabinets. She recognised the places; Sheffield, Doncaster, Leeds and surrounding countryside, all in one-inch scale. No windows looked out on the factory.

He closed the door behind them; she was trapped with him.

'A beverage, Miss…?'

'Le Croissette. No, thank you.'

'Something stronger. I have a particularly fine whisky. Brandy I understand is sought after. I have a good bottle.' He pulled a drawer out from one of the cabinets.

Whisky and brandy were rare enough in these times, certainly not offered around as this man was doing. In any event, the first rule of being captured was name, rank and serial number only. So far, he had only asked her for the first. She certainly didn't want to let her guard down by taking the alcohol. That is, if it hadn't been tampered with first.

Huxtable poured himself a glass, offered one to her, shrugged when she refused and sat down again.

'Take a seat.'

She hesitated.

'Or stand. It's up to you, but I would feel more comfortable if you sat.'

She did so, surreptitiously checking the worn padded surface for anything that could inject something into her without her knowledge. She had heard of Nazi truth serums and wasn't keen on being another tick on their list of spies. She realised she was shaking. She had always been the support, the back-up to the men, but here she was, a spy, on the front line and captured. All on her first mission and within a few hundred yards of the outside world.

Huxtable took a sip of his brandy. 'This is such a fascinating time. I always wanted to come here. The manufacturing processes, the war, even the bombings. It just creates such a thrill.' He looked straight at her, fixing her with his eyes. 'You weren't fazed by the Quark?'

Eileen stayed silent. She knew that this was an interrogation. Anything she said could tip off an enemy on tactics or intelligence. Even just acknowledging that Huxtable was right could tell him that the Fourth's intelligence was working. She stared ahead, feeling her vision blur as her breathing grew short and shallow.

Could she cope if they started vicious interrogation?

'Of course you weren't. The War Office Special Support Group must be used to such strange things. After all, that's why they exist.'

Don't nod, thought Eileen. *Nod and you've told him about a top secret military corps.* Although that was the second time he'd used the official name of the Fourth Operational Corps, so he clearly knew more than he was telling.

'You see,' he continued. 'I have a good working knowledge of your employers. It is one of the advantages of coming from where I do…'

I bet it's Munich, she thought, *he has that look about him.*

'…the year 6587,' Huxtable finished. He looked at her, awaiting a response. 'Nothing? You've been trained well. Come on. This isn't an interrogation. I'm telling you something. I need you to know something. It is vital to everyone in your time and across the galaxy in mine.'

'How do I know you're not lying?' Eileen asked.

Huxtable sat back, drumming his fingers. Finally, he reached under the desk and appeared to press a button. The lights dimmed, the centre of the desk glowed briefly, forming itself into a blue circle at the centre, which then expanded up and out of the surface of the desk, forming a hemisphere, then a globe as it rose into the space above it. It then flattened into a disc, a large bulge remaining in the middle of a swirl of glowing dots.

'There you go. I come from around there.' He jabbed at the globe, about half-way between the bulge and the edge. 'We are currently here.' He pointed again, a similar distance but about a quarter of the way further around.

'That's the galaxy.' Eileen remembered her father showing her the stars once in the back garden, the faint white ghost of the Milky Way winding across the sky. 'How did you do that?'

'A holographic map. A simple enough piece of technology in our own era.'

Eileen nodded, understanding and believing.

'So, who wins?'

Huxtable was shaking his head before she had finished asking. 'I can't tell you that. There are civilisations, far more powerful than any of us, that watch us all the time. I can get away with coming back here, just one man with a stack of blueprints and a little technology. But I know that they're watching, and I need to make sure I stay below the radar, build an army of Quarks using only the technology of the day, make a small surgical strike at the target and get out of here.' He swallowed. 'But I cannot give any of you any idea of what comes next.'

'An army?'

He nodded. 'An army. The only army that can be used against the group that I've come for. The Quarks.' He tapped another button and the holographic display turned to a picture of one of the squat little robots, looking different, weapons more streamlined and the body covered in metal armour. 'We've taken the design and the positronic brain from a race known as the Dominators. They've been using them for centuries.'

'Dominators...' Eileen tapped her fingers on the table, looking from the display to Huxtable 'Domination hasn't got the best associations right now.'

He looked sheepish. 'The Quarks are tools. They're pretty efficient ones. We are at least putting them to good use.' He pointed out of the door. 'We've had to build them from scratch here. We couldn't bring them with us, except for the "brains". Very difficult to reverse engineer them to what you have to offer. We had to keep the shape and basic function to ensure the subroutines continue to function.' He pressed a button under his desk again, the display changed to show another Quark, this one covered in metal armour. Slowly it changed, its ray gun attachments turning to machine guns, the armour falling away to be replaced by fabric stretched over a metal frame. 'But everything I heard about the ingenuity of this era is right. Apart from the brains I brought with me, everything else is the product of those brilliant women outside. The power plant was a bit tricky.'

Eileen cocked her head to one side.

'You have yet to split an atom,' Huxtable continued. 'Nuclear power is rather out of the question. Fortunately, ballistic weapons reduced the load considerably and we can run them off stored electricity. Now we've finally got a small army ready to go.' He was proud, and, Eileen noted, sufficiently so that he couldn't stop prattling about it.

She allowed herself a small smile. 'A small army? What chance has that got against what we have? We've got planes, bombs, tanks. Your robots won't last five minutes.' Eileen sat back. She was still shaking, but determined to take it all in.

Huxtable sighed. 'It's still not sinking in is it? I'm on your side. Or at least, I need you to be on mine. Here, let me tell you a story and show you what we're up against. Then, you can see for yourself why you have to help me.'

Travers had used many forms of transport in his travels around the world, but, without doubt, the motorcycle was one of his favourites. The feeling of speed and freedom when riding one was unmatched by simply sitting in a car.

The Bodians' house was already firmly on the outskirts of the city. 'Int' posh bit' as the locals said.

Nevertheless, the sense of steering into the unknown and out of civilisation assailed him as he rode out and over the

91

moors, past old coaching inns turned huntsman's haunts and now parade halls.

He passed them and dropped down again into river valleys, through the little villages of Hathersage, Bamford and Hope, surrounded by fields of cattle and sheep. Ahead, the great ridge rose, and he took a sharp left to bring him around its nose and into the Vale.

He caught himself as the bike all but slid around the corner. Why was he rushing? He'd met Eileen once and he recommended she be conscripted by the Fourth, but, as useful as she was, that was no reason to break his neck for her.

It wasn't about Eileen. This breakneck run, this was because he suddenly saw a way to approach the Boggarts and find Charles Peeves. Charles, just a couple of years older than Anne. He remembered that feeling as he saw her face on the body crucified to the thorn in his dream. He also thought of the boy's missing father. Travers knew, deep down, that man had not deserted. If the father had been lost when the son was abducted, what then could they do to Anne? And Alun?

He turned down the lane that led to Owd Hob's Meade, slowing as the bike skittered and slid across the permanently damp moss and grass that covered the dirt floor. Huge lumps of stone were thrown by his wheels as he advanced on the house. As it came into view, he stopped and dismounted. He opened the pannier and withdrew the helmet. He felt faintly ridiculous in it as he finished the rest of the walk to the farm.

Again, as he entered the farmyard, it was deserted. He paused, listening. There was a faint whisper at the edge of his hearing, a flicker in the corners of his vision. He stepped further in, straining to hear better. He approached the farmhouse now. Still nothing. As he got to the door, he spun, remembering the attack last time. No footsteps followed him now. He pushed at the door, and it gave slightly. He eased it open, hearing the hinges squeak their protest as he did so.

He stepped into the room beyond. White-washed walls and dark furniture, much of it looked like it had been reclaimed from rubbish. Thrown away, but here stacked neatly and still in use. The pictures on the wall were something else.

One showed a thousand men, women and children, turned away from the viewer, bowing before a small group who stood on a dais. Above, the sky cracked and a red scar, jagged as a flesh wound, illuminated the scene. The group on the dais were robed. He looked closer. Their faces were almost caricatures, deep creases where a normal person may have had just wrinkles. Above deep-set eyes were two small but clear horns, like the faces that he had seen here before. Travers shivered. The whispering was stronger now.

Another painting showed a field, the aftermath of a war. Bodies, some dismembered, were strewn around. The robed group from before crouched over some of them. Travers saw that they consumed the flesh of the dead, the blood and sinews dripping down their chins. This was a morbid celebration.

He listened. He had heard children laughing last time. Only children could laugh when surrounded by this. Like the urchins of the East End that play soldiers among the ruins of houses that were now graves. There was no laughter now, just the silence of an empty house.

He moved through the rooms, all spartan apart from the strange paintings. The back door was a typical stable door, but for one thing.

As he stared at it, he realised what was different. This door was designed so that the latch was on the inside. He pressed it down and the door swung outwards, to the back garden.

He checked the rear of the door. Just as he had thought. There were bolts on the outside. The door was designed to be locked from the garden. Looking around, he could see why. High walls loomed over him, ivy and other creepers clinging to them and giving the impression of tapestry.

The garden itself was wonderful. Wild flowers bloomed in a spray of colours that complemented each other from ceramic pots and wooden boxes. The grass lay thick from wall to wall, springy under his step. Small wooden toys lay on it, of a type he didn't quite recognise. Like those that predated his own childhood. Little wooden figures of people. Not soldiers, as he had enjoyed playing with, but ordinary people, bus drivers, farmers, shopkeepers.

The place was deserted. As much as it was to keep children safe, there were none here. If Charles Peeves had ever been hidden here, he was gone. Again, Travers thought of the child's mother and her challenge. Imagine if it was your child.

The whispers grew louder out here, moving from the edge of his hearing to almost a scream from a spot in front of his own forehead. He lifted the helmet, just an inch or two off his head, and the vision struck him immediately.

Anne, dressed in a white robe, bound to the altar at the centre of the stone circle and screaming, sobbing and calling for him, her father, as the figures with torches, wearing those same robes as in the paintings grew closer and closer.

He slammed the helmet back down on his head. A warning had clearly been given. One that would be churlish to ignore. And yet, this was a hint as to where his quarry was.

Now, Travers was determined to go to them.

All his adult life he had travelled. He had left England and gone abroad to adventure, to discover things that were just rumours. Eight years ago, in Tibet, he had even discovered the metoh-kangmi, the abominable snowman... and other things besides.

But those occasions had felt like escapes. Leaving the banality of England on the expenses of some newspaper baron, or university. He came home to the Royal Geographic Society, and got back to reality, even meeting Margaret Goff and starting a family with her. Margaret, Anne and Alun seemed like the safe real world, back home away from the world of adventure.

Now the War was on. And bombs fell that could kill any of them any moment. He couldn't travel anymore. There was no world of adventure out there for him. The dangerous world had come to England.

This trip had excited him to think that it could be a taste of his pre-war exploits. Instead, he felt that his family, his dear little safe family, was now at more risk than ever.

He knew he had to go to the circle. That's where they would be, as the sun started to sink on Midsummer's Eve.

CHAPTER TEN
Future History

HUXTABLE TOLD his story, images flickering into life in three dimensions above the desk as he did so. Miniature rockets flew through the sky. 'They held people,' he said. 'Thousands of people. There were hundreds like them. That's what my ancestors used to leave this planet. They went to colonise space. Then colonies became nations, became Empires.'

This was a bedtime story, Eileen decided. A simple story for children. People didn't fly in rockets. She'd heard stories of rocketry experiments. Knew that across the water, the enemy was planning something. But the cargo of those rockets would not be people. Rockets wouldn't bring hope, they would bring death.

'So, who flies these space rockets? Your little robots?'

'Robotics were forbidden,' he told her. 'We had become reliant on technology. There was no danger in life when everything is automated. We were, literally, alienated.'

He went on. He claimed his people travelled by rockets and inertialess drives, calculated in the same way that Eileen did in the Filter Room. Quickly and by hand and mind. A whole empire, covering a corner of the galaxy but hundreds of worlds, rockets arcing through the void at many times the speed of light connecting them all. Representatives of each world gathered in a vast chamber to elect and advise the Serogant who ruled the sector. Families vied for position and power in the court, all attempting to outdo each other in sycophancy and decadence. Despite it all, the system worked.

Was this serious? Eileen watched the shapes of planets, saw the cities as they grew rapidly across their surfaces. Why lie about something so unbelievable?

'I was a researcher in the Central Dome of Administration,' he continued. 'That's how the political families liked to train their children in the ways of the government.'

Huxtable would often travel to court, where he would meet the representatives, speak to them, find out what they wanted and go and get it for them. Until one day, as he hurried on an errand.

'That's when I met the first one,' he said. 'I didn't think much at first, the Empire ruled by the Serogant covered so many worlds, you got strangers with so many different styles and looks.' He nodded at Eileen. 'Like with the British Empire, in fact. You must be used to meeting Indian and Chinese people in your larger cities for instance.'

Eileen stayed silent. She had lived in London. There were precious few people from the sub-continent there. How was this man so poorly informed if he was working for the enemy?

'He looked like a follower of some strange religion,' continued Huxtable. 'He kept his head covered by a dark hood. I bumped against him in the corridor, entirely accidental, but I knocked his clothing, his hood fell back. He stopped dead, stared at me with his eyes that didn't seem to blink. He was short, squat and powerful and when he looked at me...' Huxtable paused, staring at nothing for a few seconds. 'In the future they have a technique to change your body. To add extra bits or change your skin tone. Purely cosmetic, of course. I thought that's what he had done, because under that hood was a forehead with two horns. He looked like something out of an old book.' He smiled directly at Eileen. 'I think you know the one I mean.'

She did. But she doubted the Devil appeared as many paintings depicted him. He was, after all, a fallen angel.

'I stepped back. Apologised, made to move off, when I felt this irresistible urge to turn, to look back at him. When I did, he had his hood back up. As he looked me over, I could feel his mind shifting through my own, like someone rifling through a filing cabinet. Then he simply turned and swept off.'

Huxtable continued. As he watched the newcomer over the next weeks and months, he discovered the man was the newly elected representative for the planet Hecate. Huxtable noticed that he didn't drink alcohol, he didn't try to work his way into the Serogant's favour or play the other representatives against each other. He simply waited. Huxtable looked into the policy platform that had allowed him to take Hecate. It was bland. Nothing but a list of whatever parochial requests the colony had been demanding. Nothing that made any economic sense. Others of the horned-one's family appeared at court, keeping to themselves. Their dark robes marking them out in the corridors of power as they swept past the other courtiers and courtesans.

Then there was an election on Crilia. Their new representative was another man in black robes, with horns on his forehead. They could have been brothers. Another family to join the first. They too had no recognisable policies, simply a string of promises to satisfy the colony, nothing achievable.

Finally, the world of Cydonia changed its rulers. Cydonia was a hereditary monarchy and chose its Imperial Representatives accordingly.

'I saw the rulers of Cydonia on the telepress.' Huxtable swallowed. 'They were strung on scaffolds in the city square, dangling in the breeze. Standing behind them, as the crowds cheered and hooted and hollered, were dark robed, hooded figures. The planet had fallen to the group now known as the Family.'

Eileen looked at his face. The memory seemed a raw one. Either the man genuinely believed that he had lived on a space empire in the future, or he was an incredibly good actor.

From that time, he told her, worlds fell like dominos. Always the same, a previously strong social order fell overnight, through ballot box or blood, always with the strength of feeling of the population, always replaced by the dark hoods of the Family.

Huxtable paused in his story.

'My father was the representative of Ragvarr. I remember when he lost his seat, we had to scramble to be out of the residence within an hour or so. Then *they* arrived.' He nearly spat the word, a curled lip betraying his feelings. 'Ousting our family wasn't sufficient. We had to run, but they were everywhere. We thought that we could escape, hide in the mountains. But friends we once trusted, betrayed us and led them to us. We were in a small shack, far away from any civilisation. One day, my parents told me to climb up into the attic. I had to stay quiet. Whatever happened.' He looked away. Eileen watched his face again, his lip trembled, briefly, before he turned back to her to continue his story. 'I could see through the rafters, I saw what they did.' He swallowed, his eyes sunken and haunted. 'I saw them tear the flesh from my parents' bones. Yet, I felt nothing but love and awe for them as they did it. It was like an all-pervading sense that what they did was completely right. It lasted until they were out of sight.'

Huxtable went into hiding. He'd been taught at an early age how to survive in the wild. Of course, there was an organised resistance. But the worlds still fell one by one to armies that bombed into submission and then detained and slaughtered anyone they saw as a threat. They acted without conscience. The native population of each world was all but enslaved. Each became a vassal, as the Family left a group of their own behind everywhere they arrived.

Eileen looked away from the images that accompanied this description. It was simply too real, looking at the images of the battles and the slaughter that followed. There was no film studio in the world that could have created those images. They could only be real. She began to look at Huxtable anew. But a truthful enemy could still be an enemy.

She thought of France, of her rush to escape when the German Army began rolling towards the border. Of towns, villages falling and the Jewish refugees that shared her train. She felt angry, all their efforts, all of the efforts of nearly every man, woman and child in Britain. The rationing, the hard work, the lost homes and the lost lives. All of this, and in a few thousand years, everything they had fought against would be repeated on a galactic scale.

'Didn't anyone do anything? Didn't anyone come and help your empire?'

Huxtable shook his head, looking at the floor. 'In the future, humanity is divided. Scattered across the galactic disc. We were all one empire once, but it couldn't hold. Maybe that's their purpose. To unite us all again. But they started with simple conquest.'

'What did you do next, after you escaped?'

He shrugged. 'It's a long tale. Enough to fill a bookshelf.

But the end of it is this: We found out who they are. They have been bred. They developed specialised psionic organs. On their temples, like devil's horns. They can project their thoughts. Control minds, even read them. Some can even attack the unconscious. They can drive a body into the sort of metabolic action that will literally make it burn. That's how a small Family controlled an army that covered a quarter of the Galaxy. No one can attack them. They can sense the attack coming and make the attacker take his own life. It's the perfect defence.'

'Bred…?'

'You've started doing it already in this era. There are men across a very narrow sea south of here that are perfecting the idea. They want to create a super race. But the Family weren't just a product of that. All the humans with the greatest psychic powers bred together. They were altered.' He pressed another button. A strange helix shape appeared, like two intertwining staircases. 'These, ah, elements shall we say, of their make-up have not come from humans. They have been introduced into the bloodline from elsewhere.'

'That's disgusting. They've bred with aliens?' Somehow, the idea was abhorrent. Doubly so after what Eileen had just seen.

He shrugged. 'Miscegenation in the future will be nowhere near the taboo it is now. However, no, I'm not suggesting they were crossbred like prize horses. I'm suggesting they were engineered. Like a weapon. Because that's what they are. That's all they are.'

'By who? And why?' She had no idea of the extent of the Nazi eugenic works. What did he mean, they had started already? Were they linked to these terrible creatures?

'I don't know. Possibly humans, possibly some outside force. We speculated that they wanted to turn all of humanity into some sort of army. I don't know what war they wanted us to fight.'

Maybe not the Nazis then, thought Eileen. But that hint at something going on across the channel chilled her.

'For our purposes here. It's not so important,' Huxtable continued. 'Once we discovered what they could do and how, we realised that our own taboos needed breaking. So, we went in search of a ready-made robot army.'

Eileen saw it immediately. 'Robots don't have minds to control. The Quarks could attack them!'

'Exactly. We were able to obtain them. Their masters had started using something far more terrible. I took the role of commander. I gave the orders and attacked the Family.'

The images above the desk changed again. The Dome that she had seen earlier, surrounded by sweeping roadways that soared above the pristine lakes and gardens below.

Through this arcadia ran crowds of people, a swirling mass that fled from the dome, men and women in a vaster array of clothes than Eileen had ever seen. They swept past small groups of stunted, solitary shapes standing on the walkways. After the crowds cleared, those shapes moved again. Not the ramshackle framework, firing machine guns, she had seen in the testing house. These were sleek, smooth lines of burnished metal. The doors of the dome were sealed, but the Quarks simply unleashed their weapons and melted them open.

She saw a vast council chamber, the size of Earl's Court. Space for representatives of every world inside it. And each of those representatives wore the now very familiar black robes and began firing strange weapons. She saw white fire cutting through the chamber, the members of the Family falling to the floor, Quarks exploding. Finally, masonry started falling and the roof itself fell in, dust and rubble obscuring the vision of whoever had taken this picture.

'In every world, in every palace they held. I helped to gun them down. I gave them all a quick death. As painless as possible. It was more than they had given to my family.'

'I'm so sorry.' It was all Eileen could think to say.

'So was I. And then we discovered that some were unaccounted for. They had got away.'

Eileen thought, her mind racing. So that was what he was hunting. Why he needed to build the Quarks. It came together. It wasn't for her to believe him. That was her superior's job. But she was certainly convinced.

'They came here, I mean, now? How?'

'It wasn't their technology. Three thousand years from now, and a thousand years before our time, humans will learn to traverse the time vortex in a nasty and dangerous way. Not a pleasant way to travel and you can't take much more than a suitcase with you. The Family had stockpiled the technology, ready to escape.' Huxtable laughed, briefly. 'And we thought that buying Quarks second hand was difficult. It took years to source the technology to follow them. There's no telling what they've got up to here since they arrived.'

'Why do you need our help?' Eileen felt calmer. It had been a struggle to take all of this in, but it made sense. It explained what Huxtable was doing here. It fit the evidence.

'We need to make sure that they are dealt with before they infect the whole history of Earth,' he said.

'Where are they?'

'They're close. Really close. The remnants of the Family are out in the countryside, not far from this city. And they are ruthless. They will kill anyone that comes looking for them. They've already started. You've lost a plane out there recently, I think?'

Eileen caught herself before she nodded. She was still bound by her duty. He pressed a button and the display ended. Light returning to the room.

'I'm nearly ready to send in the Quarks. But if I fail, the War Office Special Support Group must be ready to do everything they can. Believe me. This war you are fighting is terrible. But what the Family can do is far, far worse.'

CHAPTER ELEVEN

We'll Meet Again

TRAVERS STOPPED for breath as he climbed. The stone circle on his map was in the centre of a patch of moorland, high above the valley in which Edleton lay. He was now approaching the outcrop under which he had hidden from the Junker's bullets. As he breathed the hot air from his lungs, he could see the sun as it slowly dipped towards the horizon, bathing the land in an orange glow. The day had been hot, and the wind was starting to pick up, ready to cool the rocks. He was nearly within sight of the circle. Just a brief scramble up the rocks.

He pulled the iron helmet over his head, hoping that it would be sufficient. In one hand, he withdrew his revolver. If this plan didn't work, he had little doubt that he was to return home. Perhaps the images of Anne were a message, just to warn him off the scent. She wasn't in any danger and all would be well. As he placed one foot in front of the other to push up to the edge, he knew that a warning would never have been enough for the people he went to meet now.

If someone had professed the means and motivation to harm his family, he could not rest until he was certain they were safe.

As he crested the outcrop, through the rocks, scattered boulders and spikes of stone, he could see the circle in the distance, across the undulating purple heather now tinged with orange as a single hawk hovered above it and a couple of bees buzzed lazily from flower to flower. Something was wrong there and his eyes drifted from this idyllic scene to the black, blasted moors further up on Kinder, where the Bristol had come down. No vegetation had grown there for decades, all dead from the smog and smoke that blew from the cities.

Yet here was heather, and unseasonably early heather at that. It was now mid-June. The hills should not be turning that colour until August.

He put his field glasses to his eyes. He knew it. Shapes, too indistinct to see clearly, surrounded the circle. The long dresses and coats present as ever, but the bonnets and hats had been discarded. They were too far away for him to see faces.

He took a deep breath. Unsure if the hammering of his heart came from the distance he had climbed, or the task that lay ahead.

Again, the heather tugged and caught at his clothes, paths disappeared into patches of marsh and bog where foul smelling water seeped into the top of his boots. Nevertheless, he pressed on towards the circle, trusting to the qualities of the iron to keep him safe.

He saw the figures clearer as he got within fifty feet of the circle, indistinct in the growing twilight. He crouched to the ground, creeping closer, his revolver a reassuring weight in his hand. The itch at the back of his head had returned, the nagging sense of dread and loss. He was very close now. They all appeared unarmed. Travers took a deep breath and swallowed. He hoped these people would listen to reason. He stepped forward and coughed loudly.

The group all turned to him. They were the Boggarts he remembered from the farmhouse earlier. Men, women and children, all now bareheaded, their faces deeply creased and their bodies squat and powerful. Travers stared in fascination, transfixed by one feature in particular. Jutting from the temples of each and every man and woman were two, stubby, but perfectly formed horns.

They were the very image of the Christian devil and the primal gods that came before.

Matthew typed the last sentence of his report, hit the full stop and sat back, massaging his hands. It was an ironic fact that secretaries in the civil service could rarely type well. He had heard no sign of the return of Professor Travers or the arrival of the squad from the War Office Special Support Group. He stood and went to find Cownall.

Rather surprisingly, he and Beatrice were in the parlour. They were playing chess.

'No sign of the squad or the professor yet?' Matthew asked.

Cownall didn't look up. Matthew hadn't revealed his old rank, but he could at least expect some respect as a civilian. He restrained himself from barking at the man.

'The professor keeps his own timetable. He's not keen on the military,' said Cownall, slowly moving his bishop. 'As for the squad, well, I had to arrange to radio them to tell them to get some explosive ordinance on the way up. They're probably stuck arguing with the quartermaster at some base off the Great North Road. Checkmate.'

Beatrice looked down at the board. 'Damn,' she said. 'Looks like we'll need a decider then.' She set the pieces again. 'I'll say this, Matthew. Conscription does produce a better class of NCO.'

Matthew smiled, a smile that froze as he heard the haunting familiar wail of a siren howling in the city outside.

'Air raid. To the shelter!' he snapped.

Beatrice shook her head slowly and pointed at the window, where the road would have been without the blackout. 'Just up there is the biggest POW camp in England. This is one of the safest places we can be in a raid.'

Matthew relaxed slightly, lowering himself stiffly into a chair. 'What were you on civvie street, Cownall?'

The corporal sat back. 'A lot of things. I raced cars, gambled, made money. Mostly I'm in finance. Not much of a financial industry even before that little twerp invaded Poland. The point is, nothing I did was reserved. So here I am.' He shrugged and grinned lopsidedly.

'Why the War Office Special Support Group? I didn't trust them when I heard they'd been handed this job.' Matthew folded his hands behind his back, watching everything Cownall did.

'Well, that was my mistake. Saw they were based in Blighty and assumed they wouldn't see any active service. My family pulled some strings. Now I know what they're about, joke's on me isn't it?' The grin had frozen now.

Matthew pulled a chair up. 'I wasn't conscripted in the last war. I couldn't wait to sign up. My brother tried to jump the queue. He lied about his age. It didn't work. By then, they were on to that sort of thing.' He glanced at Beatrice, flicking his eyes to the door.

She nodded slightly and stood to leave. As she stepped out the door, Cownall turned to Matthew, his face taking on a less flippant look as he leaned forward.

'What was your rank?'

'Captain.'

'Sir.' Cownall made to stand.

Matthew waved him down. 'Not high enough for the family's liking. I didn't join up again this time.' He sighed and drummed his fingers before turning back to Cownall. 'I know a reluctant corporal when I see one.'

'I'm not scared,' said Cownall. 'Sir,' he added.

'I never thought you were. You ran towards machine gunfire.' Matthew remembered men convalescing in the hospital. The lucky ones who had only seen the bullets go through their legs or arms instead of perforating their torso like their comrades. 'That kind of action is brave. Like as not get you killed.' He winced inside. 'You're not so good with orders.'

'Not minded for it, sir. Not looking forward to Captain Day getting here to tell the truth.'

Matthew smiled. 'A harsh command?'

Cownall pursed his lips. 'Bit of a ball ache to tell the truth. So why not join up again?'

Matthew stared at the window. The faint evening breeze rattled it behind the blackout blinds. 'Sometimes command has to be harsh. It's difficult ordering men into danger when...'

'When they're friends,' finished Cownall.

Neither man said anything for a few moments.

'What happened?' Cownall asked, eventually.

'France; I joined up late. Didn't see a lot of action on the front. I ended up on mine duty after the armistice. Had to clear a field. The CO sent us out there, pointed at the hill he thought we had to climb and told us to get. They were our mines and that was our orders.' Matthew thought back. He had struggled to talk about it, but such a direct question was hard to ignore.

'Do and die.' Cownall's tact was second to none.

'Exactly,' said Matthew. 'I trusted our briefing. I should

have studied the maps myself, but hindsight is wonderful.'

Cownall nodded, understanding. 'The CO got it wrong.'

'Badly. Poison gas mines. I was halfway across before one of the lads stepped on one. He died in the mud. Not all of them got their masks on in time. I stood there, the gas so thick I couldn't see where to step safely.'

'It sounds so simple.'

'It was.' Matthew's heart was beating hard just recalling it. 'But it was a gross mistake. And even though I led them in, my father assumed that I was guilty of cowardice for standing there. I had only joined up a few months earlier. So that was the defining moment in my army career. Getting my men slaughtered. There was talk of a court martial but, of course, the CO would have been up there with me. Easier to brush it all away and lean on me to take a discharge.' He felt hot-faced just admitting it.

Cownall surprised him. 'How are you judging yourself?'

'Sorry?'

'What standards are you using? You and your father obviously have the same ones, a way that someone should act in war. But the way I see it, that's rubbish. There are no standards in a war. You just do whatever you can to try and get you and everyone through it.' Cownall looked around himself. 'And if you mess up, like getting a transfer to Professor Challenger's kamikaze battalion for instance, then it wasn't you. It's war. War's supposed to kill people. That's what it's for. That's why we probably shouldn't have too many of them.'

Matthew rose to his feet, ready to give the ungrateful NCO something to talk about, when he heard the door being hammered on.

'Finally. The troops. About time you had a CO to keep you in line.'

Matthew made for the door, killing the lamp in the hall to stop the light spilling out into the garden. He flung it open.

The short young lady outside with the determined set to her jaw was not Cownall's CO. He had met her before, on the hill outside the Pickering Steelworks. With a certainty, he knew who it was.

Eileen Le Croissette. He pulled her into the house, away

from the raid, and turned the hallway lamp back on. Feet came running down the stairs.

'Eileen!' called Beatrice as she cleared the final marble step. 'You escaped!'

Eileen shook her head. 'I didn't escape. After he told me about what's really going on, it's taken me ages to find you. Why on earth did you leave the address with that old lady?' She took a deep breath. She'd obviously trekked a long way.

'Old lady?' Matthew flicked his eyes towards Cownall and Beatrice who both gave slight shakes of their heads.

'Yes, she was in very strange clothes. She must have bought them abroad. She was waiting outside the steelworks, on the other side of the street. She shouted your address over to me.' Eileen looked from one to the other, clearly taking in Cownall's Special Support Group insignia. 'I think I need to remind you all of the need for absolute discretion on operations. Walls have ears after all. We'll say no more about it.'

Matthew resisted the urge to raise an eyebrow. 'So, Huxtable let you go then, miss?'

'I wasn't in any danger from Huxtable. You see, I think he's doing the right thing. He's trying to act against an enemy. A very dangerous enemy. Worse than the Jerries.' Eileen looked at Cownall. 'So where is the rest of the Group? I thought this was a major operation?'

A strange hollow thought came over Matthew.

'What kind of enemy?' He thought of orders given again. Of men dying where he had led them.

'A secretive group. Out in the countryside. In the High Peak. They've got powerful psionic abilities and are utterly ruthless.'

Matthew groaned. At least last time he had been there when his men were killed. This time he had let Professor Travers ride off to his death.

Travers held the knife in his hand, point down. The figures around him swayed and chanted as he advanced through the circle towards the altar. The steady chant, almost Latin, almost Celtic, but truly nothing of either. The air crackled, the static increasing as the tempo of the chant did. The people around him parted, letting him tread the path to the victim, tied down. He raised the knife, and loudly, clearly, said a prayer to the creators. The victim's head was turned away; that made it easier. A sacrifice was a job that had to be done, but much easier not to look into the innocent's eyes. He stepped forward for the final strike, ready to plunge the knife deep inside the chest of this unfortunate.

The head turned and again he recognised the child, the piercing eyes, the unruly black hair. Anne.

In a moment, he realised what was happening again. Another vision, breaking through his defences. A warning or a real threat. He concentrated, forcing his mind to act against it, like a signal man trying to send a runaway train into a catch point. He focused on that image, such a mundane and sensible thing, far away from the horror before him.

Anne's face faded. His hand was empty. One of the robed individuals turned to him. As the edge of his vision sharpened and the blurriness faded, he could see her face clearly.

'I think,' she said, her accent an old-fashioned English one; a hint of French and West Country, 'that we need to take a different tack with you, Professor.'

CHAPTER TWELVE
Over the Hills and far Away

THEY LED him back to their farm. Not in chains, not threatened by weapons, not even using their formidable mind control powers. They simply asked him to follow them and he did.

The men ignored him for the most part, occasionally glancing at him, as if to check he was still following. The younger members jostled and even walked arm in arm as they trudged across the moors, even children followed, scurrying between the adults. The sun was gone now, leaving only the silvery moonlight to guide their steps. It was not enough. Several times, Travers stumbled, catching his foot on a rock or tripping over the lip of a small animal's home.

The old woman walked next to him. 'You can call me Morrigan,' she had told him.

'An old name,' he volunteered.

She nodded with a small noise at the back of her throat. 'We are an old people. Both in an individual's years and since our ancestors came here.'

'So, how old are you?' Travers heard his own voice form around the words before he could stop himself. 'Sorry, madam, I don't want to offend…'

She laughed as he said it.

'I'm one hundred and fifty-three. There are treatments in our time that can extend a life, far beyond what anyone born now could hope for.' She walked in silence for a moment. 'You can take that helmet off, you know.'

'No, thank you.' Travers wasn't ready for that yet. 'I still don't trust you. As much as you have now, certainly, begun to treat me better than you treated your previous guests, I want to keep this layer of protection on and around my brain.'

'We have an oral tradition to pass our history on. The Iron Age was a difficult time for us, but we stayed here.' She gestured down to the valley, the darkness of the night encroaching onto it, bringing with it the sudden, bitter, wind that always followed a warm day in England. 'Fortunately, it turns out that it's only iron that has the effect. Strange that steel does not. Please keep that to yourself.'

'I'll be sure to,' said Travers, meaning nothing of the sort.

'This is not the first war that we have seen. We've lived through the English Civil War, the Wars of the Roses, the Norman Invasion and, before all of that, the Battle of Hope Valley.' Morrigan sighed. 'And yet, this is not our home. Long ago, we came from another world, another time.'

Travers pulled to a halt. 'You look human enough.' As he said it, it felt inadequate.

'We are.' A cold, hard stare in her eyes brought him up short.

He waved a hand airily at the horns on Morrigan's head. 'Apart from those. Positioned on the temples. That fits nicely with the frontal lobes. They assist you with your psychic abilities, I imagine.'

'We are human.' Her voice stayed level. A slight tremble and a shake of her jaw betraying her. 'We have been altered by millennia of breeding. Formed into what you see.'

Travers stood, feeling the chill wind brush over him as he stood on the plateau, surrounded by these people.

'And what is it that you have been formed into?'

Morrigan stopped, her lips pursed. 'We are weapons,' she said at last. 'The most terrible of weapons. We can turn a society against itself. Mother would kill son.' She paused and locked eyes with him. 'Father would kill daughter.'

The words hung in the air.

'Anne…'

'So that's her name,' a male voice said.

One of the young men stepped forward, short and squat like the others. He looked barely more than a boy.

'You know that you could do it, you know that we could make you do it.' He smiled as he said these words, watching as Travers slowly began to tense and move towards him.

A girl appeared behind the boy's shoulder, a soft grin on her face. The boy leaned forward before a larger man placed his hands on both of their shoulders.

'Enough, Egcbert, Arian.'

Travers could see the family resemblance as they turned to the older man, their lips curled in identical expressions of distaste. Calmly, he led them away.

Morrigan turned back and continued to lead the way through heather and sphagnum. Travers shouted after her.

'What can you do to Anne?'

Morrigan stopped dead and turned to him, leaning closer. Even in the dim moonlight, he could see her face, her piercing eyes like those of a snake, unblinking.

'We don't harm anyone without extremely good reason. And unless we have encountered them or they have been on our land, we cannot touch them. If someone like you is close enough, spent a lot of time with someone, it forms a bridge and we can see into their minds. But that's all we can do to your family. They are safe.' She paused and glanced up into the sky. 'From us at least.'

Travers realised then what they had done. They had read his mind, sent him those images of Anne, knowing full well that he cared for her more than anything else. That violation of his own mind, of his daughter's, stung like a slap to the face.

'And those airmen. The ones that crashed here. How safe were they? What about the child? Charles Peeves? What about all the other children that you have taken, down the years, from the parents and kept out here?' Travers' anger was flowing now. Despite the cold air he could feel the warmth rising inside him.

To use Anne against him, to make him think that he could harm her...

'Come with me.' Morrigan cut away from the path, over broken, undulating ground, where gorse pulled at Travers' ankles and threatened to bring him down.

Eventually, she stopped, Travers stood next to her. By her feet was a small boulder, tall, shaped by the wind into that characteristic wheel shape so common there. Others sat with it, like an inverted garden, rocks growing among vegetation.

'What's this?' he said.

111

Morrigan's voice was quiet, almost reluctant in the dark evening. 'This? Why, this is a graveyard.'

The back of a Bedford truck in transit was not the ideal place for a briefing. However, Eileen and Cownall had convinced Captain Day that an attack on Owd Hob's Meade was needed. Day struggled to make his voice heard over the rattling of the flat back and the thumping of the wind on canvas.

'The targets are a small group,' he shouted. 'We believe that they are unarmed by conventional means, but possessed of powerful psychic abilities. That means that they can control minds.' The van rocked as it rounded a corner. 'By the time we arrive, the sun will be close to rising. We'll have lost the cover of darkness if we tarry.' He pointed to Eileen, sat at the side. 'Section Officer Le Croissette has provided us with valuable information about the threat posed by this group. They are a previously unknown race, to all intents and purposes.'

Eileen shifted somewhat uncomfortably to hear herself referred to as the source. If the information she had been debriefed of proved to be wrong, she could look very foolish. Or worse, have blood on her hands.

'They are brutal sorts,' Day continued. 'The standing order is that as soon as you think you, or any of your fellow troops, is falling under any influence, you are to take action immediately. Is that clear to you all?'

A chorus of 'Yes, sirs!' rang out.

'Excellent. The plan is that the truck will drop us off at the end of the lane and from there we will move through the fields around the target farmhouse. It is vital that at all times you maintain total silence.' He looked at each of the men in turn. 'We have no idea of their capabilities. It may be that they can even sense us coming from a distance.' Day began to detail which sections of his squad should take which route towards the farmhouse.

Day, Eileen mused, was an ideal officer for the Fourth. He was experienced and intelligent. He had a keen mind that approached a mission as a problem-solving exercise. But he didn't question the information given to him. He simply took, as read, every strange thing that the Fourth threw at him as another problem to solve.

So, when the troops had finally arrived at the Bodian house, redirected by Cownall's messages to various army bases along the Great North Road, for munitions, he had calmly listened to everything he was told about robots from the future that were on their side, psychic powered horned men that once ruled a galactic empire, and the missing professor. That last one, he had found particularly easy to believe.

'Damn the man!' he had said. 'If he was a member of the Forces he would be on a charge.' It was an idle threat. Even if applying a court martial to Travers wasn't more trouble than it was worth, he was simply too valuable an asset to the Fourth to treat poorly.

Eileen had told Day of the danger that Travers was in. Huxtable had been clear to her. He would not attack until he was ready. But when he did, he would not leave survivors in that homestead. He had been very apologetic, but if they didn't get Travers out soon, he would be dead one way or the other.

Then, despite the protestations of Captain Stewart, Eileen and Cownall, Day calmly took out a map of the area and drew up a plan of attack before instructing them to leave. Eileen had even had time to change into her battledress uniform. The slacks were far more practical than the skirt she had worn to traipse around the steel works.

'Section Officer Le Croissette,' Day said, quietly, as he moved down to where she sat.

'Sir?'

'Obviously, you will remain with the truck. I want you to keep a close eye on everything that happens using the field glasses. At the first sign that anything is going wrong, that we have lost our minds or started to rout, you and Driver Warren are to return to safety and inform General Dornan at once.'

'Yes, sir.'

Day was worried then. He thought there was a real risk that he and his men would not make it out, and didn't want them to find out. She looked around the truck. Did they know? Private Barns was pointing out of the back door at the hills, telling the disinterested men either side of him about the escarpment marking the edge of one rock type and the start of another. The Fourth tended to make a grab for the more educated conscripts before the RAF got hold of them.

She looked across at Cownall. He sat still on the bench, his rifle in both hands and head bowed. The irreverent joker that couldn't even take war seriously was praying. He looked up at her and winked.

'We're going to need all the help we can get, aren't we?'

Before she could answer, Warren slammed on the brakes and the truck slid across its bare rubber tyres to a halt.

'Take a seat.' Morrigan indicated the dining table that Travers had examined earlier that day.

Travers quietly took the iron helmet off his head and placed it on the table. Not a single twinge. They were making good on their promise.

'Where's the boy? He's the one that brought me here. Is he also in a grave?'

Morrigan sighed as the other Boggarts busied themselves around her fetching cakes and bread. She pointed at one of the children, one that still wore his hat from the long trek on the moors.

'Here he is, try to keep up.'

The boy looked much the same as the rest of the children, as they ran in and out of the dining room and kitchen weaving between the legs of the adults. As he focused on the child, Travers could see that the fine downy fur that covered the hands and necks of the other family members was absent. Then the child turned to him and Travers was left in no doubt.

'You've got your mother's eyes,' he murmured. A perplexed look crossed the boy's face, then he shook his head as if trying to dislodge an insect and ambled off to follow his peers.

'He doesn't remember his mother.' Morrigan pulled a chair out and leaned against it.

Travers slapped his hand down against the table, causing the wooden bowls to jump as he did so. 'How can you do that to a child?' Again, the thoughts of Anne and Alun slipped into his mind.

'Indeed? And are you any better? Leaving them so far away. At least Charles doesn't know what is missing. Anne has only just decided that she wants to be a scientist and now...'

'Stop that.' His voice caught in his mouth, he couldn't find the words to express his hatred at the way they forced their way into his mind, into his family. The strength of the image faded away, but the sense of Anne, of Alun, playing in the Goff's garden remained. Was this a remnant of the memory, or were they still hanging at the edges of his mind with their powers?

'Our power is not absolute. He can either remember everything, including who we are, or nothing, as he is now. He is not the first that we have taken in.'

Travers thought of the list of names in Carter's book, and of the silent, still graves on the moors. A lonely island in a sea of heather with no visitors.

'What do you want from him?' Images flashed through his head of occultism and sacrifice. Surely such a thing would not happen in England.

'He was brought here. It was not a decision of all of us, but rather that of a single member of our family.'

Travers looked around the table as she spoke. Egcbert almost withdrew into himself, his bony shoulders giving him the appearance of a tortoise as it emerged from his shell.

'The fawn,' Travers said. His mind racing. 'It was on your land. You avoid meat.'

'The creature was known to those of us that have explored the area. It was taken from its mother and slaughtered. It was only fair that after we destroyed its killer, we should also take the family's child.' Egcbert leaned against the corner of the room as he spoke.

Travers could see Morrigan's eyes dart towards the boy.

'The difficulty we have, is that now this young fool has brought the boy to us, he has seen us, knows where we live and who we are,' she said. 'He, like our previous visitors, is a danger to us if he leaves with his memories intact. We will look after him as one of our own, but he cannot leave.'

Travers took this in. He thought of Chief Petty Officer Peeves, a man thought to have deserted, but who he now knew was clearly dead. 'You can stand to kill a man but not lose an animal.'

'They are the same to many of us. They feel the same pain,

want the same things. Food, companionship. And family.' It wasn't Egcbert that spoke, but the man that Travers had assumed was his father.

'Well, to us, they are cattle and game. A line has to be drawn somewhere.'

The man shrugged his huge, muscled shoulders. 'It was an explanation. Not an excuse. I didn't want my children turning up with one of yours, any more than you do.'

Morrigan looked around and beckoned Travers with her, away from the main gathering of the family, into the hallway.

'Athel is a simple man. A blacksmith. He is unusual to work so close to iron still. He is very sensitive to the threats of the outside world. His children are more curious about it. The endless battle of youth and experience.'

Travers nodded with a smile to himself.

Morrigan pointed at one of the paintings he had noted before, a black robed figure stood over a massacre. Slaughtered and dismembered women and children lay in the square, shattered food and entertainment stalls, the remnant of its previous life before the black boiler suited figures had rampaged through it.

'This is who we are. Who our ancestors are. Or will be, if you like.' She sighed and pointed to the figure at the back. 'We keep up this artwork to remind ourselves of what we are capable of. That, in turn, reminds us of our training. We don't feel empathy naturally. It has been bred out of us. We have to search for it, through contemplation, meditation.'

'And the children found it in the deer,' finished Travers. 'Very astute of them.'

'The skill to feel the pain of another does not override the ease with which we can take revenge of the worst kind, if we choose. If we are angry, or threatened. That beast lives within us.'

Travers thought of his feelings as he approached the stone circle. 'So, Egcbert...?'

'Intensive training. We need him to be with us. He has such mental skills and power. He could transform matters for people like us. He made a mistake in killing that man.'

Travers ran his fingers over the painting. The brushwork was wonderful. Such attention to detail and vibrancy of colour.

'Whoever made you, I don't think you've left your glory days behind. The thing that brought us here, brought that plane overhead, was flares. High towers of flame coming from the moors. What are they?'

Morrigan avoided his gaze. 'These are ancient islands. Riddled with settlements, worship places and graves. Think of Boscombe Moor, Devil's End, Little Hodcombe...' She looked out of the window of the farmhouse, her old eyes glazing over. 'Those places have power that we can tap into. The same with that circle up on the moors. Think what happens when you use your energy sources. Wood, coal, gas.'

'They burn,' Travers said simply. 'And the same with yours. Psionic power is something I still don't fully understand yet, but clearly whatever you are doing is creating a signature writ large across the moors. You're lucky that you haven't attracted any German bombers.'

She shrugged. 'They can't do much damage to our sites. They've dropped a couple of loads up there on the moors.'

'What happened to the British plane? You've shown me where the airmen are. Why did it come down?'

She sighed. 'Our work has caused some very localised confusion. Navigation doesn't work as it should. The plane's crew thought it was higher than it was, thought it flew straight when it climbed...'

'You expect me to believe that was an accident. After abducting a boy, after what happened to his father? What are you doing here?' That was the one aspect that Travers, maddeningly, still didn't fully understand.

'There's a war on.' It was such a simple answer. Usually used by people as an excuse for not having something, not doing something. But not by Morrigan. 'We may not have a lot of interaction with those in the village, but we will help where we can. A little nudge here, a little moment of doubt there, and a Japanese bullet meant for one of the men that has been called up will disappear safely into the undergrowth.'

But Travers knew, simply from looking at her face, that they would never interfere with the bigger picture. They would see the men from the village safely home, but they would not try to affect who would control this country when they got back.

'And you need these stone circles for that?' he asked.

Morrigan was facing away from him still, looking at the sky splashed with stars beyond the glass and crumbling white plaster of her home. He could see her nod.

He didn't accept it. There would have been no stone circles to tap into out in space. He supposed that their own innate, bred, powers could, coincidentally, link with these ancient sites placed here so long ago. But to what end? That was something he simply didn't know and couldn't ask.

'Why Anne? Why did you show me all those images of my daughter being killed in such terrible ways?'

Morrigan sat at the foot of the stairs. Her body crumpled like a sack of potatoes. 'As a warning,' she said simply. 'A warning to keep you away.'

'It didn't work.' Travers felt the building of his anger again.

'We know that now. Gender is different in our time. A man would not ignore such obvious danger for someone else just because they are a woman. Perhaps we should have paid more attention to the age of chivalry.' She shrugged. 'But then, I wouldn't be in charge, would I?' She laughed, starting as a cackle but growing deeper and more genuine.

'But why, Anne?' he asked again.

'You care about her. More than your wife. And oh, I am so sorry about her…'

'Sorry? She's ill, but far from Death's door…'

Morrigan's eyes stopped him. Sad but piercing. She knew, again, much more than he did.

'How do you…?'

'We can see into minds. The brain, if you want to be technical. That's where it is. And it will grow inside her until you lose Margaret forever. I am, truly, deeply, sorry.'

Travers sat down in the hallway with a thump. Of course, these people could say anything. They had already threatened Anne, what difference would it be if they also put Margaret in their sights? He should challenge them, call their bluff.

But he couldn't. Somehow, it fit everything that he knew about Margaret's condition that he hadn't wanted to confront himself.

'You can do something. If you can see it, you can cure it.'

His voice was flat as he said the words.

Morrigan placed a wrinkled hand, like dice wrapped in tissue paper, on his shoulder. 'We can influence the mind's actions. We can't change anything of the body and what makes it. I'm sorry, Edward Travers.'

'Why?' Travers' thoughts were fighting their way out of his mouth, ignoring the grief, leaving it curled in a corner, waiting to strike again. 'Why do you take such steps to protect yourselves?'

'We are in danger. Our ancestors made enemies.' Morrigan pointed back at the painting. Travers found it hard to look at what the figures were doing. 'Who do you think they are?' she said, pointing at the young men, black uniforms and tool belts looking like last decade's pulp spacemen, yet with hands caked in blood as they thrust their hands into the piles of bodies to bring the still living up, and dash their heads on the ground.

'The muscle for the chap at the back in the black robe. I'm guessing he's your ancestor.'

Morrigan shook her head. 'They were an army that was plotting against us after we took the post of Serogant. That is their planet of Pesgoda. The women and children were hiding, thinking they were safe. Our ancestors found out about the plot. Those men you see carrying out the massacre weren't our troops. They were their victims' fathers and husbands. Their punishment was to be allowed to see what they had done and to live with it.'

Travers breathed out slowly. 'How many generations have passed? Are any of the people that did this still alive?'

Morrigan shrugged. 'We are a long way adrift from our time and we live longer than present day humans. But in linear terms? Around two thousand years. Maybe twenty-five generations.'

'Then none of you can be blamed for this. How can anyone still pursue you for what happened so long ago.'

She put her head in her hands and muttered something about time aware cultures that Travers didn't quite catch. 'They can because to them it happened a matter of years ago.' Morrigan tapped her teeth. 'How many wolves are there in the country?'

'None, the last wolf was killed in Scotland in the

119

seventeenth century.'

'Why? Did every wolf then living kill livestock or children?' She shook her head at Travers. 'The reality is that wolves were hunted for what they were and what they were capable of. And we are no different. We all have the ability to command armies again by thought alone. We all have an instinctive compulsion to take control, to be callous, brutal. We have had to train our own mental abilities to give us that empathy. We could lapse at any stage. That is why people from our time will follow us, and kill us. No matter how many years have passed for us.' She sighed. 'To them, we are a disease that must be eradicated.'

Travers had heard such talk before, from men dressed in black, now detained for the duration. 'I think someone has already followed you,' he said. 'He has brought with him some kind of robot. Short, a little comical, but deadly.'

Morrigan was back on her feet in an instant. 'Quarks!' she hissed. 'Stories of them have been passed down to us. Those things were used to try to wipe us out before. Armies of them dispatched, with no human troops to back them up. They're small, but vicious and very cunning.'

Travers nodded. He could feel the weight of his tired limbs now. 'We faced one down in a factory in Sheffield. I don't know if they have found you yet. Their controller has a friend of mine as a prisoner. Can you help me get her out?'

'They will find us, with people like you poking their noses in.' Morrigan tutted. 'Over a thousand years in one place, working this land, and soon we will have to move again.'

She stormed back into the dining room where the rest of the family were piling their plates high with cakes and breads in a way that would have been impossible in the outside world. All eyes turned to Morrigan as she stood in the doorway.

'They've found us,' was all that she said.

The intake of breath across the room was palpable; it was an instant realisation that Travers knew well, the look on faces when the sirens had gone off for the first time. The sense that a long-dreaded day had finally come. One child ran to a woman, presumably his mother, who scooped him up into her arms.

'We need to keep a watch,' said Morrigan. 'A constant

watch on every side. Our only chance is to ensure that we see the Quarks coming and make good our escape.'

'How did they find us here? And now?' Athel stepped forward.

Travers could see the tension in the muscles across his broad chest, still visible through the eighteenth-century shirt he wore.

'The "now" is easy to answer. They have checked their records and archives and they brought the Quarks here. We can only hope that our destruction here isn't a stable time loop.' Morrigan breathed deeply. 'As for whether or how they found out that we live here.' She rounded on Travers. 'That appears to be something that our new guest can help with.'

CHAPTER THIRTEEN
Doing Nothing at the End of the Lane

'**THE HOUSE** is a mile away. Everyone out and get moving,' called Day at the troops gathered inside the Bedford, their tin helmets in place and rifles ready. Almost as an afterthought, he quietly added, 'Good luck, lads,' as they scrambled out.

Eileen was left in the back. She dropped down and made her way to the cab, the sudden chill of the countryside made her shiver. The valley was a narrow one, the hills seemingly towering over it, only visible as the stars appeared suddenly above their black walls.

Warren was enjoying a cigarette. He offered her one as she climbed into the cab. She shook her head. The truck itself might be obvious enough on its own. She didn't want to help by providing a burning match as well.

'How long d'you reckon they've been here then?' he asked.

'Huxtable said they'd not arrived long before he had.'

Warren shrugged. 'That's not what Cownall said, was it? He said that the prof thinks they're behind all this folklore.'

Eileen sat quietly. 'Maybe they came to here and now because they matched the folklore that we already have?'

'Could be.' He took a long drag on his cigarette and let its flickering glare light up his face. 'It sounds to me that all of this is rationalising. Trying to make something old look like part of this modern world. Make it look like something we can understand.'

Eileen tried to get her head around what he meant. In Huxtable's spartan office, with the hologram flickering in the centre of it, it had felt like something that was at least possible. Although powerful, the Family had been something that could be grasped.

But she was out there, in the dark, surrounded by an ancient landscape, watching men she knew disappearing into the dark and a commander who was terrified by the unknown that he faced, but went anyway. Out there, the people that lived in that far off farmstead were more than just humans from the future. They were something primal, the thing that made sure that travellers in fairy tales stayed on the path when crossing the forest. They were the ones that stole children and lured away grown men. Professor Travers was with them now, as was the poor young boy from the village.

'They're not the Devil,' she said quietly.

Warren smiled. 'I reckon they're older than that. They're what was out here before people knew who the Devil was.'

Eileen put the field glasses to her eyes, scanning the landscape. It had been a couple of minutes since the men had left. She looked for some sign of them. She shouldn't have been too concerned. If she could not see any, then that was according to plan. But she could not escape the feeling that the moors out there had claimed another victim.

She thought of the flares that Cownall had said were responsible for bringing both her and Professor Travers to this region. Mysterious lights out on the moors leading travellers astray. Even that was something from old stories and fables. All things that had seemed so quaint and un-threatening when confronted by the might of the Nazi war machine just across the sea.

'No raids here tonight,' she observed.

The all-clear had sounded over Sheffield just before they had left. It had probably been a stray squadron heading for Liverpool that had set the sirens off. She wondered how the Filter Room was tonight. It was a rare night that was completely quiet.

'They've not been bothering so much recently,' Warren agreed. 'They're still out there, mind you. Further south it's still putting out incendiaries most nights.' He thought. 'Hey! If those chaps out there really can control folks' minds, then imagine what they can do to a German bomber squadron. They could send them up and then have them all fall back down on Berlin.' He laughed at the prospect and Eileen joined in.

'That's what we're for. Finding new ways to attack the Germans.' She was silent a moment or two, glancing back through the field glasses at the still, silent, fields and moors. She thought for a moment of the downed Bristol. 'Have they already done it?' she wondered. 'To us? Have they already brought our planes down?'

Warren shrugged. Not dismissively, but as someone that was unsure of something.

'I was with the squad that had to go and find it. We trekked up there in the driving rain. The mud and the peat sucks you in like quicksand. One lad ended up to his waist in it. No idea why those rambler chaps want the freedom to tramp around up there. It's a horrible place.'

'Was it quick for them?' Eileen knew the feeling of knowing a plane had gone down. To her it was a number and a piece on a map, but she and the girls never forgot that in each one was a group of men, many of whom had wives and children.

'It had burst into flames, so I can only hope they died on impact. The bodies were missing. Maybe they burned up.' Warren sighed. 'They decided to bring us back in to look into this job. Provide a bit of continuity and make sure that there's only so many lips that can turn loose, if you catch me drift.'

Eileen didn't need to ask why this had to be kept a secret. The wartime propaganda was that the British planes were better made, better flown and more heavily armed. If people found that these planes could be used against the public, there would be mass panic. Ack-ack guns would be trained on British planes. Brits shooting Brits. It would have been a very difficult one for the Filter Room to clear up before innocent lives were lost.

The men must have been in position. She focused on the farmhouse. That would be where any action would be. Behind a tangle of twisted hazel trees, she could see the bare stone walls of the place. Warren shifted next to her. She knew he was checking where his rifle was and preparing to drive if anything went wrong.

A shape shot across her field of view. Maybe a soldier, it appeared to be carrying a pack and rifle. Still no movement from the house. She risked a glance over to the eastern horizon, past the lip of the moors that marked the edge of Sheffield. Was there a faint glimmer there of an encroaching dawn? If they did not move quickly, the enemy would no longer be benighted.

A small part of her thought that they were best confronted with the light of the sun, but she knew that the sooner these people found out they were under attack, the harder it would be.

Figures moved by the high wall to the side of the farmhouse. She focused on them with the glasses. It looked like Captain Day and Cownall. Day was gesturing, seemingly at the top of the wall. Cownall swung his rifle over his shoulder and put his hands on the wall, ready to jump over with a boost from Day who crouched and cupped his hands.

'They're making a move,' she said.

Warren stubbed his cigarette out. 'It's worse watching.'

Eileen tensed, leaning forward with the glasses in an instinctive desire for a better view, the metal edge of the Bedford's open window digging into her elbows. They were lucky. No brilliant glare of the sun today, despite it being Midsummer's day, just a latent lightening from blue black to dark grey. The men wouldn't be lit up. She found her heart thumping. She had joined to do her bit, to help out the war effort as much as possible and, ultimately, do something interesting, but this was one of the few times when men she actually knew were in danger.

As she sought Cownall's shape again, her heart almost stopped altogether as a tap came on the door below her.

She paused and looked down. It was a priest, elderly but clearly in rude health and with jowls that hung down over his dog collar.

'Reverend! You gave me a fright.'

He ignored this, pointing over at the farmhouse. 'A Private and a Section Officer from the WAAF. I've seen lots of you soldiers around. You must be the superior, Miss.' He nodded at Eileen who realised that, technically she was. Albeit she had no authority over Warren. 'What are those soldiers doing?'

Eileen thought. 'It's classified.' *And you wouldn't believe me anyway*, she thought.

'Well, they're classifying in a theologically sensitive area .

of my parish. Pull them out.'

Eileen shook her head and held her chin up. 'I can't do that, Reverend. The CO is with them.'

'CO...?' He pondered, blowing air into his cheeks. 'This isn't just manoeuvres, is it? Good Lord, you're actually going to attack the place!' He backed away from the van, turning for the road leading to the farm, the darkness of his clothes fading into the deeper gloom of the arched trees.

Warren jumped from the cab, his boots hit the ground running, sending stones and dust scattering in the dull ghost light of the morning. Eileen heard a muffled thud and a shout. Clearly the elderly priest had been no match for a trained and fit private.

'Get off me!' the reverend was shouting as Warren dragged him back, holding him firmly by the sleeves. 'I'm a man of the cloth.'

'You were running into danger, sir.' Warren was firm, keeping his voice level.

'You're all in danger. That place is evil. It is not of this Earth. I have a duty to treat with whatever those beings are.'

'We're dealing with them, sir.' There was a slight shake in Warren's voice now. Eileen knew why.

How could anyone really deal with people with the powers that Huxtable had described? Satisfied that the reverend was now under control, she went back to observing the farmhouse. As she brought the glasses back up to her eyes, she saw that matters had changed over at the farm.

Soldiers could be seen standing in full view, rifles aimed, in the farmyard. Standing in the middle were, well, she knew them as soon as she saw them... It was the beings Huxtable had called the Family. The ones that had Travers, also now had the men from the Fourth.

Shaking, Cownall peered over the wall. The rough stone blocks cut into his hands as he scanned the garden beyond, seeing nothing but scattered wooden toys and unkempt greenery. He let his gaze wander further, towards the walls of the house itself. Tiny panes of dark glass gave no clue as to what lay beyond. He wanted to simply leave that as it was and drop down, let some other silly bugger put their head over the parapet and get it shot off, but he knew that he had to stick this one out. He wasn't a coward, he was pragmatic.

To relieve the pressure on Day, he pulled his torso further onto the top of the wall, finding a pair of tiny footholds in the contours of the gritstone. He could have hung there all day. He heard Day sigh with relief beneath his right foot.

Oh, come on, sir, I'm not that heavy.

Was there movement? Something beyond the glass. Just the movement of a tree branch or bird flickering across the mirror-like surface. He reached one hand back to motion to the rest of the squad to stop where they were. They were all in position now. Most of them in the farmyard and its constituent buildings. Others were in the nearby slopes with a sniper's view-point. The hope was that anything that happened could not happen to all of them at once. Having heard Eileen's story, Cownall wasn't so sure. What were a bunch of British soldiers in a Derbyshire farm to a family that had controlled an empire across planets?

The movement came again. This time he was sure that a figure, recognisably a man, had their face pressed against the window. He could see no features, but whoever it was, was now watching him as intently as he was watching them. They knew he was here.

He let go of the top of the wall and let his feet hit the floor two metres down. The Army's best soles cushioned the impact, but not the noise.

'Shh!' hissed Day. 'They'll hear your bloody great clodhoppers.'

'Too late. They know we're here. They're already watching us.'

Just saying it gave Cownall a shiver. The feeling of something dwelling deep into the wilderness that knows you're there and waits. Like the wolf in the woods that was a real danger before it was a fairy tale. Day motioned to fall back and the two grabbed their rifles and retreated across the yard, heading for the barn in which the majority of the firepower was waiting for an order.

'Stop!'

The command echoed across the yard, bouncing off the stones like a rifle shot. It also reverberated through Cownall's head. He found it hard to refuse the order, his feet moving as if through liquid mud, his shoulders swinging back to face the house where the sound had come from.

The figure in the doorway was lit by the flickering of an old oil lamp, held above its head. It stood shock still, the light casting shadows from the folds of its black robe. The hood was back, revealing the face inside. Cownall thought that his earlier prayer had been well placed as he stared at the deeply lined visage and the two, pointed, horns that sat on its forehead. Being told that these were simply organs that enhanced a human's psychic powers did nothing. Right there, and right then, he was face to face with the Devil.

More figures joined the first, moving silently from the doorway and spreading out across the front of the house, facing the squad. Cownall braced himself, trying to force his legs to move away. As he did so, a shot rang out, shattering the silence that had fallen on the yard. The bullet missed the family gathered against them, ricocheting off the rock walls and bouncing harmlessly into the mist.

Cownall felt his head turning, with no control from himself. From the corner of his eye, he saw Captain Day turning as well. There, in the lee of the barn, stood Private Barns, his rifle still glued to his shoulder, barely moving. A stray thought entered Cownall's head. The teacher drawing everyone's attention to the miscreant. The same principle that once led to public executions.

Although still in a firing stance, he could see Barns' face, the terror in his eyes as he stood frozen to the spot. His skin grew bright red, sweat pouring off it, mingling with the tears in his eyes. Cownall felt that the man would have screamed if he had been able to.

Steam began to rise off Barns' shoulders, his red face now beginning to blister. Cownall wanted to look away, fearful of what might come next, but, try as he might, he had no choice, his neck muscles refused to budge, he was frozen in position. The steam that was rising from Barns was thicker now. Cownall realised, a moment before the flames started to flicker out of the private's uniform, that this was now smoke. Finally, the flames took hold of both the flesh and the cloth of the uniform, and Barns disappeared in the conflagration that illuminated the yard, casting shadows across the faces of the watching troops.

Cownall tried not to imagine what the man had felt as he stood there, his body temperature gradually rising and knowing what was to come.

The fire ended almost as soon as it began, what was once a man crumbling to the ground as glowing ash and embers.

'That was unnecessary.'

Cownall recognised the voice immediately as his head was finally allowed to snap back around.

'On both accounts,' Travers finished as he emerged from the door of the farmhouse.

'He fired on us,' said the leading figure. Cownall realised that it was a woman, her lined face betraying her apparent seniority among the Family.

'And now he's dead. That was pointless!' shouted Travers. 'Senseless.'

'We do not take life lightly. Only when our existence is threatened.' The women hissed her words through gritted teeth.

Travers ignored her and stalked out towards where Cownall and Day stood. 'And as for you, Captain, I imagine that you gave the order to turn up here all guns blazing.'

'We're here to get you out.'

Clearly Day was now able to speak. Cownall flexed his mouth muscles. Yes, he too could use his jaw, but it would be better to stay quiet and let his CO deal with any flak.

'You're too valuable to the war effort to throw your life away chasing fairies,' Day continued. 'Where have you been?'

'Conducting my investigation. Speaking to the *people...*' Travers made sure this emphasis hung in the air. '...who can help me the most. I didn't need you to rescue me. And now a man is dead.' Travers was face to face with Day now. 'I hope you have a good explanation for his widow. We need to leave here now.'

'A man has just been killed by people on British soil for doing nothing more than obeying orders. I will go nowhere.'

Cownall tried to move his feet. *Well,* he mused, *Day is right about one thing. We are going nowhere.*

'Your orders led to him dying. That is why you need to

leave, before every single man in your squad suffers the same fate. These people are no threat to us...' Travers jabbed a finger at the hapless captain's face. '...unless we are a threat to them. That's when they will be a very, very serious threat.'

The growl of a diesel engine grew in the distance, accompanied by the rumble of tyres crunching across unpaved road.

'Definitely one of ours,' muttered Travers. He turned to the gathered Family members. 'Please, release them, there will be no more gunfire. I will make sure that they stay away.' He walked back to the lady who still stood at the front of the group. 'Morrigan. Thank you for your hospitality. I will do my best to help.'

The Bedford rumbled into the yard, its dipped headlights barely revealing much more than the growing dawn light provided. Cownall recognised the new addition to its front seat.

'What's *he* doing here?' Travers shouted, seeing Carter about to leap out of the cab. 'Never mind. Carter, get back in the truck. I mean it; this is no time to argue. If you want to come back to die later, I will give you a lift.'

Carter knelt in the dust, raising his crucifix and reading from his Bible. Travers shrugged.

'At least that will keep him busy.' He turned to Day. 'Captain?'

Day's lip curled. 'Like the professor said, everyone fall back into the Bedford.'

The troops, freed from the embrace of whatever had held them like statues, started to run for the truck. At Travers' direction, two men scooped up Carter by his arms and dragged him, protesting, back into the Bedford.

As he moved towards the truck, Cownall caught sight of the Triumph leaning against the gatepost. He ran for it.

'Here, lads, don't leave this behind.'

The Bedford started moving as he and two others grabbed the bike and wheeled it towards the truck's tailgate. As he dragged it onboard, Cownall saw Day turn to Travers.

'Please tell me you haven't been drinking tea with the devil woman all night.'

Travers grunted. 'It was boiled nettle leaves, but yes. And

a damn sight more productive than everyone else's activities it has been too.'

Day ignored this. 'Where are we going?'

Travers shrugged. 'I don't know about you, Captain, but I could do with a stiff drink. I suggest *The Black Boar* in Edleton. Currently a Home Guard post, so there might be some extra bodies to assist as well.'

'To come back here?'

Travers shook his head as combat boots thudded past. 'I'll explain. Call Matthew Stewart and Beatrice Bodian at the Bodian residence, and get them up here too. I think we all need to make sure that we are on the same page.'

He ran towards the truck's cab, leaving Day to scrabble into the back with the troops and the dusty Triumph. Cownall saw Section Officer Le Croissette jump from the passenger side. Travers gripped her forearms.

'My dear, so glad to see you safe and well.'

Eileen wrestled free. 'You too, Professor. After all, it was you who got me into this mess.' She pointed for the cab. 'Jump in now. We've got to get going.'

CHAPTER FOURTEEN
Council of War

DEREK THATCHER was pulled out of bed by the arrival of the truck of troops. The local Home Guard captain and sergeant were slumbering by the phone line when he let Day's squad into the bar. Thatcher sprung the till open, slapped the keys on the bar and told the troops they could pick any room they wanted to sleep in.

'The only other Home Guard are locals due back off the night watch in a couple of hours. Make them a brew and treat the till as an honesty box.' He padded across the dim bar, still in his nightshirt and slippers. 'As far as I'm concerned, this place has been commandeered. It's all yours. Night all.'

Day looked at his rotund Home Guard counterpart and asked him to leave the room so that they could conduct a debrief.

'In the meantime,' he added, 'can you get your men in vantage positions around the farmstead of Owd Hob's Meade? I need a constant watch. I need to know if a sparrow falls on that land.'

'Who the devil are you?' the captain asked.

'War Office Special Support Group.' Day calmly folded his arms.

'Is that so? I've not been told that you have any authority over me.'

'I don't. But I have the troops. Troops with more than five rounds each at that. I also have a CO with direct authority from the PM.'

As the captain gaped at Day, the Home Guard sergeant beamed.

'That's awfully impressive, I'm sure we can use the

restaurant area for now.' With that, the captain had been painted into a corner.

He tutted before taking his lead. 'They're getting some rest first. They've been up all night.'

Day shrugged as he left. 'That will have to do.'

Sergeant Howard barked at the Fourth's own troops to get some rest. It had been a long night. That left Day, Cownall, Travers, Le Croissette and the Reverend Carter downstairs in the bar.

Travers was as glad to see that Eileen had come to no harm in Huxtable's factory as he was intrigued by the story she had to tell. He listened to it carefully, nursing a single scotch. Around the table in the saloon bar, Cownall, Carter and Day drank cups of tea.

As Eileen finished the tale, Travers knew better than to question her recollection, but he also knew that what she'd been told was only half the story.

'He has missed some rather important information. Things that I only learned myself last night.' Travers took a sip of his whisky. 'Firstly, they don't go by The Family anymore. Hobson is a name of convenience.' He nodded at Carter. 'They were quite tickled by Boggarts. I think it will be my nomenclature of choice when I write a paper on them.'

Day tutted. 'Firstly, that will be subject to clearance from the general, and then the PM. Secondly, and more importantly, *Amazing Stories* aren't accepting submissions right now.' He sighed and leaned back. 'And the other piece of information…?'

'Is rather more important,' said Travers. 'They have been living here peacefully for the last two thousand years. They are not the threat Huxtable has painted them to be.'

'Peacefully?' Day slapped his hand on the table. 'One of my men was killed back there. In the worst possible way. We've lost an aircraft. Do you mean to tell me that you don't consider these people a threat?'

'On the contrary. They are potentially highly dangerous. They are possibly the most dangerous beings on this planet. More so even than the Jerries. But they have shown themselves to be of little threat to us unless they themselves are threatened.'

He thought of Morrigan's stories. Of the Boggarts' pain and guilt as they saw the grieving mothers and wives in the last war and felt unable to do anything. She had given Egcbert a stern glance as she said this.

'They could be a massive help to the war effort,' said Day, snapping Travers back to the present. 'Imagine an army led by them. They could freeze the Germans in their tracks, turn them against each other. It really would all be over by Christmas.' He gazed out of the window.

Travers allowed him to do so. He knew that deep desire in all soldiers to see the end of the conflict. To come out of the other side knowing that, after everything — all the friends lost — it had been worth it.

'They would be formidable,' Travers agreed. 'They sent a Junkers after me yesterday.' He nodded at Cownall. 'I don't believe that was mere coincidence. Their psychic powers are incredible. But they aren't leaders. They're weapons.'

A silence settled on the table.

'Built by who?' Day asked.

Travers shrugged. 'They weren't built, they were bred. And by *whom* they don't know. It sounds like Huxtable doesn't know either. In time, whoever inherits the Fourth's vaults may be able to piece it together. Those responsible could be human eugenicists like those lunatics across the Channel, they could be some outside force.' He swallowed. 'But imagine what kind of war would need a weapon like them. Imagine the kind of war where a hundred planets are just a factory and testing ground for a group like the Boggarts.'

'We need them.' Day pulled out his notebook, jotting down the details he had just heard. 'And if we can't have them under our control, working for us, then we must treat them as dangerous. After all that they have done. The loss of the plane…'

'Accidental. I'm sure of it. A side effect of work they have been doing.'

'They can bring down one of our planes as a side effect? How does that convince me that they are not dangerous?'

Travers simply put his head in his hands.

'What about the child?' Cownall's question was a stab to Travers' mind.

'Anne?' he mouthed, then shook his head. 'No, the boy, Charles Peeves.' Travers sighed. 'He's safe. They haven't harmed him. I saw him, in fact. It wasn't the Boggarts as a whole that took him. It was one member. A young man.' He remembered the hooded eyes, the dark stare of Egcbert. 'You see, Charles Peeves' father was a poacher. And who can blame him in these times? The last time he was home, he caught a fawn on land around Owd Hob's Meade. It was probably the worst decision of his life.'

'Wait,' said Carter. 'The arable farming we saw at Owd Hob's Meade. Those people obviously can't eat any sort of meat.'

'Exactly.' Travers thought of the food stores at the farm. 'They choose not to because they can sense the pain of the animal for slaughter.' He gave a short bark of a laugh. 'Then can block it easily of course. Otherwise they'd be a damned useless weapon. But after knowing what they have done in the past, it's almost become an article of faith to sense all such pain. It must have caused them immense suffering to kill your soldier. As indeed Egcbert himself must have felt when he killed Petty Officer Peeves.'

'He's dead?' said Cownall. 'He's down as having deserted.'

Travers smiled grimly. 'He died the same way as Private Barns. They can interfere with the brain.' He tapped his head. 'They can use the part that regulates our metabolism, send it into overdrive. It makes us cook ourselves. Where did you say the man was last seen, Cownall?'

'On ship, Professor. It was under sail when they found he was gone. Everyone assumes he legged it from port.'

Travers sadly shook his head. 'What would you do if you were on a ship and started to burn up like poor Private Barns? You'd jump into the nearest body of water. Petty Officer Peeves is probably ashes and bubbles floating through the ocean.'

Carter swallowed. 'So, not a coward after all.'

'No, not even particularly stupid. Just very unlucky. And Charles even more so. He was lured away by the same young man. A revenge. Peeves' family took the fawn you see. The Boggarts had no choice but to keep him.'

Carter sat back. 'Then I shall have to visit Mrs Peeves.'

135

'A change of tune, Reverend?' Travers asked.

The man coughed. 'A reappraisal. That is something that we in the clergy are capable of you know. There's a lot I didn't know about these people. There's a lot that I have taken on trust. But before I go, I need to know one thing. I need to make sure she knows that her husband is gone, and that he was no coward. But what about her son? Is she going to see him again?'

Travers simply didn't know. What would he have wanted if Anne was the one that was lost? Would he want the nicety that she would be back, or the harsh truth that she may well not be? And would the loss of a child be eased if Mrs Peeves was given an inkling that it was coming?

He was a scientist for God's sake. The truth was important.

'We will do our best,' he said. 'But tell her to prepare for the worst.'

Carter nodded. A mark of respect between the two.

'That is it.' Day put his notepad away. 'These people cannot be trusted. They pose far too great a threat. You've heard the information that Section Officer Le Croissette gave us. They could destroy the Empire. Further, they could destroy every empire.'

Travers sat back. 'I have told you, Captain. That was millennia ago for these people. It was done by their distant ancestors. They are capable now, but they do not have the will.'

'That they have the capability is enough. And that will to conquer may well come back to the fore again.' Day shook his head. 'I will recommend a full bombing run to General Dornan.'

'Would you visit on them the sins of their fathers?' Carter asked softly.

There was silence around the table in the uncomfortable way that all British people had when confronted by any strong religious sentiment.

'I think it is time that you left,' was Day's only response.

'It wouldn't work in any event,' said Travers. 'They would only ditch all your planes into the nearest lake.' He paused. 'If they were feeling generous.'

Day leaned forward. 'Even so, what are we going to do about the rogue among them? He's kidnapped a boy and killed a man.'

Travers sat back and drained his glass, wiping his chin and setting the empty vessel back on the table. 'We are going to do nothing. We will have to trust these people to keep their own in check. Do you really think any cell could hold him? That any jury would convict him? And even then, what would you do? He is a child; you can hardly place a noose around his neck. To say nothing of what the rest of the Boggarts would do to get him out.'

Day banged the table. 'So, we let them get away with it?' he grunted. 'I say that we stand back and let Huxtable and his Quarks do what they want. It will rid England of a dangerous element in her midst at a time when she doesn't need it.'

Travers stood and began pacing up and down. He breathed deeply, fighting to control the flood of emotions. He knew for himself the intense fear and anger that he had felt approaching the Boggarts, but he also remembered the politeness they had shown him after he had revealed himself by the stone circle, how forthcoming they had been as they welcomed him into their home and told him about their lives, living centuries on their land, using the techniques of the future to keep sufficient food on the table. The way that adults, children and even their 'guest', Charles, would gather around the table for a meal where bowls were filled for each other, with no man taking his own share. They had lived their lives and those of their ancestors for so long in atonement. Partly atonement, but partly because they knew what they were still capable of. Knowing this, what could Travers say?

'They look after the children that they take. They treat them as part of their own. There are graves, not marked by headstones, but deep into the moorland. You'll find the odd boulder that looks like it has no business being there. That's where they bury their dead.' He turned to Carter. 'The last time I came here I was told of a boy called Smythe that disappeared long ago. That name was recorded in your church's book of those that have lacked a proper burial.' He stopped and leaned against the wall, feeling the tiredness of his limbs pulling him to the floor. 'You can cross the name out. The Boggarts showed me where he now lies after living to the ripe old age of eighty-six. The bodies of the Bristol Blenheim crew are lying in graves next to him.'

He jabbed a finger at Day. 'And if basic morals don't persuade you, then remember that Charles Peeves is still amongst them.' He could see Eileen sat uncomfortably, facing away from her commanding officer. Damn preserving discipline, he needed the help to get Day onside. 'Eileen, what's your assessment of Huxtable's army's capabilities?'

Eileen sat up straight, facing into the centre of the table as she gave her report. 'The Quarks won't discriminate, and Huxtable won't leave survivors. He will massacre them all,' she said. 'He's not evil, he truly believes that is the right thing to do. Just like the men in the bombers overhead do every single day.'

'They killed Private Barns,' said Day. 'I did not set out to lose a man today. I especially did not set out to save the people that killed him.'

'If this war is to mean anything, it's that we protect people like the Boggarts.' Travers sat down again. 'Captain. We need to preserve these people. If you truly think they can assist us in the war effort, then they will be far more willing to help us if we protect them.'

'So, I put more men on the line by fighting Huxtable's damned robots?'

Travers shrugged. 'They're an easier target for the likes of us, less so for the Boggarts. I presume you've brought those suggested explosives with you?'

Day was about to respond when Carter jumped to his feet.

'Well, if you've decided who you're going to be shooting at, it's time that I took my leave.' His hunched shoulders threaded through the room as the sound of a car engine outside cut across the morning silence.

'Captain Stewart and Beatrice Bodian.' Eileen peered past the blackout at the new arrival, blocky and dull coloured. 'They've come in the Tilly, Corporal.'

Cownall shrugged. 'Why use petrol coupons when you can help yourself to my fuel allowance? Tell him I've had to sign for that. Civil Servants don't have to account to the Fourth's quartermaster.'

Eileen watched the two climbing out of the Tilly.

'This one might,' she said. 'I'm not sure if the khaki fits

him as well as the suit.'

As Stewart entered, Day stood. Cownall and Eileen joined him just in time for Stewart to snap off a salute.

'Private Matthew Stewart. Home Guard. Able to assist, sir.'

Day slowly returned the salute. 'I thought you were a captain in the last war?'

'I was, but the last conflict ended badly for me.' Stewart glanced briefly at Cownall. Eileen made a note to herself to catch up later with the driver to see what else he knew. 'A lot of men died. I wanted to join up with the LDV, as it was then. If only to have my own rifle if the enemy were to come over here.' He paused, again staring at seemingly nothing. 'I can't imagine the Hun would have let Whitehall go unscathed if they made it over.' He made a half smirk. 'So, I stayed as a private. I don't want my platoon or the department to connect me with what happened in France.'

Day slowly leaned forward. 'I'm too young to have been there, but my understanding is that every man that took a single step towards the enemy deserves a medal and any man that didn't had good reason not to. I think you had better sit down.'

Eileen sat as well. She noted that Beatrice pulled herself a chair, the legs screeching as they were dragged across the bare tiles of the bar. Matthew shifted in his seat, seemingly distracted by the shafts of sunlight that were creeping their way across the floor and up the stained glass of the bar.

Day drummed his fingers on the desk. 'Matters have moved on since we, ah, rescued Travers here, Private. He will fill you in on his own escapades and why we must now attack the Pickering Steelworks.'

Eileen's breath caught. 'We are attacking then, sir? I thought...'

'I've got reservations,' said Day. 'Any soldier should do. But, as Professor Travers says, this is the right course of action. One senseless war on civilians is enough. We need to put a stop to Huxtable.' He stood, swaying slightly with tiredness. 'I assume that there is little chance of these Quarks attacking in daylight?'

Travers tapped the edge of his glass, lost in thought. 'I

have no idea,' he said finally.

'I don't think they would attack until nightfall, sir,' said Eileen. 'Huxtable made it clear to me that he wants to leave as light a touch on this era as possible. That's why he has built new bodies around their machine brains at the steelworks. It's to make sure that they're mostly contemporary. I think he will send them over at night.'

Day gave a curt nod. 'Thank you, section officer. I'm going to get some sleep. I advise the rest of you to do the same.'

Travers smiled up at him, a sudden grin breaking across his usually dour features. 'Do you know, I thought I didn't sleep at all last night, but I feel fantastically awake.'

Eileen yawned. If Travers' new-found energy was something that the Boggarts had given him, then perhaps they could offer the war effort something after all.

'I'll find Thatcher and see if he can find you a private room, section officer,' Day said as he left.

Cownall stood as well. 'It's hit me,' he said. 'I'll go and get my head down too, now that we've decided who the baddies are. For today at least.'

'Yours to do and die, Corporal,' Travers said with a grunt.

Eileen thought that she could detect a small amount of affection in his voice. She looked around. Travers was already giving a blow by blow account of what he had found from the Boggarts to Stewart. Beatrice stood and headed for the bar.

'Is coffee too much to ask for?' she said.

Eileen followed. 'In a Derbyshire pub? When there's a war on?'

'I think that's answered my question.' Beatrice poured herself a cup of tea.

'Does that not bother you?' Eileen indicated Beatrice's patch, covering her eye.

Beatrice laughed, briefly. 'Not as much as it bothered my father. He thought I'd be a hard one to marry already. Too many women, not enough men left after the last war, and me a little suffragette at that. I think he'd almost given up hope, then when I came out the hospital with this, well. He was just happy to have got Nancy matched with Matthew over there.' She nodded at him. 'Tea?'

'No, thank you,' Stewart said.

'It's given me more freedom, I think. No expectations on me anymore. And, of course, it's nothing compared to what Matthew brought back with him from the trenches.'

'What was that?' Eileen asked.

Beatrice checked that her brother-in-law was well out of earshot. 'He made a mistake. A stupid one. And men died.'

Eileen thought of her role with the WAAF. She knew the sick feeling when you could have erred, sent planes the wrong way, or missed an enemy engagement. Pilots could be shot down or civilians killed. In her line of work there was always a distance. She knew that it happened, but it wasn't the same as seeing it for herself.

'Not easy.'

'Worse when his father found out. Matthew is from a famous and well-respected military family, not that you'd know as he won't use his full name as long as the war is on.' Beatrice smirked slightly. 'No wonder he married into spoons.'

Eileen giggled, knowing that the sound would cut across the room. She stifled it as soon as she started.

'What will you do when the war is over?' she asked Beatrice quickly. 'Won't you feel lost when all the men come home? I'm sure you can find a good one. Eyes aren't all they're cracked up to be.'

Beatrice swilled her tea round in her mouth, as if turning the question over. 'Marriage isn't for everyone,' she said at last. 'I'll probably help get the cutlery works back up and running. Leave it in a good state to hand over to one of Matthew's daughters. Perhaps travel a bit.' She smiled. 'Matthew is right, woman power is a rich girl's game.' She looked at Eileen, lowered her head. 'What about you? Find a man and start listening for the pitter patter of little feet?'

Before Eileen could reply, Derek Thatcher had appeared at the door. He held up his hand.

'There's one room,' he said. 'But I should warn you. It's got a bad history.'

Without looking around, Travers butted in. 'I know the one. Tell the ghosts that I've found their son. That should keep them quiet.'

It was early afternoon when the Bedford and Tilly left

Edleton, their roar echoing around its edges before fading into the mist and sunlight.

'They'll be back,' remarked Athel, his face showing no happiness at the prospect.

'Perhaps.' Morrigan gathered her cloak around her. The excitement of the midsummer celebrations, with their uninvited guests, had faded. The children had retired, and she felt her own bones aching in the sun. 'Should we be here when they do?'

They had been here so long. This landscape felt like a part of her, as it had for her mother and grandmother and further back, for generations.

Athel shrugged. 'We can't trust them. And you know that they are close to the development of robotics. The first computers are already whirring away a couple of hundred miles away.'

Morrigan knew this. The tales that had been passed down through their community for centuries were a warning. *One day, they will be able to send the robots again.* When that day came, they could no longer protect themselves. The time would come to make the Great Shift again. She had hoped not to be the leader that took her people through that to another new beginning. It was looking difficult to avoid.

'How do Egcbert's pure telekinetic experiments go?' She knew she was changing the subject, but Athel's son's gift for mental manipulation of the physical, rather than just the mind, was a new horizon for her people. The penance for his transgression in killing the Peeves man was to spend his time engaged in study and meditation of it.

Athel breathed air out between his gritted teeth. 'It changes everything,' he said eventually. 'Everything about us. I'm not sure if we are ready for that yet.'

Morrigan smiled grimly. 'Remember your history. We're not the only people that will be in that position come the end of this war.'

CHAPTER FIFTEEN
When You Come Back, I Won't Be Here

HILDA GRAVES returned home early that morning after another night shift.

It was strange walking into the works again, so soon after the special project, the Quark, had gone haywire and started spraying the place with bullets. There were still casings and shards of metal on the floor. The main sections of the works remained abandoned; no work was being done on parts for tanks or planes today. Only the special projects shed was open and, inside, less than a third of the girls were working.

They had spent the night finishing off the Quarks. Not as many as Huxtable had planned, but, he had said, enough. Every girl worked a number of posts through the night, from buffing to crane operator to welding. Even as the sirens had howled outside, they had carried on working, Huxtable promised to move them to the shelter as soon as the bombs started falling. It was crucial, he said, that the Quarks be finished that night. The girls all knew how important the job was for the war effort and threw themselves into the work.

The roar of the diesel engine on the street outside pulled Hilda from her sleep. She looked through the net curtains to see an Austin Tilly outside. Two figures climbed out. One was a stranger, a soldier in khaki with mud stained ankles. The other, she recognised. She threw on a presentable smock, or as presentable as she could find, and ran downstairs, taking them two at a time to reach the door before her landlady.

'What are you doing here?' she hissed as she cracked the door open.

Eileen stood there, in some sort of military uniform, like the WAAF but with no insignia. The soldier behind her was clearly from the same service.

'We need to talk to you,' Eileen said. 'About the Pickering works.'

The last time Hilda had seen Eileen, the woman had just snuck her way into the works and caused a Quark to start attacking indiscriminately. Who was she working for?

'Look,' Eileen continued, leaning in and glancing side to side. 'I know I didn't tell you the full truth last time. I'm not with the WAAF anymore. I've moved into a special top secret operations corps. We deal with highly secret, scientific matters. Huxtable isn't working on a weapon for the war effort. He's using those Quarks for his own purpose.'

Hilda eased the door open further, raising a finger to shush Eileen. She stepped through and slowly closed it behind her. She pointed away from the house and walked towards the vehicle in silence. She slid into the front seat, Eileen squeezed in next to her and the soldier dropped into the driver's seat with a sigh.

'You're going to help us then?' he said. 'Somehow I thought it would take a bit more than that.'

Hilda looked at him with what she hoped was a quizzical look on her face.

'Sorry, ma'am,' said the soldier, holding his hand out. 'Corporal Felix Cownall.'

Hilda reached out shakily and offered her own hand, which he took, briefly.

'I didn't want to be seen with you. Mr Huxtable is still my boss. What can you want from me that you don't already know?'

'For a start, what happened while we were gone last night?' Eileen leaned in close, but her voice was clipped, the tones of a lady that was used to giving instructions.

Hilda looked out to the city, laid out like a quilt as the hill fell away in front of the car. Sheffield was new to her, with its strange accent and bizarre layout. As a 'mobile', she had come here to be placed with an unpleasant landlady in a guest house with five other girls. She had been so alone until Huxtable had taken her to one side after a late night shift at the steelworks.

She had been terrified that the owner had singled her out, but he hadn't spoken to her as a girl, or an inferior. He had spoken to her as an equal. As someone who he thought understood what he was talking about. That's when he had taken her into the testing station and told her the truth of the autonomous weapon that he was developing for the government.

Yet, here was Eileen, her close friend from training and a section officer at that. Even now, as Eileen worked with a top secret organisation, Hilda still knew little about the Quarks that Huxtable had told her were such a vital part of the future war effort. Did that mean that Huxtable was lying, or was it more than that? Was it Eileen that was somehow working against the government, the possessor of an extremely good cover story and not actually a part of Britain's Armed Forces at all? Fifth columnists were not an illusion, but could her friend, plain-speaking Eileen Le Croissette, have been bribed, or worse, indoctrinated?

'I can't talk here. I still don't know who you represent.' Hilda lowered her head, sinking into the seat.

Cownall turned to Eileen, who nodded.

'We'll take you to where we're stationed. We need to know what's inside the works.'

Cownall gunned the engine.

Around the car were shells of buildings. After the Sheffield Blitz, over a year ago, the city had swept up the debris, but there had been better things to do than pull down what was left. A building might have three walls, half a floor on each level and no roof. No stairs led to upper floors and furniture remained on them, rotting in the elements. In places, a table cloth still fluttered pathetically. The place looked like an enormous abandoned doll's house. It was one of several shattered homes in the area. Some nearly intact, some were mere piles of rubble, pushed away from the road to be dealt with another day. Where the Luftwaffe had missed the factories, it had hit the houses hard.

Cownall pulled up the Tilly behind a Bedford lorry that was hidden in the dangerously overhanging lee of one of the buildings. Around it clustered soldiers preparing for battle, rummaging through pale green boxes for equipment and swapping cigarettes and stories. Like misshapen metal lollipops, the sticky bombs were being carefully counted and issued. Corporal Ellington and Sergeant Howard stood overseeing the activity and talking in low voices.

Eileen offered a hand to Hilda to get up into the back of the truck. Inside, crouched on ammunition boxes, sat Day and Stewart. Travers was tinkering with something that looked like a dismantled radio. Eileen saluted Day and reported that Hilda was a worker at the factory. Travers turned and coughed.

'What frequency do the Quarks communicate at?' he snapped. 'What level of autonomy have they got? Clearly not full, otherwise they would have overthrown their masters like all those tedious scientific romance novels.'

Eileen saw Hilda stay standing still.

'Who are you all?' she said at last. 'What are you doing there? And why do you want to know?' She didn't betray any indication of deference to Day, beyond her shaking hands.

Eileen tensed; how much would they reveal? Day was famously cagey even about the work he did for the Fourth. He didn't want people thinking that he had spent his war chasing after foo fighters and men from outer space. He drummed his fingers.

'The Quarks are a weapon,' he offered. 'But they have gone wrong and threatened troops in our Group. And, indeed, they threaten innocent civilians.'

Eileen thought of the private that had been lost, the chief petty officer that would not be seen again. She still didn't buy that these were the acts of innocents. The Boggarts could and were willing to use deadly force when needed. The only reason the Fourth was involved now was to stop a further massacre.

'How can I trust that you are who you say you are?' asked Hilda. She was still shaking slightly. Clearly, she thought that she was caught and trying to make a stand so that anything she revealed afterwards would be obtained under duress. It was a sensible thing to do, but with time pressing, Eileen knew that it ran the risk of driving Travers up the wall.

'How can you trust Huxtable?' he growled, dropping the components he was working on.

'Because he ran a factory approved by the Ministry. You chaps have simply turned up outside my house several times and then turned my place of work upside down. Now you're going to, what?' Hilda took a deep breath. 'Invade? Go running in, all guns blazing?'

Eileen glanced across to where Stewart sat. He may be a private here, but in his day job he could easily outrank any of them. And, once upon a time, he would have outranked everybody but Day. He didn't look ready. It was probably out of place for a section officer to do this, but…

'Perhaps Private Stewart can assist us?' she asked.

She saw his slight jump as she said it. Good. Hilda stayed silent. Stewart shifted. He was uncomfortable and Eileen felt a flash of regret that she had made him so, but he was a civil servant in the department that had left Huxtable to amass this little empire. It was time for him to do something about it instead of sending his sister-in-law and her to spy on the man.

'We took our eye off the ball,' he said with a sigh. 'He was keeping the goods flowing into the war effort and that's all that the Ministry expected. It wasn't until I dug a bit deeper that I spotted the discrepancies and the missing material that was going on the Quarks.' A realisation slowly dawned across his face. He went to his top pocket and produced a sheaf of papers, on Ministry note paper. He crossed to stand next to Hilda, placing the papers in front of her. 'These are official MAP documents. You'll notice they are stamped as secret.' He pulled out his ID card and showed it to her. 'They are provided to us by the individual factories that work for us. This is the Pickering Factory.' Eileen saw him tap the columns. 'This is the section that should detail the Quarks that were completed. It doesn't.' He tapped another. 'This section details those where the work is in progress. Again, no Quarks.' He handed the paper to Hilda. 'Read it if you want. You will find that the work you have been doing for the last six months is not work either required or sanctioned by the War Office. The Quarks are a load of mobile machine guns with no man operating them that are now free to roam this nation.'

'And they have a target,' put in Travers. 'A group of men, women and children whose ancestors caused much suffering but who themselves are blameless.'

Hilda sat in silence, leafing through the papers, casting each one aside as if it was a particularly unpleasant love letter from an unwanted suitor. Finally, she put them down. The set of her face had changed. It was a breach of protocol, but Eileen reached out and put a hand on her shoulder. Hilda appeared to relax.

'He has finished eight of them. He had them all done and ready to go by this morning. The factory is closed for the rest of the day.'

'He's going to move them to the farmhouse tonight,' Eileen said, to raised eyebrows all around. 'He won't do it in daylight because they can't be seen here and now.'

Travers pulled out his pocket watch. 'We have two hours,' he announced. 'What capabilities do those assembled Quarks have?'

Hilda looked confused.

'Well, have they been armoured?'

She shook her head.

'Are they all armed with SMGs?'

'Machine guns,' interjected Eileen.

Hilda nodded again. 'Each Quark has two. They can fire anywhere within 180 degrees in front. I've seen the tests.'

'What about mobility?' asked Travers. 'The one we saw looked like a drunken child.'

Hilda agreed. 'They give that impression. But they can pick up a surprising speed. They can manage to move faster than a human can. And they can jump. They can leap over thirty feet into the air and land with no damage. They're like little, vicious, jack in the boxes.'

Eileen shuddered at the image.

'Where are they all now?' asked Day.

'When I left a few hours ago, they were all in the testing house.'

Eileen nodded to Day to check that he understood that she knew where to find it.

'Anything else you can remember.' Travers' voice had become gentler now. 'Anything at all?'

Hilda shook her head.

'You've been very helpful,' said Day. 'At least now we know what we're up against.' He nodded at Cownall, who jumped up. 'Corporal Cownall will take you back to your house.'

As the Tilly disappeared back through the ruined

neighbourhood, Travers banged his fist on the lorry's cab.

'You can come out now.'

Beatrice emerged.

'Did you get all of that?' Day asked.

She nodded. 'It's not to say that the Quarks will be where she left them. By the sound of it, Huxtable wanted all the girls out of the way today. And let me tell you, most of them will have only been too happy to get out. They're all hopeless. No sense of curiosity about their work, no pride in what they're doing. They come in, do their shift and then disappear.' She sighed and shook her head.

'As should you,' said Day. 'It will be no place there for a lady when the bullets start to fly.'

Beatrice hesitated, she looked from side to side and from each of those gathered around. Travers, Day, Stewart and Eileen. She looked at the direction that Hilda had left and then nodded.

'Not really my field anyway,' she agreed.

'Excellent. And when the professor finishes whatever he's working on, you can take him too.'

Silence weighed into the back of the truck with a sudden oppression.

'Three points, Captain,' said Travers, finally. 'Firstly, I have already finished what I am working on, and it is a device that may save the lives of your troops in our upcoming battle. Secondly, I don't have time to teach anyone else to use it, so you will need me. Lastly, and most importantly, I am the world's foremost expert in robotics and I simply must see these machines in action.' His eyes nearly gleamed at the prospect.

Eileen was sure that Captain Day could have ordered Professor Travers to remain out of the battle. However, Eileen also knew that it was vital for any military officer dealing with Edward Travers to know the difference between having authority and exercising it.

Beatrice stood. 'I'll go.' She clambered out of the Bedford.

Eileen caught Day's look as he flicked his eyes after her. She was clearly dismissed. She jumped out of the tailgate, following Beatrice through the hubbub of soldiers checking munitions and cleaning their rifles to the tin of Golden

Virginia resting on a wall. The G the O and a number of other letters had been scratched off the top of the tin in the traditional soldier's joke.

'Private!' she snapped. The owner jumped to his feet. She could feel the blood rushing to her face. She shouldn't take it out on this young man and, in any case, she had little real authority over him. She pointed at the tin. 'I suggest you get scratching until that reads something more palatable.'

Dutifully, he reached for his bayonet and began to scrape away the remaining paint from the tin.

Eileen placed a hand on Beatrice's shoulder and led her away.

'Why do you want to be in battle so badly?'

Beatrice gave a short, sharp laugh. 'I don't. I just want to be useful. It's been a terrible couple of decades for women like me. The ones left behind and then left out. What is a woman if not a wife?' She smiled briefly, without humour. 'Well, this war has put right the wrongs that the last one gave us. We have a purpose now, I just wanted to actually be there when the men go back to the steelworks. When they fight the Quarks. I know that place inside out.'

'It will be dangerous. I'll be kept right back out of it. Just like I was in the assault on Owd Hob's Meade. That's the thing, I can be ordered to stay back. Day can order you too, of course.'

'I'm not so likely to obey.'

Eileen smiled. 'There is that.' She looked around her. 'Look. I haven't said before, but thank you. At the factory, I was completely out of my depth. You found me and got me into the right place to find out what I needed to know.'

Beatrice turned and looked back at her. 'I have a feeling that women like you are going to be needed in this war. Maybe undercover work isn't your forte, but I think that your skill with figures will be what we are going to need.'

Suddenly, she seized Eileen in fierce hug. 'Be careful out there. Those Quarks may have dumb alien brains, but they're armed with Sheffield steel. That makes them very dangerous indeed.'

Eileen smiled. 'I'll look out for the hallmark.'

Beatrice's voice dropped. 'Keep an eye on Matthew please.

His father is gunning for him right now. I was surprised that he pulled out that gun and uniform. I don't want him to do something stupid to try and impress his old man.'

'And how can I stop him?' Eileen shrugged.

'I don't know. Distract him with some double entry bookkeeping maybe? That's his real love.' Beatrice started to walk away, stepping carefully over the rubble, heading for a gap between the buildings.

'Wait!' called Eileen, glancing around the ruined buildings and rubble. 'How are you going to get home?'

The other woman smiled. 'The usual way. There's a tram stop just around the corner.'

Travers placed the final screw in his new contraption. It was mostly a collection of wires and aerials. He hadn't had time to give it a casing. He was fairly sure that it would work as it was.

'What does that do?' Day leaned in.

Travers knew the reason for his question wasn't pure curiosity. Day wanted to know exactly what his arsenal was and what his options were.

'If I'm right.' It was only in the direst of circumstances that Travers left open the possibility that he wasn't. 'Then this will help me to control the Quarks. It should seize up their tiny little electronic brains in a way that the Boggarts can only dream of.'

'And…?'

Damn the man. he could always spot a flaw coming from a mile off.

'I don't know the range. Nor do I know how long it will take to work. I'm going to need to get in close. I'll need a good distraction.'

'Happy to oblige,' muttered Day.

A shout came from outside.

'Field telephone up and running, sir.'

'Bring it in here. Stewart, you're not in the Special Support Group, please wait outside. Professor, you stay here. General Dornan may want to hear your story.'

He dialled the number once Stewart had disembarked.

'Sir?'

A brief burst from the other end. Travers recognised the clipped tones even if he couldn't make out the words.

'My report, sir. We have two factions. Both may be helpful to the war effort. The trouble is, they want to wipe each other out.'

Another pause while Dornan took this in.

'The first one is based at the Pickering works. Human commander. He is using autonomous robots. They are very fast and accurate.'

There was some excited noise from the other end.

'Well, tell the PM that the professor thinks these ones are pure robots.' He nodded as Dornan continued. 'No, we don't want a repeat of that business in the bunker. We'll try and get parts rather than whole units.'

He covered the receiver as Travers added, 'He'll be lucky to get either by the time the explosives have finished.'

'The second group, sir, are based out in the countryside. They've been there a long time, living…' He grimaced. '…mostly peacefully. They're human too, mostly. But they have been bred for psychic characteristics and command a lot of power. They can manipulate minds, turn people's bodies against themselves.'

Dornan replied.

'Not willingly, sir. That's the professor's view.' A lengthy riposte followed, fairly loud by Dornan's standards. 'Understood, sir. One last warning, then detain them.'

Travers laughed and reached his hand out.

'Give me that phone.' He took it. 'Travers speaking. Now see here, General, there is no way that you are going to hold these people.'

'Give them an ultimatum then,' said the voice at the end of the phone. 'We can have an RAF squadron there in an hour to wipe them out. It's in their interest to help us anyway. They've been living in our country.' Dornan was as matter of fact as ever. Anything that got between him and achieving what he wanted was an inconvenience, never a moral quandary.

'It won't work. Your squadron would be very quickly flying themselves backwards. And they're not scared of Nazis any more than they're scared of us. Only autonomous weapons will work.'

'They brought down one of our planes.' It was a factual statement.

'They claim not. Not directly anyway. Whatever they are doing at that stone circle up on the moors, it's affecting the navigators on the planes. They didn't know their own altitude.'

'And you believe them?'

Travers drummed his fingers on the handset. That was the million-dollar question. 'Yes,' he said eventually.

The general was silent. 'Then you need to seize control of the robots and use them for leverage. Good luck in the raid.'

A click sounded at the other end.

'Damn,' said Travers. He felt caught; disobey a general, or betray the trust of the Boggarts. 'Best to leave the Home Guard up there,' he said. 'That will at least make sure we have some warning of them doing anything.'

'The war effort is everything,' said Day. 'Let's see what we can do about Huxtable first.' He moved to the back of the truck. 'All right, chaps, time to move out!'

CHAPTER SIXTEEN
Quark to the Future

COWNALL HELD his breath as, for the second time that day, he raised his head over a high wall. This time, after a long look, he was certain there was no sign of life in among the maze-like alleyways and buildings of the Pickering works compound.

'All clear,' he whispered behind him. He dropped a rope onto the other side and shimmied down. He was followed by Privates Morrison and Doyle. He glanced to the left. The main gate was there, the security lodge in darkness and the main body of troops waiting outside. He brought his rifle up, and moved slowly towards it, checking each doorway. Evening, but the sun hadn't set, its orange rays providing them with just enough light to see into each and every doorway they passed. He nudged each one with the barrel of his gun. All were closed and locked.

They reached the main gate and Cownall gave a quick glance inside the lodge. He could see nothing past the high kiosk window beyond a few pin-ups. He was in luck; the security officer had left a key lying on a hook right next to the window.

'Jackpot,' he whispered waving it at the other two.

Doyle grinned back. Morrison, glanced, then turned his attention back to his rear-guard action of keeping his rifle trained on the various roads that led to the gate. Cownall shifted his rifle over his shoulder and went to it, grabbing at the padlock and wriggling the key back and forth inside it, trying to get the rusted mechanism to turn. It had been a long time since the works last needed to be locked. Maybe last Christmas was the last time the forges and press closed overnight.

Eventually, it clicked and the chain rattled through the bars, shattering the silence. Cownall winced as it coiled itself into the ground, grabbing his rifle and spinning back around.

His heart thudded in his chest as he waited for any sign of movement, of an impending attack. The works remained silent. He breathed out, trying to stifle the pounding that he felt. He hooted like an owl, the prearranged signal. Booted feet approached from behind, Day and the rest of the squad. He risked a glance backwards. Sure enough, there was Travers, almost leading the pack. In a way, it was good to know that he wasn't so keen for the rest of the squad to act as cannon fodder.

'Good stealth work,' hissed Day, nodding at the coiled chain, now mercifully silent.

'Sorry, sir. Never broke into a steel works before.' The look that Cownall received in reply was one from a gutter.

'Everyone got the sticky bombs ready?' A chorus of nods. 'Good, stay quiet and split up to approach the special projects shed. Be careful.'

Travers stood next to Cownall now. The rest of the squad dispersed through the works. Cownall and his section were to remain by the secured gatehouse with the professor until they had gained entry. Stewart stayed back too. Day hadn't wanted to throw a civil servant into battle.

'Damn stupid, keeping me back here like this. I should be up at the front. I'm the only one with a weapon that can incapacitate them.' Travers was shifting from one foot to the other.

'We've all got explosives, prof.' Cownall was determined not to stop scanning the area they stood in, a T junction between three internal roads, all meeting at the gate.

Each of the three men was to keep their eye on a different road.

'Explosives are no good until you can get close enough to use them.' Travers waved his device in the air. 'This will let them get close enough. It scrambles the robot's brains. Like the Boggarts did to us. There's no point in me standing back here with it. The chaps at the front could all be slaughtered by the time I get there.'

'Then run,' said Cownall. 'Anyway, right now, we don't know if your little box of tricks has any more range than our bombs.'

'Only one way to find out,' said Travers and Cownall heard him start forward. He took one hand off his rifle, just long enough to place it on the professor's arm.

He turned to remonstrate further, facing away from his posting and back towards the gate.

He would later reflect that it was this that saved his life, as it was then that the security lodge door exploded outwards, shards of wood flying from it. Cownall grabbed at Travers' arm and pulled him as the squat machine lumbered out.

No wonder I didn't see the damn thing in there, Cownall thought, *it must have been under the counter, inches away from my hand when I grabbed the key.* The thought filled him with a sense of guilt and horror.

Travers grunted, turning to see the shape. The Quark, its metal frame now covered in military style fabric, had two arms, both pointed straight out in front of it. A further hail of bullets sprayed in a forward arc. Cownall saw Doyle go down, puffs of red blood fountaining into the air around him. He had not survived. Morrison dived behind a nearby barrel. Bullets ricocheted off it. The robot spun smoothly. Again, Cownall grabbed Travers and yanked him roughly away into a doorway, sunken into a solid brick wall. Stewart followed them, breathing heavily. Cownall didn't know if the older man was spooked or out of condition.

Travers' swearing as he landed next to Cownall told him that the pull had been a bit too rough. Cownall followed his gaze and saw the reason. The fool had dropped his device in the path. Travers started back for it, before a further hail of bullets forced him back into cover.

'Glad you're here to scramble their machine brains with your know-how, prof.' Cownall realised, as he said it that, this was not his usual wisecrack. He was genuinely angry at the loss of Doyle. He was expecting a customary 'shut up' from Travers. All he got was a death glare that told him all he needed to know.

'Machine guns,' hissed Stewart. 'Never been a favourite weapon to face. They were pretty inhuman before the robots

156

started using them.'

Eileen sat in the van alone. Day had wanted everybody he could get to attack the factory, including Private Warren. Being left to sit there was no different to her previous role. She did the background work so that the men could do the fighting. That was all any girl could hope for in this war. Somehow, knowing that they would be fighting, and possibly dying, just on the other side of the brick wall made this seem more real, more immediate. She tried to see what was going on, through the arch, but her angle of vision was such that she could only see the side of the tunnel running through the archway, now empty after Day had taken his men in.

Silently, she cursed the steelworks' own trucks marshalled together in the road outside. All six arrayed in one line, blocking her view of what was happening.

She thought for a second, back to her first attendance. There had been seven on that day, including the one that was backed into the Special Projects building. Would that not have been parked at the front with the rest, if the factory was closed down? There was only one vehicle gate, she remembered; it led to the only road, through the works, wide enough for a truck to pass down, onto which the loading bays for the finishing sheds opened.

She slid out of the van, keeping an eye around her, quiet so far. She could hear nothing from the inside of the factory. A brisk jog around the corner took her to the vehicle gate, still the massive and imposing edifice it was before. Through the gap for the padlock chain, she could still see into the factory proper. Where the flatbed truck had once blocked her view, there was now nothing. She could see the length of the broad road through the steel works, past the empty loading bays of the sheds. Here and there, she saw movement as the soldiers crept through and around. All were too far away to attract attention.

She stood back, thought for another second and quickly strode back the way she had come, towards the gate.

The maths was simple. One truck was missing. The factory was used only for making Quarks last night and today, and was now completely closed down. The conclusion was also simple. The Quarks had already been taken away, rather than waiting for the cover of night.

She reached the workers' gate, stepping through quickly, now that she knew the robots had already been taken elsewhere. As she passed the security lodge she looked around. From the briefing, she expected Travers to be there with a group of privates. Typical of the man, he simply could not obey a direct order.

She stepped towards the nearest doorway to see if it was open.

'Eileen!' hissed Travers as the woman headed away from the Quark. It was no good, he realised, she was walking into an alcove. The only way out was to run towards the thing. It knew that, he supposed. It would be logical, if your prey can't escape, to close the distance and make sure of your range and accuracy. Still, that may buy him a chance.

With one eye on Eileen, he darted for the device he had made, now lying on the floor a number of yards away. As his hands closed on it, he heard a shout from the gateway.

'Eileen, run!'

He turned to see a civilian. More than a civilian, an elderly lady, wearing a beige suit. She managed to look more stylish than most of the young ladies did those days. How and why on earth was she there?

Then, his worst fears were realised, as a rasping rattle saw puffs of smoke emerge from the Quark's guns. His eyes fixed back on Eileen.

The bullets thudded into the soft bricks behind her, sending shards of brick dust flying. Eileen had turned and ducked. But Travers knew that it wouldn't take long for the Quark to adjust.

She was back now and facing the Quark, whose head was spinning furiously as it swivelled back and forth from Eileen to the old woman, squawking in its sing song voice.

'Identical wave form! Burrigan protocol required!'

She was gone. Travers had only looked away for a second and the woman was gone. He didn't hold out much hope of the Quark taking too long to reach the conclusion that it needed to send some more bullets Eileen's way.

'Eileen, run!' Travers shouted. 'Cownall! Stewart! Sticky bombs!'

Eileen ran towards him. He saw Cownall pass her in the other direction, a sticky bomb already in his hand. He firmly pressed it onto the Quark's back. Cownall waved Morrison and Stewart back and ran back towards Travers. Clearly the man could be courageous when he needed to.

'Take cover!' he yelled. 'That thing will have loose cogs and shrapnel going in all directions.'

Travers realised he was right and dragged Eileen with him away from the Quark.

The machine's head abruptly stopped spinning. It squawked in its childish voice.

'Total destruction needed!' It rocked back and forth on its oversized feet. Then it turned suddenly, both guns facing towards Eileen and Travers.

'Down!' he yelled as bullets ripped through the air again.

He dragged Eileen towards the security lodge, noting that the soldiers had already managed to get under cover.

The heat of the explosion hit them first, just as they were leaping for sanctuary. After it, came the noise and the shrapnel, pinging around them and clattering off the walls, until all was silent.

Travers emerged. All that was left of the Quark was a twisted frame and scrap metal. The fabric covering for the frame smouldered.

'Good salvage there, Professor,' Cownall said. 'Jerry will be terrified when we set that against him.'

'Thank you, Cownall.' Travers sighed and bent down, poking the wreckage with the barrel of his revolver. 'Keep an eye out for the head. That might still be useful.' He straightened and turned to Eileen, his mind working quickly. He took her gently by the shoulder and ushered her away from the soldiers, now looking around themselves for any sign of another Quark, and over to where Stewart stood.

'Right, two questions,' said Stewart, stepping forward. 'Firstly, why come into the compound? This is no place for a lady.'

Eileen had, impressively, already composed herself. Her unflappable demeanour that had impressed Travers in

Gulliver Base was back. 'A truck is missing. The factory has shut down so it can't be out on delivery. The Quarks must have already been taken out to the Boggarts.'

Travers thought for a moment. He trusted Eileen. But he had also felt very strongly that Huxtable would never attack during the day.

'Whatever is happening, our best bet is to get into this chap's office and check his papers. We need to stop these Quark things before they reach the Boggarts' farm.'

Stewart nodded. 'Agreed, but secondly, what happened when that thing shot at you? Who on earth was that woman?' He faced Eileen once more. She said nothing for a second or two.

'I heard something. I'm not sure if I saw anyone. It all happened very quickly.' Eileen sighed. 'Well, it missed, didn't it?'

'And that's the important bit, Private Stewart,' said Travers. 'Come on, Section Officer Le Croissette. There's no telling where another of those little sods is hiding.'

The remainder of the squad were in positions around the Special Projects shed. All entrances were well covered and also locked.

'What the hell happened back there?' hissed Day as they caught him up. 'And why are the civilians up here?'

'Sir, they were both instrumental in destroying the Quark that attacked us.' Stewart snapped off a salute. 'I am sorry to report that Private Doyle has not made it, sir.'

Day sighed. Stewart knew from his face that he was feeling the loss of another good man.

'It will be worth it,' Stewart said quietly, so that the others didn't hear. In his own heart, he was far from convinced. The familiar guilt of not having done enough was there.

Day clenched one fist and Stewart watched him stride up to the door. He motioned for the rest of the soldiers to pull back, and nodded at Travers who held up his device. Stewart pulled back behind an oil drum. It would be a terrible piece of cover when the bullets started to fly, but it would at least keep him hidden for a few moments. He checked the safety on his weapon.

Day turned back to the door and hammered on it.

'Huxtable!' he called. 'I've lost a good man already. This property is under the command of the War Office Special Support Group. I order you to stand your robots and troops down.' There was no answer. 'Huxtable! I will give you thirty seconds to confirm that you have stood them down or I will use explosives to break into this building.'

Stewart started to count under his breath as Day stood back a yard or two. As Stewart reached thirty, Day walked away from the doors.

'Give me a grenade, Private,' he barked at a nearby soldier.

And that was when the doors exploded.

This wasn't the simple shattering wood of machine gun fire. This was a high explosive charge. Stewart saw Day thrown down by the blast and Travers immediately clamp his hands to his ears behind the crate he had jumped behind with Eileen.

Stewart's mind flashed back to France. Day had done the right thing to lead his men from the front, but he now lay in a heap surrounded by dust and debris. Stewart tensed and prepared to dash out with his rifle. The smoke from the explosion started to clear.

That was when the rattle of machine guns began again. Stewart threw himself to the floor. The bullets sprayed across the courtyard through the smoke and dust. He could feel his blood pounding in his ears, trying to train the rifle at something in the smoke, anything, with every soldier's hope that what he fired at would stop firing back.

His hands shook. Damn. He was going to be his father's son if it killed him.

The shapes in the smoke coalesced, became machinery, drills, lathes. Where was the aggressor?

There was a gap in the air around him. He could no longer hear the sound of the bullets clattering against the brick walls. He brought himself up to a crouch. Could he risk moving? He saw Day, still lying prone, a trickle of blood from one ear. Frozen moments from France flashed past his mind's eye; a young man lying in the mud after a mine blast.

'Chaps, give me a hand with him.' Stewart hoped that his voice of experience would overcome the ill-fitting private's uniform.

Staying low, he dashed across the open ground. Two others darted from cover at the same time, also heading for Day's fallen shape. Stewart looped one of Day's arms around his neck and pulled the captain upright. He could feel the man's breath on the back of his neck as he started to drag him away from the shed. Morrison had taken Day's other side. He could hear one of the NCO's, possibly Ellington, shouting orders to stay back and cover the entrance. All Stewart could think about was getting the man to safety. Unbidden, his mind filled with the images of the young men in France, some killed by the initial blast, some coughing and gasping as the gas filled their lungs.

He heard running feet behind him, falling close together. A true sprinter's pace. He was about to turn, when he heard the familiar, high pitched squawk. A thump next to him and he suddenly found himself supporting all of Day's weight. He looked around. Morrison was spread-eagled against the nearby wall. It took a moment for Stewart to realise that he had been thrown there, thrown by a blunt object moving very quickly. The man slowly slid down. Stewart had no chance to check on him before he saw what had hit him.

The Quark stood a few yards in front. It had run on its tiny legs, clearly at the speed of a fast car, taken out Morrison and was now seemingly preparing to charge again at Stewart and Day. There was no way that he could get them both out of the way. The thing was going to run at him as it had to Morrison. He braced himself.

The Quark screamed in its high-pitched voice again. Stewart knew that this was a war cry. It was a robot, but it knew how to create fear in those that it attacked. Involuntarily, he closed his eyes.

No attack came.

He became aware of a new noise, an electronic whirring, like an out of tune wireless, coming from next to him. He opened his eyes again to see Travers standing next to him, playing with his box of tricks.

'What the devil are you doing, man?' Stewart yelled. 'That thing's going to run us down!'

'Yes…' mused Travers. 'It is fascinating, isn't it? Clearly

it has a secondary attack when it runs out of, or needs to conserve, bullets. The thing is, I think it has only recently learned to fire bullets at all. So, I think this little number is actually an example of machine learning. Absolutely fascinating. Unless Huxtable programmed them with a death wish of course.'

Stewart shook his head. 'Travers. We're the target of this "secondary attack",' he said through gritted teeth.

'Oh, I shouldn't think so,' said Travers, waving his box back at him. 'Not with this thing in my hand. I rather think that's why it's screaming at us. Not that I feel a lot of sympathy right now.' He turned to the remainder of the squad. 'Come on, you chaps, help the captains.'

Running feet behind Stewart again and he felt the weight of his shoulder lift as two privates took Day between them. Stewart watched as the man's eyes flickered.

'Howard has the command,' he murmured as they dragged him away down the path, past the still screeching Quark. Stewart looked across at Morrison. One man crouched next to his prone form. He looked over at Sergeant Howard and shook his head.

'Leave him for now!' snapped Howard. 'We'll have to come back for him.'

'We need to deactivate this one,' said Travers. 'Send a man in to try and take its head off.'

It was as if the robot had heard him. Cownall stepped forward and it stopped screaming for a brief moment. The head stopped spinning. Stewart felt that the robot was now staring straight at him. Cownall had paused for only a second or two, but was now running towards the machine again. As he reached the machine, the voice chirped again, before the whole unit hunkered down, turning itself into even more of a mobile jack in the box.

Then it leaped, its legs had concertinaed together, giving extra strength to such a small character. The bulky body sailed up through the air, arcing over the roofs of the two factory buildings either side of it.

Stewart was bewildered. He pulled his helmet from his head and rubbed both eyes.

'Damn thing could be anywhere now,' muttered Howard

next to him.

'No more than about fifty yards that way.' Both men turned slowly to see Eileen Le Croissette. 'That is,' she continued, 'a bit of an estimate based on its angle, speed and direction.' They stared at her for a split second.

'Right!' said Howard, turning away from the woman to his troops. 'You lot heard the girl. Half of you take the left-hand side, half of you take the right with me.'

CHAPTER SEVENTEEN
Last Hunt

MATTHEW STEWART hugged his rifle to his chest as he slid along the wall, the rough stone scraping the back of his uniform shirt. The thought of Morrison, Doyle and Day being taken down by the thing he was stalking left him strangely numb. He reached the corner. Half of the squad were lined up alongside him, strung out along the length of the wall. Travers was the closest to him.

He risked a quick glance around the corner. There it was, the squat little shape was now rummaging through a pile of scrap metal. Its back was to him, the canvas covering fluttering in the breeze from the ragged holes that the troops had filled it with. Its strange spiked head continued to rotate. The thing could easily still be watching him.

He pulled his head back in and whispered what he had seen to the rest. Travers nodded.

'They make munitions here. It's probably looking for some replacement ammunition.'

'Do you think it's out of ammo or just low?'

Travers shrugged. 'I have no idea. It seems pretty resourceful.' He appeared almost admiring of the creature.

'It's a model boy scout,' Stewart hissed. 'Any chance your box of tricks can work on it again?'

'It's possible. The trick is to get the sticky bombs on quickly before it does another Springheel Jack on us. And getting close enough, of course.'

Stewart risked a quick look around the corner again. The machine hadn't moved. 'Follow me, Professor,' he said. 'I've got a plan that might just work.' He paused and picked up the sticky bomb on his belt. 'Maybe just give me a second or so head start. There is little sense of us both getting caught in the blast, is there?'

Travers grunted a reluctant agreement. Stewart took a deep breath, then nodded.

He darted out from the corner, immediately racing across the internal road to the opposite wall. The road that he now found himself on was yet another high sided, windowless, death trap. If the Quark turned, it would be able to cover the area with any bullets it had left and slaughter them all.

He moved low and quickly up the wall, holding the bomb at arm's length. He judged that he was now within a second's worth of a dash from the Quark. He pulled the covering off the bomb. The thin metal cover clattered as it hit the ground. The Quark spun around so quickly that pieces of the metal it had been rooting through were flung across the alleyway.

'Disturbance. Sufficient arms to eliminate!'

Stewart took his chance as the machine's head spun with confusion. He should have retreated, but all that would have done is led the machine to the rest of the squad. Instead, he ran past it, praying that this would, at least, give the rest of the squad a chance to get behind it.

Further squawking followed him down the alley. He threw the sticky bomb in the Quark's general direction, hoping that it would at least catch the damn thing in its blast. The Quark was low on bullets, not completely out of ammo. It fired indiscriminately in his direction, the shots ricocheting and shattering around him. His luck was too good to last. He felt the tell-tale sudden sharp pain in his shoulder that threw him forward and down. The damn thing had managed to hit him.

Stewart lay on the ground, his shoulder feeling both numb and a sharp sting at the same time, waiting for the end to come, for the creature to totter over to him and finish the job. Splatters of his own blood dotted the concrete in front of his face, bright red against grey. Little spots were good, his mind told him, he might survive such a wound. But could he survive the Quark when it came to put one more bullet in his body?

It was then that the bomb went off. The sound impacted on his ears at the same time as the heat washed over him. Shards of metal carried by the blast wave carved striations across his back. He grunted with the pain as it hit.

All was quiet bar the muffled pounding of blood in his ears. He risked flexing his arms. They moved, the stinging pain in one shoulder was agony but matched the same in his back; his muscles moved nevertheless. He turned to face the creature, to see what was left of it.

It had been flung against a brick wall. As it turned unsteadily around, he saw that the canvas covering it was now even more tattered and sat over a buckled frame. It wobbled slightly, as though it was suffering a major defect in the parts keeping it upright and giving it that dramatic turn of speed.

The hammering of boots on the ground heralded the arrival of the rest of the squad, approaching from two different directions. Almost immediately the Quark started firing bullets around itself. Their accuracy was now even worse than before. The bullets flew over the troops' heads and tore chunks out of surrounding masonry.

Stewart saw what he needed to do. He raised his rifle and sighted on the barrel. His arm told him that he couldn't lift the damn thing, but he forced himself to fight against it.

He squeezed off one, two, three shots straight at the Quark's spinning metal head. At least one impacted and the machine's body lumbered around to face him.

Stewart stood his ground.

'Bomb it now!' he yelled, hoping that it would be too distracted by taking him out to care what was happening around it.

As the machine focused on him, and Cownall approached from behind, Stewart forced himself to stay stock still. His rifle dropped to his side, his arm unable to keep it up any longer.

The Quark's bullets flew almost as soon as Cownall slapped the sticky bomb to its exposed framework. The bullets, as Stewart had hoped, flew wide. He dived left and kept running down the alleyway away from the Quark. He heard it screech something about weapons calibration before he rounded the corner into the embrace of his fellow soldiers.

The bomb then went off with another loud blast.

Stewart staggered to the ground as two soldiers on either side grabbed him under his arms. He winced when their fingers closed around his wound.

'Get him bandaged, then get him out of here!' yelled an NCO's voice.

He was lowered to the ground. 'It's all right,' he heard a voice say. It was a woman. That rather narrowed it down in this group. It had to be Section Officer Le Croissette. 'It's winged you, but hasn't caused any major damage. We just need to get you stitched.'

That sounded hopeful to him. Of course, he'd rather get a doctor to check him out properly than relying on a girl. More running feet and a voice he recognised. Travers.

'You got lucky,' he said.

'They're lousy shooters,' muttered Stewart.

'I think they're used to a weapon that requires more power and less finesse. Let's hope that we never meet a Quark armed with it. Huxtable wouldn't need as many troops as he seems to have made here, for a start.'

Stewart grunted, the exertion and pain hitting him.

'Right,' said Howard. 'We're heading into the special projects building. Le Croissette, Jackson. Get the injured out of here and get an ambulance down to the front.' He glanced up at the setting sun. 'It won't be long before Jerry comes along to keep them busy. So, let's get our job done and jump the queue, yes?'

Stewart's hopes were raised. An ambulance may have some morphine, although right now he would take a damn fine Scottish malt. Not that such things were easy to come by these days. He allowed himself to be led back towards the gate.

Travers watched Stewart walking away, supported by Private Jackson on one side and Eileen on the other. The man had acquitted himself better than many officers he had encountered through the years. Another bark from Howard called Travers back. He gave the man just enough time to remind him that snapping orders at professors was a pretty poor way to win his attention. Howard turned and pulled his revolver out, although what use it was against Quarks, Travers had no idea.

'Let's head inside,' he said. 'I strongly suspect that we have seen the end of the Quarks that have been left here, but keep an eye out.'

Travers marched for the door. The smoke had cleared

now, but there were no lights on inside. All that he could see was the same maze of machinery and benches, all now quiet, tools left discarded, hanging off the edge of benches or sat on stools like incongruous cushions. Skeletal drills and cranes cast shadows across the walls.

The squad followed him, rifles scanning every corner of the shed. Travers motioned for the door at the far end, now hanging open. As they advanced, the light dimmed with the distance from the door, occasional dots of sunlight in the ceiling failing to make it down to the machinery below. Beyond the doorway, however, the blackness was complete. Howard caught up with Travers, who cast him a look.

'Torch?'

The sergeant passed one over.

'Excellent.' Travers switched it on, causing the shadows of the place to move. He stepped again towards the door, casting the torch around inside the testing area and holding his breath as he did so.

He had been right, there was no sign of any more Quarks in the testing house. Off to one corner was a small brick building with a steel door. Huxtable's office. Travers marched up to the door and tried it. The handle turned but the door failed to budge a single inch.

Howard nudged him to one side, aimed his rifle and pulled the trigger once. The shot echoed in the vast empty chamber and Howard gave the door a swift kick. It swung easily.

'Stand guard, everyone!' snapped Howard.

The two men stepped through into the small dark room. Travers swept his torch around. The room was as Eileen had described it, spartan, a desk set on a dais and a few cabinets.

'Fascinating.' Travers peered at the furniture. 'My understanding of the man's time travel technique is that he can only bring what he can carry. A few bits of tech and some Quark heads is all. He must have designed and built this from scratch. We are dealing, sergeant, with a man who is both a designer and an artist.'

Howard tutted. 'We are dealing, Professor, with a man who has further wasted money for the war effort on his own vanity.'

Travers thought for a second. 'A different morality. He

sees himself as having one mission and one alone. He wants to destroy the Boggarts. To him that takes precedence over anything and everything, including the war effort.'

'Well, I live here and now. The man has scammed the nation and his machines have killed two good mates and flattened my CO. Where the devil is he?'

Travers started walking around the room, tapping the cabinets. All locked, as he had expected.

'The truck is missing. He's gone and there are a lot less Quarks stationed here than I expected.' He sighed. 'I should think it's now obvious. He's taken his army to wipe out the Boggarts.' Into his mind swam his wife's face and the sinking guilty feeling that the best possible cure for her was about to be wiped out. 'Back to the gate.'

An ambulance, bell ringing loudly, was already arriving, as Jackson and Eileen arrived back at the gatehouse with Stewart balanced between them. Eileen waved frantically at the girl driving, who drew to a stop and jumped out.

'What's happening?' she called breathlessly. 'We'd been told about explosions, gunfire. How many injured?'

Eileen thought quickly, Official Secrets topmost in her mind as always. 'Training exercise. It's gone wrong. They thought they were firing blanks and discovered that they weren't.' Day wouldn't thank her for this cover up. It made him look even more incompetent than if she'd said he was chasing spacemen in a Sheffield steelworks. Between that and her failed trip undercover, she wasn't making friends in the Fourth.

'Let's have a look at him then.' The girl took Eileen's side of Stewart, guiding him back to the van.

'There's another man here,' said Eileen. 'Captain Day. He was brought out earlier.'

'Over here,' came the captain's voice.

Eileen turned to see his booted feet hit the cobbles behind the Fourth's Bedford. He took two steps towards them and then stumbled back against the side of the truck. Levering himself upwards, he kept moving towards them.

'I'm good to go. That blast knocked me for six, but I need to get back in there.'

'Oh no, you don't.' The ambulance driver had the look of a ward matron to her. She managed to support Stewart and face down Day. 'Both of you, back of the ambulance now. I don't care what's really going on behind those walls but neither of you is fit for duty. You, girl.' She pointed at Eileen. 'Give him a hand to walk.'

Eileen tentatively took a step towards Day, fully expecting the brush off that he then gave her. He wasn't for being helped. She stood back hopelessly.

It was this sense of hypervigilance that meant she heard the throaty roar of another engine approaching before the others. She turned as it rounded the corner onto the street, recognising the blue colour and flatbed shape at once. It was the missing lorry from the Pickering Works.

It stopped dead in the road and the engine cut out instantly. The driver she knew as soon as he alighted, with his strange shiny overalls and gun-like apparatus. She was happy to see that the flatbed was empty. The Quarks were not with him.

'Glad to see that you're all still here.' Huxtable kept his sidearm firmly down, appearing to still be trying to present a non-threatening face.

Eileen felt the blood rush to her face. Two days of being lied to and kept out of the way like a little woman. Two days of being flung into the deep end and left to swim or sink. All of it came bubbling to the surface as she stormed towards Huxtable.

'You've got a damn nerve!' she thundered. 'Two men lie dead in there from your...' She struggled for the word. '...your toys! Good men are out of action, and everyone else wasting their time because you want to pick a fight that has no meaning here.' She took a breath. It didn't help. 'We are at war! Our survival as a country, as people, hangs in the balance and we are wasting money, time and, most importantly, lives chasing after you because you've got some vendetta over what these people's ancestors did a million miles and five thousand years away.'

He stood back, shocked at the small inferno before him. 'They are not people,' he said. He wasn't defiant, but kindly, as if explaining to a child why their dog had to be put down.

'They are a stain. They can control us. They may already be controlling you.'

Eileen had heard that talk before, across the sea and before the war. She felt the bile rise in her throat as she faced the man. Her hand lifted involuntarily. She pulled it back, well aware that the man likely held in his hands a weapon that was millennia ahead of any technology that any party in this war had. In one movement, she brought it across his face, hearing it make a satisfying smack as skin hit skin.

His only response was to nod and smile. 'And ask yourself this. When all this is over and the dust has finally settled on this conflict, how long will your feelings against the German people last? Will it end with your children? Your grandchildren? Will the resentment ever end? Can you ever trust them after this?'

Eileen thought of the German planes. Of seeing one hit, falling in flames and of only being able to think 'good'. She could also remember, more faintly, as if in a different life, the friendship and care of the Germans she had met before the war. Had the war changed her so much. Would peace, if it ever came, heal?

'Then remember,' Huxtable continued, 'that what we have endured from the Family can match that and that those things you call people are really just weapons.' He stood back. 'That is what they were, weapons deployed against our empire by another race. Maybe in that race are people I can treat with, negotiate with.' He shook his head. 'But their spawn is nothing more than the artillery and vehicles you burned when you escaped Dunkirk.'

'I never met a troop carrier that could paint and write poetry,' Travers' voice snapped across the street as he exited the steelworks. 'Not even your Quarks can do that.' He strode over to where Eileen and Huxtable stood, ignoring both Stewart and Day who were now sitting in the double doors at the back of the ambulance. 'And that's the difference, isn't it? That's what makes the Boggarts something more than you give them credit for. Whatever you think of what their ancestors have done, whatever you think about what they could do if they put their minds to it, you have no idea what they are now. Maybe they won't bring us peace or cure

172

disease...' Eileen saw Travers' face fall slightly. '...but they are still living beings, and their very being here has shaped history and folklore in these lands.'

Huxtable fixed him with a glare. 'I'm not willing to risk the effect they could have on the future history that I call home, to assuage some well-meaning academia. They need to be wiped out. It is not pleasant...'

'...And that is why you have sent the Quarks. They don't just get past the Boggarts' mental controls, do they? They keep your hands clean.' Travers swiftly brought up his revolver. 'Now tell me where you have placed them. It's still light. They must be hidden. So where is it?'

Huxtable snorted. Somehow Eileen had expected a manic laugh, but this man was no villain. He sincerely believed that he was doing what had to be done.

'Come on, Professor. Do you really think I'm going to tell you so that they can be destroyed? They are already on their way and will reach the farm during nightfall. Then they will complete their task and I will be out of your hair. I'm afraid I will be taking most of this technology with me. I simply can't allow you to use it.'

Travers raised his revolver again to focus squarely on Huxtable's chest. 'Location. Now.'

Huxtable raised his own weapon, incredibly quickly to point at Travers. Eileen ducked for the ground as Travers squeezed the trigger. She saw the barrel rotate and heard the crack of the shot. It was shortly followed by the quiet plink of the bullet hitting the ground.

'Personal shield, Professor. Sorry, a bit of a cheat.' Huxtable pulled his own trigger with an apologetic look.

A silver beam shot backwards from the gun, striking Huxtable in the chest, and quickly developing into a patch of the same colour that rapidly spread across his whole body, glowing with a bright light that steadily built until Eileen closed her eyes against the glare. Just as suddenly as it started, the light dimmed, leaving only a space where Huxtable had stood.

'Damn,' said Travers. 'No residue of any kind. I can only presume that he has used some kind of teleport.'

The clattering of boots and rifles heralded the arrival of

the rest of the squad. Howard in the lead, followed by Cownall. Howard took one look at the Pickering truck sat in the middle of the road.

'Now what?'

Travers sighed and pocketed his revolver. 'Huxtable is missing. The Quarks are somewhere we don't know, and this jaunt's been for nothing.'

Howard folded his arms. 'Then we leave them to it. There will be no more troops sent in to save those people. They'll just have to deal with it. People are dying across this country in bombing raids every night. What makes them so special?'

Eileen coughed. If Howard was now taking the lead, then it may be worth a reminder that, as a section officer, she technically outranked him. She spoke directly to Travers. Something had been playing on her mind since the conversation in *The Black Boar*.

'When we drove through Edleton, there was no war memorial.'

Travers nodded. 'A Thankful Village. They've lost a couple of men this time around mind.'

'It must be harder for the Boggarts to save men from the new weapons in this war.' Eileen needed to press him, get him to spell this out to Howard. She didn't want the confrontation, but she would give as good as she got if it came to it.

'Indeed, their psychic powers are of limited use against torpedoes, bombing raids. Whereas before...' Traver snapped his fingers. 'How did I not notice! For a village that size to have lost no one in the Great War is a miracle. They might have saved a dozen men already, twenty in the last conflict.'

'You mean...?' Howard's expression softened. 'They've been saving the men of that village for two wars.'

'More!' said Travers. 'We haven't got time now, but you go through the parish records. See if you can find anyone dead in the Crimea, the Boer, the Napoleonic Wars, I'd wager you wouldn't find a single man.'

'That's all very well, Professor.' All four turned to see Day approaching, the ambulance orderly following with an exasperated look on her face. 'But the question remains as to how my men are going to confront them without being massacred. We're four down out of twenty already. We don't

174

even know where to start looking.'

'If we can solve that conundrum, we might be able to stop them.' Travers unrolled his map across the back of the flatbed. 'This shows the area around Owd Hob's Meade. Where looks like a good place to hide an army of robots?'

'Professor Travers?' Eileen nodded to where Huxtable had stood. 'He said that the Quarks were on route. That suggests that they are walking towards the farm as we speak. Not already hidden nearby.'

'Damn,' said Travers. 'Well, we can assume that they aren't moving through the road network, so that doesn't give us many options.'

'They must be moving at night,' said Day. 'Even the Home Guard would have spotted a fleet of those things marching through the countryside.'

'Caves!' said Eileen. 'There's a network of caves under much of Derbyshire. Lots of it is unexplored. Anything could be hiding down there.'

Travers snapped his fingers. 'Of course!' he said. He pulled the map towards him. 'But look here.' He jabbed at it. 'Owd Hob's Meade is surrounded by moorland and gritstone edges. No cave systems there. The nearest entrances to the cave systems are here.' He tapped the map again. 'Speedwell or The Devil's Ar--' He caught sight of the ladies nearby and stopped short.

'Devil's Rear End?' suggested Eileen, looking over his shoulder.

'Possibly,' said Travers. 'Base folk entomology is a subject for another time. If they come through either of these, they have to cross this ridge to get to Owd Hob's Meade. This saddle looks the most likely place.' He tapped a point equidistant between the caves and the farm.

'Have we got enough explosives to rig a trap?' asked Cownall.

Day shook his head. 'Nowhere near. And no way to detonate them remotely.'

Eileen thought for a moment. 'Have we got flares?'

'Flares? Yes, there's a few in the back of the Bedford and a Very gun for firing. Why?' Day looked confused.

Eileen swallowed. 'We could direct a couple of

Wellingtons from Finningley. We'd only need a couple and their payload. That's likely all that we would be spared. Set them on the correct bearing and set the flares as soon as the Quarks appear.' She looked at Day for confirmation.

'Someone needs to set the flares,' he said, looking around.

'I'll do it.' Travers straightened up. 'Cownall, get the Triumph out of the back of the Bedford, will you?'

'Sergeant Howard?' Day said.

'Sir!' The man snapped a salute.

'Get on to the Home Guard post. I want them to give us instant updates on everything that happens in the valley from now on.'

Howard saluted again as Day nodded at Eileen. 'Section Officer, I'll give you authority to request and direct the planes. If the top brass give you any lip, send them to General Dornan.' He turned and started to limp back to the ambulance.

Eileen saluted and turned to Cownall. 'Corporal, I'll need the nearest telephone and a map.'

'Both this way, I'm afraid.' Cownall led the way back into the compound.

Behind them, Travers picked up his own map, checked he had sufficient flares and the gun, and climbed onto the Triumph.

Back in the ambulance, Day turned on Stewart.

'What the devil happened to you anyway?'

Stewart smiled weakly. 'I got shot and then hit by shrapnel. Took one of them with me, mind you.'

Day turned to Howard for confirmation. He nodded.

'All true, sir. Private Stewart took the Quark on almost single handed. His first explosion knocked him and it flying, and he distracted it long enough for Corporal Cownall to take it out.'

Day whistled through his teeth. 'Action like that will see at least a mention in dispatches. Who is your Home Guard CO?'

Stewart smiled through gritted teeth. 'I would take it with the hugest of kindness if you could send it to Alistair Lethbridge-Stewart, former Military Intelligence, at Glen Cladach. And perhaps mention that Matthew Lethbridge-

Stewart is ready to take up the family name again.'

Day nodded. 'Ah, a Lethbridge-Stewart, eh? Yes, well, that explains a lot.' He smiled. 'I think you already have.'

CHAPTER EIGHTEEN
Those Magnificent Men

EILEEN TOOK in the spartan surroundings of Huxtable's office again. When she had last been here, there had been maps pinned to the wall. He had clearly found what he was looking for and they had been tidied away.

'Find the maps,' she told Cownall. 'We need to give the boys from Bomber Command a bearing to the ridge rofess Travers is heading for.'

Cownall nodded curtly, no time even for a wisecrack. She decided she was grateful for small mercies.

She started on the drawers herself, finally feeling that she was achieving something. Doing her bit. That's why she had joined the WAAF and why she thought she had joined the Fourth.

Now, she was standing in some future man's office and she knew that the future held people that were no better than the enemy that England faced now. One side capable of such terrible crimes that she could scarcely imagine them. The other so consumed by hatred for the first that they would wipe them out, men, women and children, generations later. Now, her blood having cooled since her slap on Huxtable, she wasn't sure at this point that she wanted any part in their struggle. She knew there was a right side to be on, the Boggarts alive now were mostly innocent, but in attitude and morals they seemed so alien.

They hadn't done their bit. That was what galled her the most. The Boggarts lived here too, and they had the power to be able to help the whole country, not just one little village. Instead they had kept themselves to themselves and promised nothing. She remembered what she had said out by the gate to convince Howard. If they could be persuaded onto the side of the Allies, they could still help. They could do their bit, just like everyone else. And she would feel that she had achieved something for the war effort on this assignment, because right now, it felt like a sideshow to what was truly important.

'Here!' shouted Cownall, pulling a drawer open.

'The maps?' Eileen dropped the wires she had just pulled out of the drawer she was searching.

'Nope. The phone.'

There, like something from a Bugs Bunny short, he was pulling out a Bakelite receiver from the cabinet. She took it from him and dialled the operator.

'Now, find the maps!' she hissed at Cownall. 'Finningley. Commanding Officer, please,' she told the operator. She knew that it would take some time to get through to the correct person and even longer to get him to do as she asked. She could only try her best.

Cownall continued to rifle through the drawers. Huxtable had amassed a huge collection of rubbish; there were sweet wrappers, empty food containers, posters. Eileen remembered his comments about always wanting to live during this war. The man had obviously fetishised and collected everything he could lay his hands on.

The voice at the other end turned out to be another WAAF.

'Section Officer Le Croissette, on attachment to the War Office Special Support Group, under the aegis of the prime minister. I need to speak to the base commander.' That was probably enough rank pulled, she decided as the line went quiet after a hurried 'ma'am'.

A crash across the room alerted her that Cownall had probably still not found the maps that she needed.

'What is it?' A clipped upper-class accent came down the line.

Eileen could imagine the owner with a moustache waxed and trimmed. 'Sir, I have authority from the War Office Special Support Group to requisition as many planes as you can spare immediately.'

'As many as we can spare?' A sigh. 'That number is zero. Who are you anyway?'

'There should be a standing order regarding assisting us.

Perhaps one of your aircraftwomen could dig out the folder relating to us?'

'Call back in five minutes.' A click.

Eileen swallowed. It would not take Travers long to reach the ridge. It would likely take the Quarks the same amount of time to exit the cave systems and advance on Owd Hob's Meade. The planes needed to be up in the air soon.

'He can have two minutes,' she said out loud. 'Any luck, Corporal?'

Cownall held up one sheet. 'Found a large-scale sheet for Sheffield and Owd Hob's Meade.' She took it, flattened it. At any other time, the lights of Sheffield would have given the pilots something to navigate with. Now, during the blackout, they had no chance of using them.

'Try to find a sheet with Finningley on as well.' She marked the location of the farm, and the ridge that Travers was headed towards. 'Please,' she added as an afterthought. Absent mindedly she reached for the phone again and asked for the base once more.

This time, the commander answered immediately. 'There's a code word,' he said. 'Tough luck if you've forgotten it. I don't take kindly to losing two planes for the night.'

'Blue Box,' Eileen said after racking her brains briefly. She had asked what it meant, but all she'd been told was that it was one Churchill himself had come up with. With some amusement, apparently. 'Sir, I hope that we will only need your pilots for an hour or two. We don't need the air gunners either.'

'I have them ready and their planes are good to go. What do you need?'

At that moment a further map sheet was placed in front of her. She could have hugged Cownall. It showed Finningley and abutted exactly the edge of the map that she already had.

'Ruler and compass,' she hissed under her breath.

This one was easy to find; Cownall appeared to struggle with the other. Eileen drew the line quickly while explaining.

'They'll need to fly into the countryside on a bearing that I will give you when my assistant finds the right equipment. Distance is approximately...' She guessed, 'Forty miles.' She swallowed. 'When you arrive, there will be a flare showing.

You need to drop the bombs on, or as close to, the flare as possible.'

And try to miss Professor Travers. So much could go wrong, the Quarks could get there too quickly, or too slowly. Ditto the planes. And then there was the professor. His best chance at getting the planes to hit the target was to wait until the Quarks were approaching and then set off the flare. But then, how did he get free?

'You may have to circle around for a few minutes, sir,' Eileen finished lamely.

Cownall slapped something down on the desk in front of her. It was the compass that she needed to give a bearing. She quickly used it, passing the information to the commander.

'What's the purpose of this mission?' he asked. 'Will there be any enemy fire?'

'Small arms only,' she said. That was true, at least. Of course, the small arms in question were being fired by robots that could leap over a building. The planes may not be entirely safe. She decided not to mention the fact that the Boggarts could easily persuade either pilot to crash their plane into a mountain. Her only hope there was that they wouldn't. Self-preservation, after all, seemed to be one of their virtues.

Travers took the Triumph as far as he could, up the grassy track that connected the Boggarts' lane to the ridge that he had marked as the likely route for the Quarks. Around him the light failed, and the smooth, close-cropped grass slowly gave way to pebbles, then rocks and finally boulders. The dust of the path was already working its way into his nose as he rode his way around the obstruction, kicking the smaller stones out of his way, more with frustration than anything else. Finally, he abandoned the bike altogether and pocketed the Very gun to continue on foot. Ahead, a mere few hundred yards away, was the top of the ridge.

The moon still cast a silvery sheen across the landscape. An occasional shape would stir beyond the path, the sudden white dash of fear skittering past him, letting out a tell-tale baa.

As he continued, he felt that someone was with him, keeping with him. It wasn't a noise, or even a glimpse from one eye, it was simply a sense, a sense that he was walking with someone else when all logic told him that he could not have been. He rubbed his eyes. He was tired. He knew he was. He had barely slept for nearly forty hours. It was a common feeling among mountaineers to report the feeling of having another person with them. Something he'd experienced himself in Tibet during his return from Det-Sen to the village of Tsongkhar on his first visit there. That was all this was. A common phenomena. Travers continued walking.

The feeling stayed with him, a prickling at the back of his neck, a constant sense of the *other* being present. He felt a fool as he stopped and turned, slowly. Somehow, he was unsurprised at what he saw, even as it shifted to the corner of his eye. However, he moved, she remained just out of sight, something he could only see as his eyes passed over to somewhere else.

'Morrigan,' he breathed. 'You are here?'

'What are you doing up here?' He heard the voice in his head. That answered his question.

'Helping you. Saving you.' He didn't go into the details of the plan. He was beginning to doubt it himself. He turned and started scrambling back up the path.

'Why?'

'A lot of reasons.' Travers was almost speaking under his breath as the exertion of the climb started to hit him and the dust of the path swirled up in the evening breeze to stick in his mouth and to his hair. He doubted the Quarks coming in the other direction would have as much difficulty. 'Firstly, because you are the innocent descendants here. Secondly, because the boy is still with you and I am determined to bring him back.' He swallowed. 'And lastly, because you could help cure my wife.'

He let the wind roll over the exposed grass as he paused for breath. Had he driven her off with that last comment?

Finally, she replied.

'We cannot affect the physical world with the powers we were given.'

'You can find it.' For now, he didn't want to give it its name. 'That means you can help direct surgeons to it.'

He could almost sense the head shake, the blast of helpless

negativity in his head.

'It doesn't work that way. In any case. We are soon to leave.'

That hit him; all of this could be naught.

'Leave for where? And why?'

The next thought that hit him was almost a giggle, a sensation that washed over him like sand pulling away from bare feet as the sea retreated.

'*When*? We are not bound by time. *Where* is more difficult to determine, sadly. As for why… We are weapons.'

'You are people.' That sound was definitely not one made under his breath. Travers had to be careful. Between that, and his clattering through the stones and pebbles, the Quarks would be only too alive to his presence. The first he knew may be a bullet to his head.

'We know what we are. And so will others. You don't know the future. The first man-made object to enter space has already been launched by your enemies. Others will follow and they will be like a beacon. A light that can't be extinguished. In little over twenty years, this planet will be a battleground. Like England is now in one war, the Earth has unique strategic importance for the galaxy and the timelines. We cannot be here when that happens.'

Travers turned, looked out across the valley below him, the settlements that dotted it, farms, villages, even towns. Even with the blackout they could be seen, grey shapes, ghostly against the dark landscape.

'So, if we survive this war, a greater war will come, one that we can't survive,' he said.

'You will. Many won't even know that it is happening. Ignorance will be blissful. Help will come. Men already alive will rise to the challenge. You have recently met a man whose family, alongside yours, will be on the front lines. But that place is not ours.'

Travers shivered. The wind was picking up. Who could she be speaking about? He'd met many lately. As for his own family… There were no soldiers in his family. Unless Morrigan meant the Goffs…? He quickened his pace. He could keep talking as he walked. He only had to think his replies.

'How do you know all of this?'

'It's ancient history. For our time at least.'

A stone skittered down the path and bounced against the toe of his boot. The discussion forgotten, his gaze travelled up the path. There remained enough light to be able to see what was ahead of him. The spherical but spiked shape on the box-like body that lumbered up to the horizon. Around him, the rest of the sky was empty of any sign of the bombers. There was no one to signal.

The Quarks would come through him and then onto Owd Hob's Meade and begin their massacre.

He dropped to the floor, rolling off to one side of the path, cursing under his breath.

'Morrigan,' Travers thought. 'Are you still there?'

The only sound, inside or outside his head, was the whistling of the wind and the slowly increasing thud of oversized metal feet on the pathway ahead. His mind raced. They may well go past him, may well not fill his body full of lead. But after that they would continue down the hillside, then down the lane and into the farm. The men, women and children, young and old, innocent and guilty, including the little boy from the village, would all lie dead and his wife would remain in her bed with no hope on the horizon.

A slim chance was better than none.

Travers steadied himself, tried his best to slow his breathing. Slowly in, and slowly out.

Where are those damn bombers?

As much as fear, he felt anger and, lurking at the back of his mind, embarrassment. This plan had failed.

'Morrigan,' he tried again, searching for her, like a child lost in a snowstorm. 'Please, if I don't make it, find Margaret. Make her well again.' He realised, with a choke, that *that* was what he wanted. He wanted her out of that bed; he wanted Anne and Alun holding her hands as they walked down the road. He wanted them all together and laughing, with no bombs and no doctors and no war.

Travers darted out of cover. The Very gun and its flares would have no effect, but if he could run between them, they may injure each other, may topple down. It may give him just a bit more time for the bombers to arrive.

The first Quark was just a few yards away.

He tensed. Its guns were flat to its chest as it stopped, swaying slightly.

'Conserve power. Analyse hostility.' Its head spun.

He should have realised earlier. What power did these things run on? Batteries most likely. Even with Huxtable's know-how, they most likely wouldn't be able to travel much further than the farm at this stage. They must have laid dormant in the caves and then started advancing as the sun had set.

He tensed again, and ran at them. Remembering his time with his college's rugby team, he lowered his centre of gravity and threw himself headlong at the first body, wrapping it with sufficient force that he hoped its weapons were pinned into its body, bringing it to the floor.

'Hostile action detected. We will destroy!' chirped the next in line.

They were strung out like Arabs in the desert all the way up the path to the ridge. He rolled off the one he had tackled, giving it a swift kick as he did so. He doubted it would have any effect, but it was satisfying nonetheless.

The first bullets hit the rocky ground by his feet, sputtering out in a line as the Quark tried to find its range and angle. What they lacked in accuracy, they more than made up for in ferocity. A shame, he mused, as he pulled himself to his feet and lunged feet first down the grassy slope to the side; the munitions they carried would have been valuable to the war effort.

Travers skewed as he went down, hit the boulder at the foot of the short slope with his shoulder, and yelled with pain as it jarred him to a halt. He pulled himself to his feet, looking behind him to see the Quarks all stood in a line. Without a word, all but one turned and started to lumber down the hill.

So that was how they would save their energy. Leave him to get killed by one of them while the rest went to massacre the Boggarts. He admired their efficiency.

Travers grabbed a rock from the ground, hefting it in one hand. His cricketing days were longer ago than his rugger days, but it was worth a go. He lobbed it, a fielder's throw rather than a bowl, and heard a satisfying clunk as it struck a Quark wobbling down the path. It immediately halted and turned, its weapons springing out of its body.

Travers looked around. The hillside was bare, the rock he had hit nowhere near enough to hide behind. He prepared to run.

CHAPTER NINETEEN
The Bomber Always Gets Through

HE HAD no idea how it started. For those brief minutes, it had been him, Edward Travers, against the robots. Perhaps it was when the bullets didn't come. Maybe he had caught something out of the corner of his eye and turned, just for a brief second.

It was a credit to his knowledge of folklore that he breathed its name out as he saw it, rising up into the sky from the opposite hillside, from the stone circle that the Boggarts had used for their gatherings. Legs like a goat and with two long straight horns in place of the Boggarts stubby short versions.

'Owd Hob,' Travers breathed, remembering Carter's description of the figure from folklore.

A character that was supposed to represent the father of the Boggarts, but who had the appearance of something very different, that of the Christian Devil himself.

Travers stared at that figure, standing on the opposite hillside, unable to tear his eyes away, numb to all that was around him. It must have been only seconds that he stood there, feeling like a boy caught in his headmaster's torch beam sneaking out of the grounds at night, but it felt like minutes, even hours had ticked by. It was only slowly that he became aware of what was wrong. Or rather, what was right.

The bullets of the Quarks were failing to rip his body apart. It was a further supreme effort to tear himself away from the beast on the far hill, and even with that done, he found that his feet felt like he was wading through the worst sucking swamp imaginable.

When Travers locked sight on the Quarks again, they were stock still, shaking. As he stared at them he saw the rivets popping from their body; shells, springs and sprockets had already fallen from them. One opened its gun arm. The swivel mechanism opened out and then continued to open, nothing stopping it, until the arm, hanging on by perhaps a screw or two, dropped to the floor with a clang. The Quark chirped up, its voice even more garbled than usual. Travers could make out very little of what it was saying, but the thing was clearly in distress. As it spun on the spot, a further clang heralded the loss of its left leg. The entire machine toppled to the floor, where its voice became deeper and even less intelligible than it had been before.

It was then that Travers realised what was happening. That figure was no entity itself. It was a creation of the Boggarts, either through amplification of their own powers to create a psionic force, or through harnessing some latent technology from whichever ancient astronauts put the circle there in the first place.

That meant... Travers forced his feet forward as he realised. The Quarks collapsed and disintegrated behind him, rivets and beams falling to dust as the fabric that covered and camouflaged them flapped away in the breeze.

The Boggarts could affect physical objects. Not just sentience, but inanimate matter like robots.

Like, he realised, whatever was eating away at Margaret and taking his wife away from him, Anne and Alun.

He had to get to them. He had to plead with them one last time. They may not help, they may have already gone, but he owed it to himself to at least try.

Ahead, the great satanic figure started to fade, dissolving into the stars behind it. He supposed that behind him the Quarks were now nothing more than scrap and bolts. The Fourth would have to recover them later.

The Triumph still lay on the ground where he had left it, a dull shape among the rocks and grass. He pulled it up, scrabbling to find the ignition.

The blow to the back of his head came out of the blue, a heavy thump that threw his face forward and into the bike's handlebars. He felt himself rotating and hitting the ground, landing again on the bruised shoulder that collided with the rock.

The figure, recognisably human but blurred from the blow and the dark, knelt next to him, rummaging in Travers' pockets. He flailed uselessly at the man, his hands unable to close to a fist. They were quickly pushed away.

'Easy there, Professor,' growled the mid-Atlantic accent. 'This will be much easier if you just let me pick up what I need.' It was Huxtable; the voice was instantly recognisable.

Travers tried to respond, but his voice could only manage a slurred mumble. Huxtable's hand closed around the Very pistol.

'Ideal,' he said. 'With any luck, those magnificent men in their bombers will be along shortly. Let's give them a target, shall we?' He pulled Travers by his coat, rolling him to the side.

Still groggy, Travers tried to lever himself to his feet as he heard the Triumph engine start. A spin of wheels and a spray of pebbles showered onto him. At that moment, he realised that the bike was heading down the path, back to the valley floor and from there, to the Boggarts' farm.

As the motorcycle noise faded away, Travers heard another sound, similar, but with a constancy to it; a drone of engines from the far end of the valley. He didn't need to guess what it was. He knew that the Wellington bombers had arrived and were cruising down the valley. They would drop their payload wherever the flares appeared.

Travers stumbled forward, his head still swimming. He was concussed, he knew. The best thing would have been to sit down and drink water. He snorted with a half-laugh.

He took step after faltering step, picking the pace up, feeling himself stumble backwards, his feet sliding on the pebbles and dust. He dropped to the floor as he went, sliding undignified for a few inches before pulling himself upright and moving back down. The roar of the bombers increased as they approached, the pitch rising as they inexorably led their way down the valley.

So often he had heard and seen German bombers doing the same. The dread rising in his heart as they moved over London, waiting to see where they were heading, which neighbourhood they would destroy that night. He felt the same dread now, mixed with the hollow feeling that he knew what was going to happen.

He could still hear the motorcycle's engine under that of the planes, its rasping buzz fading into the distance.

The smallest sliver of hope entered his head. The farm was a long way away, the motorcycle barely more than a man's running pace, no match for an aircraft engine that barrelled through the sky so swiftly. He dared think, in his confused delirium, that the planes would pass the farmstead long before Huxtable could get there and mark it. Even now, he could see the shape of the two planes, black against the dark blue of the night sky. They were close to where he thought the farmstead sat. Much closer than he had thought.

Travers paused, caught his breath and watched as they flashed past, their engine noise dropping again as they did so, pausing again and then throttling up to climb out of the valley. He breathed out. They had passed by. The people were saved.

His head now calmer, the unsteadiness leaving him, he started again for Owd Hob's Meade, to try to meet them before the Boggarts disappeared for good. He could catch them, convince them to help, to come and meet Margaret, to help the surgeons cure what was inside her. Then, when the war was over, he, Margaret, Anne and Alun could play outside, take long holidays, walk along an empty beach with not a shred of barbed wire or mine in sight and no demands on his time from generals or the unnatural. They could be a family again.

That was when he heard the engine noise change again. First the pitch stopped dropping, then it started increasing again, growing louder as it did so. The hope that had filled his heart shattered into a thousand pieces.

The planes had turned and were heading back down the valley to pass once more over Owd Hob's Meade. That was when he realised that he could no longer hear the sound of the motorcycle's engine.

As if on cue, a single orange smoking ball flew up into the night air from across the valley floor. A second followed, then a third. The flares from the Very gun erupted from the centre of the farmstead.

Travers stared, frozen to the spot, his mouth half-open, knowing what would come next.

The bombs fell in four lines, two from each plane, offset like footsteps. He watched the orange flowers bloom in a steady line, starting where the flares had erupted, marching through the marked point and then continuing after it. The second plane flew slightly to the side and behind the first, the bombs falling accordingly, as if mopping up any survivors. Travers saw no gaps in the pattern, no dud bombs.

He should be glad, he thought, of the skill of the British pilots and factories.

The Bakelite in Huxtable's old office rang. Eileen looked at it, reaching out one tired hand.

Cownall got to it first, snatching the receiver up. Eileen was angered for a second. She had always been the conduit for news.

Cownall listened to the voice at the end. Then nodded. 'I'll tell her. When are we moving out?'

He replaced the receiver.

'Well?' Eileen asked.

'We can get some sleep finally.' Cownall gave a wan smile with little enthusiasm. 'The Home Guard have reported explosions.'

'Good.' Eileen breathed out. At least they had succeeded in wiping the damn tin soldiers out.

'Not so much. They didn't hit the Quarks. Who knows where they've got to…' He paused, gazing at the map. 'They hit the farm. Obliterated it. It's just a burning ruin. We'll go and find out what happened there tomorrow.'

Eileen slumped in her chair. She had failed.

She gazed at the maps strewn around the office, empty of the man that had caused of all of this. Blueprints for robotic soldiers from the future now loose in England's green and pleasant land. She opened her mouth to say something, but with only Cownall to hear it, she let the phrase fall into silence.

Travers reached the gates of the farmstead. The posts still stood at either side of the entrance. Everything behind them was in ruins. The Wellingtons hadn't dropped any incendiaries, so nothing was still burning, half an hour on from the bombing. The bombs had hit the ground, exploded and their work was done. Travers could see the four lines of smoking craters which ran through the centre of the farm, where once the house had stood, with its moss-covered stonework that seemed to make it half stone and half alive.

There was only rubble there now, scattered across the yard. The dark and smoke hid the worst of it, but as Travers picked his way through, he could see no sign of a building, nothing that remotely resembled somewhere that people could have lived, learned and shared food with each other. There was only stone, shards of plaster and what might once have been furniture, burned and shattered out of all recognition.

His foot landed on something that gave way immediately with a loud crack. He jumped at the sudden noise in the silence. Looking down he could only see a vague outline and knew that he had shattered the canvas of one of the vile paintings that had adorned the walls of that house. He shook it off his foot.

'Good riddance,' he said out loud, taking another step into the ruins, desperate to find some sign of life, some survivors. He heard a cough behind him and spun around. 'I had hoped you'd be dead. Scattered here like the rocks.' He bit his tongue, fighting the rising tide of hatred that was enveloping him.

'I ran,' said Huxtable, pointing in a direction perpendicular to the line of the bombing, 'that way.'

'I wish you had broken your damn legs. What are you doing here? Gloating?'

'I don't gloat.' Huxtable's head dropped. 'I'm doing a difficult job, thousands of years from home. It is not one that I enjoy.' He looked up, and Travers saw that the man was wearing dark glasses, like flight goggles. 'But it is necessary. And I will continue to do it.' He lifted a chunk of rock, looked it over and then threw it to one side. Travers heard it knock against the other stones, a cracking noise that faded into the night.

'Haven't you done what you wanted? Disappear from here. Let us find them and bury them. No one could have survived this.' Travers bit his lip. Holding back the despair and anger that he felt. 'Is this a victory in your time?'

Huxtable looked around. 'This is what a victor is in our time. A man who does his job.'

Travers kicked the ground in front of him, his foot connected with a round object that created a hollow clang as it rolled across the rubble. The iron helmet from the Bodians' house.

'See. You feared them too.'

Travers closed his eyes. He had. He had worn that ridiculous thing because he hadn't trusted the people that had lived here. 'I never attacked them.' It was a weak argument.

'Evidently I haven't managed that successfully. Look around you.'

Travers tried, still seeing nothing but stones in the darkness.

'Ah yes. I forget. I have night glasses. They help me see without casting any light. And they are showing me no bodies and no survivors.'

Travers took this in. They had survived then. But they were gone and with them, Margaret's best hope. When the sun came up, he expected to find, somewhere here, the body of Charles Peeves, the boy that he had set out to rescue. When he did, he would have the final confirmation that he had failed in what he had set out to do. So had Huxtable.

'You don't know where to look for them do you? They've got away from you. They could be anywhere. And anywhen.'

Huxtable laughed. 'Their time travel technology will be long gone by now. According to what you have all told me, they've been here for hundreds of years.'

Travers sat down on a piece of rock, taking the weight off his feet. He picked up a piece of a stone wall, hefted it in one hand and threw it in the direction of the moors, and the stone circle.

'Up there, they seem to have found technology that has been here for thousands of years. There must be examples all over the world. If they already know how their ancestors travelled, they could be able to use it to travel through both time and space. Probably a one-way ticket, but where? And when too? And how can you ever hope to find them again? Can you track them through such a void?'

Huxtable kicked a rock, it followed after Travers' own hurled stone. It landed short of it. 'Not instantly. But eventually. All we have to do is read long enough and find the footprints they leave. That's what led us here.'

Travers sighed. 'And then you will try to murder them all over again. I hope you fail.'

Huxtable smiled sadly. 'So speaks a man who has not seen what I have seen.' He shrugged.

'You can stay here and see some more,' said Travers. 'There was a child living with these people. Do you think he has gone with them?'

'He is of no use to them in another time. Why would they need him as a hostage in a time and place where he may not even look like the natives?' Huxtable tutted. 'I doubt that their technology could even have taken him anyway.'

'Then use those goggles for something useful and help me find his body.' Travers sighed with a weary resignation. 'His mother should be allowed to bury at least one of her family in this war.'

Huxtable didn't say a word; he simply stepped over the rubble and walked towards the larger pile. Travers followed, scrambling up the mound. Beyond it was an area of grass, itself untouched by the bombs but no longer enclosed by the high walls. Stone bricks lay where children's toys had been only last night.

Huxtable dropped down onto it. Travers followed, shining his torch around what was left of the garden, the shrubs and small trees that the children had played around just hours earlier. He was glad they had escaped.

'Here,' said Huxtable, prodding something on the ground with his foot.

Travers swallowed, preparing himself for the worst. A child dead from bombing was something he had never wanted to see. He approached with his torch.

There was no body. There the turf was loose and had clearly been blown back by the bombing. Beneath was a solid stone slab with wooden ring through the centre. Huxtable gripped it and heaved. The slab moved, scraping across the detritus of the garden that had hidden it and revealing only darkness beneath. Travers stepped forward, shining his torch down the hole that it revealed. Bare stone steps led down, but there, at the very bottom, his torch beam fell on a face that he knew from his last visit.

'Charles!' he called down, holding out a hand.

The boy began to climb back up the steps.

'Wait!' snapped Huxtable. He levered the slab to the entrance again, balancing it in such a way that it could fall back and cover the hole, trapping the young boy underground again. 'Now,' he said. 'Where did they go?'

Charles Peeves' lip wobbled as he stared up.

Travers wasted no time. He dropped his weight to his back foot and threw all of his weight into a single punch to the back of Huxtable's head.

The man dropped instantly, the slab falling harmlessly away from the hole.

'There,' said Travers. 'Favour returned.' He held his hand out to the boy again and helped him from the hole. 'What do you remember?' he asked. 'Your mother? Father? The people that you have stayed with?'

The boy stared around him, confused. 'They gave it all back. I can remember everything.'

'Everything?' Travers crouched next to the boy, a hand on his shoulder. 'What was happening before you were in the cellar? Before the bombs dropped?'

The boy looked distant, detached. 'I was... I don't know,' he trailed off. 'I was safe. I remember that. But they were going somewhere. And before that...' Charles swallowed. 'Before that I was in the woods. With Jacob, by the bombs.'

Travers stood slowly. He stole a quick glance down at Huxtable, who groaned. Clearly that personal shield didn't stop everything. He stopped himself from delivering a swift kick at the man and took Charles by the shoulders, leading him away from the place that had been his home for the last week.

Footsteps across the farmyard, crunching through the gravel, stopped him. He brought his torch around to locate them.

There, in the yellow light and serviceable overalls that wouldn't have looked out of place on a Land Girl, stood Vivian Peeves, the boy's mother. Travers let his arm drop to his side as Charles wrenched away from him, tottering at first, before breaking into a fast stagger and finally a run that took him into his crying mother's arms. As she gripped her son tightly, his clothes scrunched into her clenched hands, she opened her eyes to look at Travers.

'I came. I felt a weight had been lifted from my head. Then I heard the bombs.' She almost spat the words out between sobs.

Travers nodded. 'They must have put a lot of effort into keeping your mind away.' He shrugged. 'But they're gone now. He's all yours again. In just as good a state as when he left you. Maybe better. The people that lived here didn't much care for rationing.'

'Good riddance to them.' She stood, her eyes hardening. 'I'll chase them off myself next time.'

A thought occurred to Travers. 'How did you know where to find him?'

She pointed behind her. 'She showed me.'

Travers shone his torch into the gloom. There, standing by the gateway was an old woman, still wearing the same beige trouser suit she had worn when she had appeared at *The Black Boar.* As he started towards her, Travers' foot nudged against a rock. It knocked him slightly off balance, not for long, but enough that the torch-beam slid away from the woman.

When he brought it up again, she was gone. He shook his head. It seemed like a mystery that wasn't going to be solved tonight.

'Go home,' he said to the two reunited figures behind him. 'You're together and alive. That's all any of us can ask for these days.'

As he watched them walk off down the lane, Travers heard a strange laughing cough behind him.

'See, Professor?' He turned to see that Huxtable had pulled himself to one knee. 'The real people in this time know what is important.'

Travers waited until he was sure that the Peeves family were out of earshot.

'They're scared. There's a lot to be scared of. That's no excuse for what you tried to do.'

'I'm still trying. For a good cause, believe me.' Travers could see him raise up his weapon-like implement. 'Goodbye.' Huxtable pressed a button and was gone into a silver mist. A pebble hurled by Travers passed through where he had stood.

'Damn him!' shouted Travers.

The man thought he was right, that was what really angered Travers. Once he had decided that the people that had lived here were not human, were mere weapons, then anything he did to them became morally acceptable. Now, he was off again, to Lord alone knew where. Travers tutted to himself. Lord alone knew when.

CHAPTER TWENTY
Home from the Front

MATTHEW LAY in the bed in the hospital, his wounds stitched and scrapes salved by something that had stung worse than the shrapnel, and with a smell and colour that still lingered in his senses. He could hear the groans of those with lost limbs, deep open wounds and with lungs full of dust, outside his cubicle. After the sun had set, there had been a raid. Not a Blitz, nothing so dramatic, but enough to make sure that the people of Sheffield remembered that Hitler was still there. He felt lucky to have been treated at all; the benefits of the uniform he guessed. He would soon be sent on his way.

The curtain was pulled back and a nurse stood there, her uniform starched and shoes shining.

'Visitor, Mr Stewart.'

'It's past visiting time,' he tried to say, his voice hoarse from the dust and cordite that he had breathed in two days ago.

'Not for me.'

He recognised the voice immediately. His father, Alistair Conall Lethbridge-Stewart, swept past the nurse. How he had already found out what had happened and where his son was, Matthew didn't want to know. Military Intelligence obviously continued to function long after apparent retirement.

His father dropped a bottle of brown liquid on the bedside table. 'Brought you something medicinal from the still.'

Matthew chuckled, despite their differences. 'Maybe later.'

Father puffed his cheeks out. 'I was hoping you'd be the guinea pig. We've only recently got it set up with the shortage of good whiskey.'

Matthew eyed the bottle with even more trepidation. The

198

nurse withdrew, closing the curtains behind her. It provided very little privacy.

'You've come a long way, Father.'

'The trains are dreadful.' Father helped himself to the wooden chair next to the bed and sat, looking around, as if searching for a place to start the conversation.

'I've heard from Gordon,' Matthew said.

His father grunted. 'I hope he's well. He's flying a Halifax now, did you know?'

Matthew did. He had been involved in ensuring delivery of the planes to Gordon's airfield.

'You've come here to see me, Father?'

His father grimaced. 'I was travelling from London to Glen Cladach, I thought it best to check up on you.'

Matthew closed his eyes. This sort of conversation was not a strong point for either of them. His father seemed to gather his thoughts.

'After all, it seems you're not the coward you were.'

Matthew levered himself up in the bed. He'd been wanting to walk around, there was nothing wrong with his damn legs, but the sisters wouldn't allow it. 'I don't think that I ever was. But I wasn't cut out to lead men.'

His father tutted. 'Then we will have to work on you then, won't we?'

'Father?'

'Well, in time, you'll have an estate to run.'

The old man smiled across at Matthew Lethbridge-Stewart, who returned the gesture.

'It didn't go too well, did it?'

Eileen held her typed report about six inches above Miss Roberts' in-tray. How had she known what was in it? General Dornan's secretary followed her gaze.

'I haven't read it, dear, but Professor Travers has already given his report.'

'He must have typed it up quickly.'

Miss Roberts laughed and returned to filing her nails. She looked over the edge of her glasses. 'The professor never writes his reports for us, dear. He says that he's too busy working on journal papers. He gives them orally. That is, he

199

and the general have an argument and I type it out in a form that is suitable for Mr Churchill to read.'

Eileen swallowed. Her failings were already with the general then. Worse still, it was on its way to the prime minister.

'What did he say about this one?' she asked.

Miss Roberts pocketed her nail file. 'Best go through,' she said briefly.

Inside, the general was engrossed in the paperwork in front of him. She snapped a salute off. He paid no attention and continued reading, finally setting the paper down carefully when he reached the bottom.

'Well,' he said. 'I've already got Travers' report, of course. Yours will be with Miss Roberts I imagine. Sit down.'

Eileen did so. The room was now mercifully clearer of papers than it had been a few days back. Although, she reflected, that merely meant that Dornan could give her his full attention. She waited for him to speak.

'Well, as far as I can tell, your undercover work was spotted within a few minutes, which is unfortunate. Having been discovered, you then took it on faith from the target of the operation that we should direct our attack elsewhere at a group of mostly innocent civilians.' He ticked off each point on his fingers. 'Finally, once we had established the correct antagonists and which people we should be helping, your chosen form of attack was easily intercepted and then led to the total destruction and loss of a settlement. Did I miss anything?'

Eileen gave a curt shake of her head. 'No, sir.' She felt a yawning chasm ahead of her. The Filter room was beckoning, but strangely, she would have welcomed it. She just didn't want to arrive back there under a cloud. Then Dornan did something she hadn't expected. He laughed. She looked at him, questioningly.

'On paper it looks terrible, doesn't it? That's the problem with a lot of what we do. Look at it this way, one half of this future conflict was never going to help us. That hasn't changed, but at least we have the moral satisfaction that they survived and we managed to get the boy out.' He drummed his fingers on the desk. 'The other, well, he left us with a lot of robot brains. I don't think we can fully replicate the Quarks, but we have some plans. Our boffins are going to try and work them into the Panjandrum. I dread to think how that will turn out.' He gazed up and blinked, before turning to Eileen.

'I'm glad something good came out of it, sir.' Eileen felt strangely hollow. She was used to feeling that she had contributed. That she had done her bit. Planes in the sky being shot down was something real, tangible. All she had done here was give Britain a possibility, a small one, that something might work out well in the end.

'Something very good came out of it.' Dornan smiled. 'I have a new operative who makes mistakes, learns from them and shows grit and imagination in approaching her tasks.' He held up the paper that was in his hand. 'This one is your next assignment. Assuming that you're not heading back to the Filter Room anytime soon of course?'

Eileen smiled and held her hand out to take the paper. Maybe both she and the Fourth would give each other a second chance. For now.

In another part of London, far away from the Fourth bunker and the bombs, Travers carefully opened his front door, stealing past it onto the red tiled floor beyond and closing the wood and stained glass against the night. He was finally home. He took in the surroundings as he dropped his overnight bag and coat to the floor. The bills he had expected were neatly tidied away. Clearly Margaret had managed to get up and about somewhat. He was glad to see it. He hung his hat on the hatstand and took a candle from the side, lighting it quickly with a match.

He padded quietly up the stairs to the bedroom, sheltering the flame as he went, to prevent it showing through the windows. He knew that the blackouts were up in the bedroom windows and he let the light shine across the room.

Margaret was in bed, propped up on the pillows. As always when he found her asleep, his eyes automatically went to her chest. It was still moving, going up and down rhythmically. He carefully placed the candle on her bedside and sat in the easy chair on her side of the bed.

Gently, he took her hand, held it between his own. She

didn't wake, stirred slightly and then resumed her sleep. He sighed heavily, feeling the emotion drain from him.

He had already felt his frustration at losing the one chance that could have made it all right and given him his wonderful family back again. But now, sat here and watching her face as it dozed on the bed, he didn't feel anything else. It was as if his mind was pulling him away from the woman on the bed, preparing him for the worst.

He brought his lips down to her hand and swore to himself; even if sometimes he couldn't wholly trust his mind, he knew that he would not give up on her.

As she stepped out of the bunker entrance, into the busy London street above, Eileen had a new spring in her step. She weaved between middle-aged women, dressed in their dowdy tunics, baskets of limp veg and liver clutched in their hands.

Among them all was a lighter shade, an old woman, someone she thought she had seen before, in the shadows outside the steelworks. When she should have died.

Now, the woman stood in the middle of the pavement looking like a rock as the river of history streamed past her.

From her trouser suit, the woman pulled out a coin. She turned to Eileen, lifted up her head and looked the younger woman straight in the eye.

The woman's own eyes widened as if in surprise, she pulled back. The coin dropped from her hand, rolling on its edge in a perfect circle, one minute heading away, then curving towards Eileen. She bent to pick it up, feeling a strange pull as she closed her hand around it, absorbing her whole body and yanking her in a new direction, not up, down or sideways.

Eileen Younghusband, nee Le Croissette, stood in the street, staring at the spot where the young woman had just vanished. No one else had noticed. Everyone had more important things to worry about.

It had been a shock to see her younger self, a face she had become used to only seeing in photographs. Dangerous too. She tried to recall the name of the effect. Named after some Russian chap.

Her instructions were simple. Find Travers, and when he

was alone, away from her younger self, give him the temporal beacon. At all costs she had to avoid herself. Time was fracturing, another instability would only quicken its collapse.

Eileen couldn't pretend she understood half of what the man had told her; but she got the gist. The future and the past depended on her fulfilling one more mission. But remaining in the past had proven difficult; the man had explained that the essential timeline was fracturing counter-chronologically, and keeping her in its past would prove difficult. Even for him. But she had remained in the past long enough to guide that woman towards Travers, and her son. And now, in London, she was sure she had timed things right. When Edward Travers would be leaving the secret HQ of the Fourth Operational Corps.

Typically, you could never rely on him being in the right place. Even when there was a war on.

She picked up her stick and started to walk away, but she felt something strange happen. She couldn't quite find the words to explain the feeling, just a sense that she was... falling apart.

EPILOGUE

THE GUARDIAN watched as Eileen Younghusband was erased from the essential timeline, just like Brigadier Lethbridge-Stewart before her. Her own time period was no more; the work of the fracture point as it strained under the weight of the temporal collapse.

Still the Guardian needed agents. Traverses and Lethbridge-Stewarts from the strongest divergent timelines, those that were closest to the essential timeline. They could fix things, acting on his behalf.

The Guardian of the Quantum Realm turned to face the young woman who had been brought to the nexus through her contact with the temporal beacon. It had not been the Guardian's intention to bring forth her. Standing before him should have been Edward Travers. Still...

He smiled with his manufactured mouth, a movement of the muscles that seemed to put corporeal beings at ease.

She would have to do.

'Eileen Le Croissette, your realm needs you...'